Heett
after seven long years had
flustered her more than
she'd expected. This was
the same arden...
man she remem...
changed him in many ways.

The pitiless Indian sun had darkened his
skin to the colour of a Barbary pirate's. The
wild black curls she had once loved to twine
around her fingers had been cropped to short,
severe stubble. His mouth, once so mobile,
was now set in an unyielding line. The years
had chiselled his features into a visage of
stark, savage beauty. Eyes once the warm, soft
green of new moss were now hard and cool as
jade.

Had all those changes been wrought by the
passing years and his experiences in the
Orient? Or had he always been such a forceful,
ruthless man, while she'd been too naïve to
see it?

Part of her itched to turn and flee from this
formidable man, while another part felt
irresistibly drawn towards him…

Author Note

Welcome to the first book of my new series, *Gentlemen of Fortune*, about the self-made men of Vindicara Trading Company! After I wrote this story I decided to give Ford Barrett a couple of business partners. Since I needed these men to have made their fortunes while still young, I looked for a time and place when opportunities were ripe. I saw it at the end of the Regency era, when the trading post of Singapore was founded. Born of a flamboyant risk, its early existence under constant threat, the tiny settlement brought together people of very different cultures united in their drive to succeed. I have relished the opportunity to learn more about Singapore's fascinating history and culture.

Ford Barrett, Hadrian Northmore and Simon Grimshaw all left Britain for various reasons, going halfway around the world to make their fortunes. Now, though they have money, power and success, they discover those things mean nothing without a special person to share them. As destiny throws three unique women into their paths, these driven men discover that achieving material success was easy compared to the challenge of forging a close, passionate relationship that will last a lifetime.

MARRIED: THE VIRGIN WIDOW is the story of Ford Barrett, who inherits a title and estate from his late cousin. Returning to England to put his affairs in order, he must confront his cousin's beautiful young widow— the woman whose betrayal broke his heart and drove him into exile. Ford believes that by possessing her at last he can free his heart from her thrall. But Laura will not be possessed. Tested by hardship, she is haunted by wrenching secrets, including one that could destroy Ford and their rekindled love!

I hope you will enjoy MARRIED: THE VIRGIN WIDOW and look forward to those of the other Vindicara partners!

MARRIED: THE VIRGIN WIDOW

Deborah Hale

MILLS & BOON

All the characters in this book have no existence outside the imagination of the author, and have no relation whatsoever to anyone bearing the same name or names. They are not even distantly inspired by any individual known or unknown to the author, and all the incidents are pure invention.

First published in Great Britain 2010
Harlequin Mills & Boon Limited,
Eton House, 18-24 Paradise Road, Richmond, Surrey TW9 1SR

© Deborah M. Hale 2010

ISBN: 978 0 263 87594 2

Harlequin Mills & Boon policy is to use papers that are natural, renewable and recyclable products and made from wood grown in sustainable forests. The logging and manufacturing process conform to the legal environmental regulations of the country of origin.

Printed and bound in Spain
by Litografia Rosés, S.A., Barcelona

In the process of tracing her Canadian family to their origins in eighteenth-century Britain, **Deborah Hale** learned a great deal about the period and uncovered plenty of true-life inspiration for her historical romance novels! Deborah lives with her very own hero and their four fast-growing children in Nova Scotia—a province steeped in history and romance!

Deborah invites you to become better acquainted with her by visiting her personal website, www.deborahhale.com, or chatting with her in the Harlequin Mills & Boon on-line communities.

Novels by Deborah Hale:

A GENTLEMAN OF SUBSTANCE
THE WEDDING WAGER
MY LORD PROTECTOR
CARPETBAGGER'S WIFE
THE ELUSIVE BRIDE
BORDER BRIDE
LADY LYTE'S LITTLE SECRET
THE BRIDE SHIP
A WINTER NIGHT'S TALE
   (part of *A Regency Christmas*)

Look for more in
Deborah Hale's
Gentlemen of Fortune
BOUGHT: THE PENNILESS LADY
WANTED: MAIL-ORDER MISTRESS
Coming August and September 2010

Thanks to the smart, talented, generous members of *Romance Writers of Atlantic Canada* for their continuing support. Extra-special thanks to Julianne MacLean, Ann Cameron and Anne MacFarlane, who tutored me in the mysteries of alpha-males and romantic revenge.

Chapter One

June 1821

Ford Barrett's spirits soared as he read the letter he had been waiting seven long years to receive. A letter he had often despaired of ever seeing. A letter that would end his long exile and allow him to reclaim everything that had been stolen from him.

Including his heart.

After a voyage of five months and many thousand miles, the letter had arrived earlier that day in Singapore. Ford and his business partners had been so busy it was after sunset before they had a chance to read their mail.

Now the three men sat pouring over their correspondence by candlelight, on the deep veranda of the wooden bungalow they'd helped build beside their warehouse. Overhead, raindrops from the south-west monsoon pattered softly on the roof, thatched with palm fronds. The distant commotion of a cockfight mingled with a haunting wail summoning the Maylays and Arabs to their evening prayers. Pungent odours of fish, mangrove swamp and burning joss sticks hung in the sultry night air.

Hadrian Northmore glanced up from one of his letters to fix Ford with a penetrating stare. "Bad news, is it? I've never seen you look so sour."

Ford made a strenuous effort to relax the clenched muscles of his face into his usual neutral expression. He hated it when others could guess his true feelings—even the tough, proud man who'd helped him make his fortune.

Hadrian's remark drew the attention of Simon Grimshaw from his own correspondence. "Not more debts, is it, Ford? I thought you paid off the last of those ages ago."

"I did." Ford kept his tone offhand, yet deep inside in rankled to be reminded of the debts that had driven him from his homeland to this tropical purgatory.

So much had happened since then and he had changed so much from that foolish, feckless youth, it often felt like another lifetime. But when thoughts of Laura Penrose stirred his smouldering outrage over her betrayal, it seemed like only yesterday. The letter on his lap had brought all that back like a fresh blow to an unhealed wound.

He had been betrothed to her and deeply in love. Laura knew he could not afford to wed until he inherited his cousin's title and estate and she had agreed to wait. Then one day, Ford had received a terse note breaking their engagement and informing him she intended to wed his cousin Cyrus instead. The jilting alone had been hard enough to bear, but there was worse. By marrying his cousin, Laura had also jeopardised his expectations. If she'd borne Cyrus a son, Ford would never have inherited the title and estates that had been in his family for centuries. What tormented him worst about her betrayal was the poisonous suspicion that she had only used him to ingratiate herself with his wealthy cousin.

"If not your debts, what is it about then?" demanded Hadrian in a deep voice, rich with the cadence of his native Durham. He was a big man whose tightly coiled power and fierce nobility reminded Ford of a tiger on the prowl.

"It isn't bad news at all." He rubbed the edges of the thick paper between his fingers to reassure himself it was real. "Quite the contrary. This letter is from a London solicitor who begs to inform me that my cousin Cyrus died over a year ago, leaving me to succeed him as Lord Kingsfold."

"Congratulations, your lordship!" Simon rose from his seat and bowed to Ford. Though not quite as imposing as his two partners, he had the pragmatic toughness of a tested survivor. "I say this calls for a celebratory drink."

He headed off to fetch the bottle, favoring his left leg as he often did at the end of a long day.

Meanwhile, Hadrian stared at Ford with one dark brow arched. "I suppose from now on you'll expect us to tug our forelocks and address you by your proper title, your *lordship*?"

His partner's wry levity shook Ford from his bitter brooding. "Why, of course," he quipped. "Though, as a token of particular favor, you needn't fully prostrate yourselves on the floor."

"You are too kind, exalted one." Hadrian gave a mocking chuckle.

They were still engaged in deprecating banter when

Simon reappeared bearing three glasses and a bottle of potent Batavia arrack. "I was so elated by your good fortune, Ford, I did not think to offer my sympathy on the death of your cousin. Were the two of you close?"

"Not really." Ford took the glass Simon offered him. "Cyrus was older than my father, so I thought of him more as a distant uncle. A solitary old codger."

Not so solitary that he'd been able to resist the flattering attention of a pretty young woman, but foolish enough not to realise she was only after his fortune. Had Laura feigned the least show of grief when her husband breathed his last? Or had she celebrated *her* inheritance with a glass of something more bubbly and expensive than arrack?

Simon uncorked the bottle and poured a liberal measure of clear, yellow liquor into each of their glasses. Back in England the stuff was in great demand for compounding *rack punch*, but Ford and his partners preferred it undiluted.

"What will you do now?" asked Hadrian as Simon handed him a glass. "Sell up and get out of trade? Sail home and forget you ever knew how to work for a shilling?"

Ford fixed his partner with a level stare. "I shall never forget that, I hope."

Work had been his salvation—an opportunity to prove he could succeed at something. It had provided a welcome escape as well. His aim had been to work so hard every day that he would collapse upon his bed in exhausted sleep, before bittersweet memories or dashed dreams had a chance to haunt him.

Though hard work had made him rich, it had failed to break Laura Penrose's pernicious hold upon him.

Whenever he caught a stray whiff of orange blossoms, his nostrils flared and his breath raced. Whenever he heard the strains of certain music, an ache of longing gnawed at his flesh. And whenever he'd lain with a woman, he could not prevent himself from picturing Laura in his arms.

"I *do* intend to go back to England," he continued. "For a while at least. I shall need to put my affairs there in order. We have often talked about opening an office in London. This might be the right time."

Ford did not tell his partners the other reason for his return to England, though he had been planning it for years, hoping this opportunity might arise. He recalled his long voyage of exile, his heart and pride mauled to such tatters that he'd yearned to hurl himself overboard to escape the pain. All that had saved him from despair was his unquenchable thirst to reclaim everything that had been stolen from him.

Bolting a drink of the fiery liquor that tasted like potent rum laced with rice wine, Ford pondered his plan.

By forcing Laura into marriage, he would regain control over the fortune she'd inherited from his cousin— a fortune that should have been his. Once he possessed her, the last tangible symbol of his youthful failures, once he bedded her to sate seven years' thwarted desire, she would no longer exercise her infernal fascination over him. His life and his heart would be his own again.

Hadrian lifted his glass in a toast. "This just might be the right time to open a London branch of Vindicara Company. I don't trust those smarmy Whitehall diplomats not to hand Singapore over to the Dutch in some treaty or other. We need to be ready if that happens."

"And until it happens," Simon raised his glass, "we keep on making money hand over fist."

They all drank to that.

"Speaking of money," said Hadrian as Simon refilled their glasses, "when you go back to England, will you take some for my brother? Now that Julian's out of school and reading law, it's time he thought about standing for Parliament in the next election. A seat in the Commons doesn't come cheap."

"I'll be happy to do whatever I can for your brother." Ford had often wondered why his partner never spent a penny on himself. Any profit Hadrian did not plough back into the company went to give his brother the best of everything money could buy. Though he and Ford never spoke of it, perhaps they'd both sensed a secret hunger in each other. The wealth they'd worked so hard to secure was only a means to some deeper end.

"Since you mention it—" Hadrian leaned back in his chair and regarded Ford gravely over the rim of his glass "—perhaps once you're settled, you might use your connections to help Julian find the right sort of wife."

By now Ford had drained his second glass of arrack and was feeling a trifle less guarded than usual. "And what sort might that be? I am hardly one to give sage advice about women."

Hadrian considered for a moment. "One with good breeding and useful connections who can help him rise in the world. Sturdy enough to bear lots of strong sons, but pretty enough that he won't mind bedding her to breed them. Above all, see that he steers clear of fortune hunters."

Ford's hand clenched around his glass. "I can give you my word on that."

He would do everything in his power to put young Northmore on his guard against women like Laura Penrose.

With a rumbling chuckle, Hadrian drained his glass. "No need to settle everything tonight, though, is there? It'll be months before the winds shift to take a ship back to England. Anything could happen by then."

His partner's words sent a chill of dread down Ford's spine. Cousin Cyrus had been dead for more than a year already and it would be a further nine or ten months before Ford could hope to reach England. What if, in that time, his cousin's widow cast off her transparent charade of mourning to wed another old fool for his fortune?

If that happened, Ford feared he might never be able to free himself from her thrall.

April 1822

"Please, Mama, you need to eat more." Laura whisked the cover off the plate she was holding and leaned over the bed to wave a dish beneath her mother's nose. "Dear Mr Crawford caught this lovely trout not three hours ago and fetched it here expressly to tempt your appetite."

And perhaps hoping he might catch a glimpse of Belinda? Much as Laura appreciated his gift, she wished Sidney Crawford would conquer his bashfulness and propose to her sister. Then they could afford to eat fish as often as they liked, purchase the occasional new gown, and perhaps take Mama to Bath for a course of waters.

Best of all, her family could vacate the house that had been their home for almost seven years, before its new master returned from abroad to evict them. Laura would give anything to avoid an encounter with the man who'd once promised to make her his wife only to abandon her in her hour of need.

"How kind of the…dear boy." Mrs Penrose struggled to pull her frail frame into a sitting position. The effort made her gasp for breath. "You are all…much too indulgent…of a troublesome…invalid."

"Nonsense." Laura tried to ignore the stark evidence of how much her mother's health had declined during the past winter. "Nobody goes out of their way to give *less* trouble than you."

Sometimes she feared Mama would like to slip away from life altogether and be no more bother to anyone. Laura would have moved heaven and earth to grant her mother any wish but that.

Having caught her breath, Mrs Penrose inhaled the succulent fragrance rising from the plate. "It does smell good. And Cook has prepared it just the way I like— poached in a very little water, without rich sauces to smother the delicate flavour."

Laura gave a rueful smile. Did Mama truly believe Cook possessed the necessary ingredients to compound a rich sauce even if she'd wanted to?

Perhaps so. Even when Papa was alive, she'd had a remarkable ability to overlook anything that threatened to dim her rosy view of the world. Now her air of fragile bemusement made the entire household conspire to shield her from any unpleasantness. That protective conspiracy was growing harder to maintain as the number of such worries grew month by month. Laura did not have the luxury of pretending all was well. A faint sigh escaped her lips as she set the dinner tray in front of her mother.

Mrs Penrose glanced up with a look of vague but fond concern. "Are *you* feeling quite well, dearest? You look tired and you have grown thinner over the winter. I know how hard it must have been for you since poor Cyrus died."

"It has been a long winter." Laura avoided mentioning her late husband for fear her tone might betray her true feelings.

Even with the hardship his death had brought upon her family, she was happier as Cyrus Barrett's widow than she had ever been as his wife. No doubt it was wicked of her to harbour such feelings, but after the way he'd treated her, she could not summon a jot of sincere grief for the man.

"But spring is here at last," she added. "That is the only tonic I need. Now, eat Mr Crawford's trout before it gets cold."

They had survived the winter, Laura reminded herself with a faint glow of pride. Now that the nights were growing milder, she and her sisters would no longer have to share a bed for warmth. The kitchen garden would soon yield vegetables and herbs to augment their rations.

But spring might also bring a less welcome event. The winds of April and May often blew ships from the East Indies to England's shores.

As her mother took a tiny bite of fish, a brisk knock sounded on the door.

"Come in," Laura called, a hint of wariness tightening her voice.

The door swung open and Hawkesbourne's butler, Mr Pryce, strode in with an unaccustomed bounce in his step. A wide smile lightened the usual solemn dignity of his features. "My lady, Master Ford…that is, *Lord Kingsfold* has just arrived! He is waiting in the drawing room. I told him I would summon you at once to welcome him home."

Laura tried to form a reply, only to come over as breathless as her mother had been a few moments ago. A tempest of contradictory emotions raged within her at the prospect of facing the man who had forsaken her after she'd naïvely given him her trust and love.

If her family had not been dependent on her for their survival, she would have taken great pleasure in denouncing Ford Barrett for his past behaviour. But she did not have the luxury of venting her hurt and anger. For the sake of her mother and sisters, she would have to behave with as much civility as she could muster. A man with so few scruples surely would not hesitate to turn her family out of *his* house if she provoked him. But if he expected to find her the same helpless, gullible girl he had abandoned seven years ago, Lord Kingsfold would soon discover his mistake.

What in blazes was going on?

Ford wrenched open the heavy window curtains to let a little light into the drawing room. Its murky dimness made the linen-shrouded furniture look like a party of musty-smelling ghosts. Had the whole place been shut up for the winter while Laura gadded off to London or the Continent?

If so, she must have returned recently. The moment he'd entered the house, the faint scent of orange blossoms had beguiled him with the most vivid awareness of her. She seemed to hang about him, no more than a breath or a kiss away.

Even before he could demand to see her, Pryce had bustled off, saying he must fetch her ladyship to welcome the new master. At least that provided satisfactory answers to Ford's most pressing questions. Laura was in residence and she had not yet found a new husband. During his voyage home, he'd been haunted by the possibility that remarriage might place her beyond his power. How could he have endured it, if she'd slipped through his fingers again to continue plaguing him for years to come?

The soft patter of approaching footsteps made Ford feel like a volcano—his core of seething emotions encased in a shell of cold, hard self-control. He dared not erupt, as he longed to do, spewing accusations and reproaches. Even a hint of his true feelings might make Laura flee. And that would spoil all his plans.

So he steeled himself to withstand the sight of her and betray nothing of the fury that smouldered inside him. The years he'd spent struggling to make his fortune had given him plenty of practice. Indeed, he owed much of his commercial success to his skill at concealing his emotions. But nothing in the past seven years had tested his iron self-control as severely as his first glimpse of Laura.

She entered the room carrying a candle. Its light glinted over her fair hair, which had darkened to a shade that reminded Ford of sweet cider. Most of it was pinned up in soft ripples, but a few stray curls clustered around her face like the kisses of a gentle lover.

The moment she crossed the threshold, she swept him a low, formal curtsy. "Welcome home, Lord Kingsfold. You look very prosperous. You must have made gainful use of your time in the Indies."

Nothing she could have said would have whipped Ford's wrath up so quickly. It took all his self-control to school his tone to one of cool irony. "You sound surprised. Did you expect me to return from the Indies in rags? I will have you know, I amassed a considerable fortune during the past seven years."

"I congratulate you." Laura could not disguise the silvery glint of avarice in her eyes. "What made you leave all that behind and travel so far for the sake of a modest country estate?"

Did she despise the place? Was that why she had not hesitated to deprive him of it? "Hawkesbourne and the family title have always been more important to me than any amount of money, Lady Kingsfold. That sounds awkward, doesn't it? Perhaps you would prefer I call you something else?"

He could think of a great many things he would like to call her, none of them flattering.

His suggestion set Laura in motion. Or perhaps it was some menace in his stare that he could not fully conceal. She hurried about the room, lighting candles with the one she had brought. "We were once on friendly enough terms to call each other by our given names. Could we not continue?"

She still moved with rhythmic grace, as if every step were part of some bewitching dance. Once she ran out of candles to light, Laura came to stand a few feet in front from him and fixed him with an inquiring look. Jolted out of his bemusement, Ford recalled her question. Did she mean they should take up again as if the past seven years had never happened? Though that would play perfectly into his plans, the heartless audacity of her suggestion infuriated him. He paused for a moment, weighing his reply.

Meanwhile his gaze ranged greedily over Laura, comparing her present appearance with the golden ideal of his memory. He had once thought her eyes as clear and candid a blue as the summer sky. Now they were clouded with secrets, perhaps even capable of passionate storms. Her face was thinner than it had been, making her wide jaw look stronger. But her lips were as full and potently inviting as he remembered—like some succulent tropical fruit at the peak of ripeness.

"I must confess, I never think of you as Lady Kingsfold…Laura." He found it impossible to say her name without his tongue caressing it.

Though her features betrayed no sign that she noticed or cared, the flame of the candle she held suddenly flickered out. "I must apologise for offering you such poor hospitality. If we had known you were coming, we would have contrived something better."

The gall of the woman! Welcoming him into his own house when it was clear she considered him as welcome as the plague. No doubt she'd hoped he would stay half a world away so she could continue to play the lady of the manor at his expense.

"Perhaps you wish I had *warned* you of my arrival." Ford spoke more sharply than he intended. "So you could have contrived to be elsewhere."

"No, indeed!" A flash of distant lightning blazed in the summer sky of her eyes. It must vex her that he saw through her mask of courtesy to the disdain she truly felt for him. "Though I will admit, that is partly because I have nowhere else to go."

"You cannot mean that." Ford drew back abruptly and began to stalk around the room, circling her at a wary distance. "According to the solicitor's letter, you inherited all my cousin's personal assets, while the estate fell to me by entail. Surely a beautiful young widow possessed of such a fortune is at liberty to go wherever she wishes."

Damn! He had not meant to call her beautiful, even if it was truer now than ever. From there it was but a short, treacherous step to admitting her beauty affected him.

Laura refused to acknowledge his compliment. "I assure you, what I inherited from your cousin was no fortune and now it is almost gone."

Her words stopped Ford in his tracks. If she was telling the truth, what had become of his cousin's money?

Chapter Two

So Ford thought she'd been living in luxury on his cousin's fortune. Had he cultivated that belief to assuage any bothersome twinges of conscience over his past behaviour toward her?

Even from several feet away, Laura marked the sudden jump of his dark brows and the brief slackening of his tight-clenched jaw. This was not precisely the way she'd meant to surprise him. But it would do. Anything to jar him out of his frosty composure.

Perhaps then she might not feel quite so vulnerable in her own unsettled feelings. Her first glimpse of Ford Barrett after seven long years had flustered her even more than she'd expected. Not that he was the same ardent, charming young man she remembered. Time had changed him in many ways.

The pitiless Indian sun had darkened his skin to the color of a Barbary pirate's. The wild black curls she had once loved to twine around her fingers had been cropped to short, severe stubble. His mouth, once so mobile, was now set in an unyielding line. The years had chiselled his features into a visage of stark, savage beauty. Eyes, once the warm, soft green of new moss, were now hard and cool as jade.

Had all those changes been wrought by the passing years and his experiences in the Orient? Or had he always been such a forceful, ruthless man, while she'd been too naïve to see it?

"My cousin's fortune all gone?" Ford spoke in a bemused murmur. "How is that possible?"

His tone of disbelief galled her. Did he suppose she would continue to live in this decaying old mansion, crammed to the rafters with painful memories, if she'd possessed the means to go elsewhere? Did he imagine she would have stayed to be subjected to his mocking condescension?

Staring at him over the hump of a dust-draped *chaise-longue*, she refused to be cowed. "Losing money is a great deal easier than gaining it. Rising expenses. Bad investments. The years since the war have brought hardship to many in this country. Perhaps you were not aware of it, being so far away, in lands where luxuries are cheap and fortunes easily made."

Harsh laughter burst from Ford. "You have no idea what you are talking about."

His scathing tone reminded Laura so much of his cousin's, it made the flesh on the back of her neck prickle. The deep timbre of his voice, once a mellow caress upon her ears, now had a hoarse, raspy edge.

"Those items you consider luxuries may be cheap in the East, on account of being so plentiful. If cinnamon came from the bark of elm trees or cloves from the buds of myrtle bushes, no one in England would think them such rare extravagances. In the Indies, items you might hold of little value—iron cooking pots, glassware, printed cotton—are the costly luxuries."

Every word struck Laura like a stinging blow, driven by contempt and sharpened with ridicule. That Ford was correct in everything he said did not lessen the insult. That his handsome, arrogant presence over-whelmed her with such intense awareness made it ten times worse! She did not dare reply for fear of saying something so offensive he might take out his anger on her mother and sisters. She'd been relieved to discover he was wealthy, only because it meant he might not grudge her family houseroom.

Ford emerged from behind the draped *chaise-longue* and approached her with deliberate, intimidating steps. "As for my fortune being easily gained, you could not be more mistaken. There *are* opportunities in the East, but for a man to take full advantage of them, he must work hard, take risks and be ruthless when necessary."

As each word brought him closer, Laura stood her ground against his steady, menacing approach. On no account must she let Ford see how his nearness affected her. And how was that, exactly?

It filled her with alarm, of course—a sensation no less distressing for being so familiar. Though her husband had been dead for more than two years, her throat still tightened and her insides knotted whenever a man came too close to her. The faint whiff of spices that hung about him made her mouth water, while his air of tight-leashed power made her light-headed. When his glittering green gaze roved over her from head to toe, Laura's flesh prickled as if responding to a feathery touch.

She managed to stand firm. But that owed less to her resolve than to being caught between two contrary inclinations. Part of her itched to turn and flee from this formidable man while another part felt irresistibly drawn toward him.

Willing her voice not to tremble, she replied, "No wonder you made such a success of your ventures. Two of the three necessary qualities come so naturally to you."

Once he came toe to toe with her, Ford stopped, unable to advance further without knocking her down. As Laura glared up at him, he loomed over her, his gaze fixed upon her lips. Was it her imagination, or was he leaning toward her?

"Which two qualities might those be?" he demanded in a husky murmur.

Ford *was* leaning closer, inch by inch, forcing her to tilt her head back. If the candle in her hand had still been burning, its flame would have scorched the breast of his coat.

Her voice did not come out in the brisk snap she intended, but rather a breathless whisper. "Surely you can guess."

As his lips bore down on hers, Laura opened her mouth to protest. But before she could speak, a volley of girlish giggles erupted from the doorway.

"Pray don't let us interrupt!" cried her sister Belinda in a teasing voice.

"I believe we *must* interrupt," chimed Susannah, the younger of the two, "for the sake of Laura's reputation."

As Ford jerked back from her and spun about to face

her younger sisters, a wave of relief swamped Laura. But in its wake came a fleeting sting of frustration.

The sound of high, twittering laughter broke over Ford like a cold sea wave upon scorching sand. Jolted back to his senses, he shook off the bewitchment Laura had cast upon him. He turned toward her sisters with a vexing mixture of gratitude and annoyance.

"Who are you two snooping chits?" he demanded in a bantering tone. "And what have you done with the sweet little Penrose girls?"

His question was not altogether in jest. The sight of Belinda and Susannah drove home the reality of how long he'd been away and how much had changed. He remembered a coltish girl of barely fifteen and a child of twelve with oversized front teeth that had made her look like a little brown rabbit. In his absence, they had blossomed into a pair of lovely young women who had not yet lost their childish impudence.

"The Penrose girls?" A hint of turquoise mischief flickered in Susannah's eyes. "Those silly green gooses? We locked them in the west attic until they learn to flirt properly with young gentlemen."

Ford felt his mouth stretch upwards in an unfamiliar way while a strange sound rumbled up from his chest, stiff and hoarse from disuse. He marvelled at the effortless way Laura's sisters lightened his mood. While he bantered with them, the past seven years seemed to retreat like a bad dream from which he'd been relieved to waken. "I thought flirts were the ones who got locked away until they learned proper decorum."

Belinda shook her head, making her chestnut curls waggle. "I fear you are sadly behind the times, sir."

Both girls laughed, wrinkling up their pert little noses as their sister once had. It was a mannerism Ford had found particularly endearing. Now, as she brushed past him to stand behind her sisters, Laura looked as grim as any strait-laced spinster.

"Mind your manners, you two," she chided them with only the flimsiest veneer of jest, "or Lord Kingsfold may turn us out of his house. Is that not so, my lord?"

Behind her pretence of wit, Ford sensed fear and desperation. But the proud tilt of her chin issued a challenge. He was not certain how to respond. Nothing at Hawkesbourne Hall was what he'd expected.

"I said no such thing," he replied. "Your sisters are welcome to visit for as long as they wish."

"Visit?" cried Susannah as she and Belinda swooped toward Ford, each taking hold of one of his arms. "You're joking again, aren't you? We live here, of course, and so does Mama. How pleased she will be to see you again."

Belinda let out another infectious giggle. "I hope you won't turn us out before we've had a chance to hear about your adventures in the Indies. Did you ever see an elephant? Or a tiger? Did you eat lots of curry?"

"Too much." Ford strove to conceal his surprise at Susannah's off-hand announcement. How long had the girls and their mother been living at Hawkesbourne and why? "But just now, I could eat a whole tiger or a haunch of roast elephant. Join me for dinner and I promise to fill your ears with tales of the Far East."

"Dinner?" Laura looked as if he had demanded her

head on a platter. "Of course, you must be famished after your journey."

Casting a glance at her sisters, she nodded toward the drawing-room door. "Susannah go help Mr Pryce fetch in the master's baggage. Belinda, come with me to help Cook prepare dinner. We have the rest of those trout dear Mr Crawford brought. I hope fish will suit you, Ford, since we are fresh out of elephant?"

Her question made Ford grin before he could stop himself. It surprised him to discover she still possessed a spark of wit beneath her mask of cool restraint. A great number of things about her surprised or mystified him.

One minor mystery provoked him to inquire. "Who is this Mr Crawford who furnishes food for my table?"

"Only a kind neighbour," Laura replied as her sisters released Ford's arms and headed away with obvious reluctance. "Without his generosity, we would have had a poor meal to welcome you home."

Now that he thought of it, Ford recalled a Crawford family who occupied one of the neighbouring estates. They had made quite a fortune in the brewing business. "I suppose I should be grateful to him, then."

He did not feel grateful, no matter if the fellow filled his whole larder. He did not care for the fond way Laura spoke of their *kind neighbour*. Might his cousin's fortune-hunting widow have her eye on a fresh matrimonial victim?

That would never do.

What a disturbing encounter!

Laura's fingers fumbled as she tied on her apron. Prior to Ford's return, a stubborn corner of her heart had nursed the foolish hope that she would find him still the same eager, amiable man she'd once known.

But the cold, severe creature who'd confronted her seemed quite capable of turning his back on anyone who became an encumbrance or an obstacle. At first she'd questioned the flashes of hostility she glimpsed behind his mask of aloof restraint. After all, she'd never done anything but free him from an inconvenient obligation to her. Was he angry with her for marrying his cousin? What choice had he left her?

And why on earth had he tried to kiss her?

Laura wished she had some private time to puzzle it out, but at present she had her hands full trying to prevent Cook from having hysterics.

The poor woman was well on her way. "Lackaday! How am I to put a fit meal on the table for the new master with the larder so bare? Why did he not send word he was coming so we could have prepared things decent?"

Laura wondered that herself. Did Ford enjoy setting the household in an uproar and her life in turmoil?

"Don't fret." She patted Cook on the arm and tried to reassure them both. "His lordship has been away for seven years and finally come to the end of a long journey. Little wonder he wanted to get home without delay. Besides, he says he's very hungry, so he isn't likely to care what we put in front of him as long as it fills his belly."

"He complained about spicy food, too," Belinda piped up from the hearth, where she was adding a few scraps of coal to the fire. "So I doubt he'll mind plain fare."

Cook fanned her ruddy face with her hands, but seemed to be recovering her composure. "We do have the rest of Mr Crawford's trout and there's plenty of sprouts and carrots in the cellar. That still isn't much of a meal."

"I promised his lordship dinner within the hour," Laura muttered. "We have lots of eggs, haven't we? What about a batter pudding? I'll have Mr Pryce open the wine cellar. If we ply his lordship with enough to drink, he may not notice *what* he's eating."

"Have Mr Pryce fetch me a bottle of brandy while he's at it." Cook grabbed a copper mixing bowl and a long wooden spoon. "If I hurry, I can poach some pears for the sweet course."

Having finished stoking the fire, Belinda snatched a basket from its peg by the cellar door. "I'll go fetch the pears and vegetables."

For the better part of an hour, they chopped, stirred, filleted and fried. Meanwhile, Mr Pryce fetched bottles from the wine cellar, unlocked the silver chest and supervised Susannah as she set the dining table.

With only ten minutes to spare before the meal, Laura herded her sisters up the servants' stairs for a quick change of clothes.

"This is so loose in the bust," complained Belinda as she donned a gown that had once been Laura's. "If we must dress for dinner from now on, I'll have to take it in."

Susannah brushed one red-brown curl around her fingers. "Now that Ford has come back, perhaps we can all have new gowns that won't need to be let out or hemmed up or mended."

Her sister's delight at Ford's return made Laura's tightly suppressed feelings boil over. "Why should Lord Kingsfold spend money on new gowns for us?"

Susannah set down the hairbrush, then turned to fasten the buttons on the back of Belinda's gown. "Perhaps so his new sisters-in-law won't look shamefully shabby at your wedding. You are going to marry him, aren't you? When Binny and I caught the two of you in the drawing room, I thought he must have proposed."

"Proposed? What nonsense!" Laura turned away from her sisters, to hide her foolish blushes. "That would be the last thing on his mind, I'm sure. He hasn't set eyes on me in seven years and he didn't want to marry me then. Nothing about me has improved in the meantime."

Back then theirs had been a fairly equal match. She'd been a young lady of good family, though limited prospects. he'd been a young man with nothing but his expectations. Now she was a penniless widow with a family to support, well past whatever beauty she'd possessed in her youth. By contrast, Ford was more attractive than ever, in a dark, dangerous way, with a fortune and a title. He could have his choice of women.

Susannah gave a defiant sniff. "Are you certain Ford didn't want to marry you? As I recall, *you* were the one who broke the engagement to marry his cousin."

"You were a child then," snapped Laura. "How could you know anything about it? I only broke our engagement because he could not."

A gentleman was legally bound to stand by his offer of marriage, while a woman had the prerogative to change her mind. Laura wondered how any woman could insist upon wedding a fiancé whose feelings toward her had changed.

"Let's not spoil such a happy occasion by quarrelling," Belinda entreated the other two. This was not the first time she'd played peacemaker between her responsible elder sister and her rebellious younger one. "Ford is home at last and scarcely seems changed from how I remember him. No matter what his feelings for Laura, I'm certain he'll be hospitable."

Laura wished she could be so sure.

One thing she could not dispute—Ford's manner toward her sisters was altogether different from the way he'd treated her. When he'd bantered with them, she caught a bittersweet glimpse of the man she'd once loved. That had shaken her more than his earlier severity, which she'd been better prepared to confront. The last thing she needed were any of her old feelings for Ford complicating her life more than it was already.

Halfway through the main course and after three glasses of wine, Ford continued to ponder the situation he'd found at Hawkesbourne. Nothing was as he'd expected. His uncle's fortune appeared to be gone. Rather than revelling in the lap of luxury, as he'd imagined her, Laura was living under strictest economy with her sisters and widowed mother in a corner of *his* house.

Though this presented him with an unforeseen opportunity to compel Laura to wed him, marrying her would not restore the fortune he should have inherited. Perhaps he should cut his losses and forget the whole thing.

The hell he should! Seeing Laura again, more alluring than he had left her, Ford knew the debt she owed him was far greater than money.

He sat at the head of the long dining table opposite

Laura, with her sisters seated halfway down each side. The ladies made a pretty trio in spite of their ill-fitting gowns.

"Give my compliments to the kitchen, Pryce." Ford raised his wine glass. "This dinner is far superior to shipboard food. I cannot tell you how I have longed for the taste of plain, fresh English cooking."

All the same, it was rather humble fare for a baron's table. Well prepared, but not much variety. From what he could tell, there were only a handful of servants looking after the place, with Laura and her sisters acting as maids of all work. Her claims of poverty seemed genuine, but where had his cousin's money gone? Frittered away by a young bride with no thought for the future because she could always snare another rich husband? That was how Ford's stepmother had behaved, bringing his father to ruin.

"Cook will be most relieved to hear the meal met with your approval," replied the butler. "More wine, my lord?"

Ford shook his head. "I have already had more than I am accustomed to at meals. Perhaps for the ladies?"

Belinda and Susannah looked toward their sister, who gave a discreet nod. "Only a little, though. We are not used to taking wine with our meals."

Since Pryce must know that, Ford assumed the comment was meant to enlighten him. All through dinner, Laura had addressed her conversation exclusively to her sisters and the butler.

Not that she had much need to speak. Belinda and Susannah kept him busy answering questions about his experiences in the Far East. At first, he hadn't known quite what to say. He had never thought of his years away from England as anything but a sweltering perdition of work and festering bitterness. Yet the young ladies seemed fascinated by the most commonplace customs of those far-off lands.

"Do they drink wine in the Indies?" Susannah savoured a sip from her glass.

"Only the Europeans," Ford replied. "When I was in India, the local people drank sweet coffee or tea brewed in a mixture of milk and water. In Singapore, where I've been lately, many of the traders drink arrack instead of wine."

"Tell us more about how they dine in India," begged Belinda.

"Dinner is usually served around midday," said Ford. "After that, most people retire to sleep for an hour or two. Supper is served late in the evening."

"Sleep?" Laura sounded if she thought he was having a jest at their expense. "In the middle of the day?"

"In the *heat* of the day." Ford relished a flicker of satisfaction for having compelled her to address him. "I assure you, it is impossible to accomplish any useful work, then. The only thing you want to do is lie naked under your bed netting and hope you may escape to some cool place in your dreams."

A sudden vision of Laura lying bare beneath a flimsy drape of netting sent the sultry heat of the first monsoons sweltering through his flesh. What had possessed him to say such a thing, in the presence of her innocent sisters? He should never have let Pryce ply him with so much wine.

"Naked!" Susannah clapped a hand over her mouth to stifle a burst of giggles.

Laura stared down at her plate as if she had not heard

Ford's provocative remark. But even from the far end of the table, he detected a blush blazing in her cheeks.

"Bed netting?" Belinda shot her giggling younger sister a fierce glare. "Is that like bed curtains?"

"Rather like." Ford seized upon Belinda's helpful diversion. "But instead of the thick cloth we use to keep draughts out, they use very fine netting to let the air in but keep the insects at bay."

"Fancy!" Susannah stopped giggling as abruptly as she'd begun. "Now what about the elephants? You said you'd seen some."

"Mostly in festival parades. Then they are decked out in bright, colored silks and paint, with plates of gold hanging over their foreheads and *howdas* on their backs." In reply to their puzzled looks Ford added, "A *howda* is a sort of saddle for riding on an elephant. They can be quite elaborate, lacquered and gilded, with canopies to protect the rider from the sun."

That description invited more questions, which provoked more stories. The ladies seemed to hang upon his every word, including Laura. For the first time in seven years, he found himself making an effort to be sociable. To his surprise, it brought him an all-but-forgotten sense of enjoyment. Was it possible his experiences in the Far East had enriched him in more than material ways?

"India sounds so much more exciting than cold, dull Sussex." Susannah turned toward Laura. "Don't you wish you could have gone to India with Ford?"

"No indeed." Laura fumbled her spoon. "It may sound fine in stories, but I expect the discomforts and dangers far outweigh the pleasures."

Her sharp retort pierced Ford's high spirits and sent them plummeting to the ground. During his first years of exile, whenever he'd beheld a scene of exotic beauty, his first unguarded impulse had been to wish Laura could be there to share it with him. Her disdain for those brief, yearning moments was an insult to every tenderness he'd ever felt for her.

"Your sister is fortunate not to have lived in India." Though he addressed his words to Susannah, Ford directed a contemptuous sneer at Laura.

"Why is that?" She lifted her napkin and swiped it across her mouth. "Do you suppose I am a frail flower who cannot withstand harsh conditions?"

"No." He dismissed her suggestion with a thrust of his lower lip. "Because it is the custom in some areas to burn a widow upon the funeral pyre of her dead husband."

In unison, Laura's sisters gasped.

"How dreadful." She spoke in a cool, dismissive tone. "You must be weary after your long journey. We should not pester you with so many tiresome questions."

Before Ford could protest, she rose from her chair, beckoning to her sisters. "Let us leave his lordship to enjoy his brandy in peace."

Belinda scrambled to her feet at once, but Susannah gave a mutinous scowl and followed her sisters out of the room with obvious reluctance.

After they had gone, Ford tried to convince himself he was relieved to have a bit of peace and quiet in which to reassess his plans.

Laura had stolen his inheritance and he meant to find out what she'd done with it. If, as he suspected, she'd squandered it beyond his power to recover, he deserved compensation more than ever. He could imagine few forms of compensation more satisfactory than her presence in his bed.

Chapter Three

Two days after Ford's arrival, Laura found her mother holding court from her bed. Ford and the girls sat on either side while a vigilant Mr Pryce hovered nearby.

Feeling like an intruder, she was about to slip away when Ford suddenly glanced her way. She could not allow him to think he had the power to frighten her off.

"Are you hosting a party, Mama?" She affected a cheerful tone as she entered the room. "I hope too much company will not tire you."

"Quite the contrary, dearest." Her mother's voice sounded stronger. "I have not felt so well in months. Come and sit with the others. Ford was telling us the most amusing story about the time a pack of monkeys got into his baggage."

As Laura approached, Ford rose from his chair. A fast-fading smile still lit his dark features and once again she caught a glimpse of the man she'd loved. Even as a gentle ache swelled in her heart, the moment passed and he became a stranger once again.

An attractive, compelling stranger, but still a danger-ous enigma.

She wished she could keep a safe distance from him, the way she did at mealtimes with the long table and her chattering sisters between them. But there was only one chair left—the empty one beside his.

Warily, she sank on to it. "The poor man may soon long to sail back to the Indies to escape these constant demands for stories of his adventures."

As Ford resumed his seat beside her, his nearness overwhelmed her senses. The dark arch of his brows and the jutting crests of his cheekbones lured her gaze. Her skin prickled whenever he made the slightest movement, anticipating an accidental nudge of his knee. Every time she inhaled, the faint, spicy tang of his scent tickled her nose. Her ears strained to drink in his low, husky voice.

"Never fear," he replied, a hint of frost cooling his tone, "I would far rather *talk* about the Indies than return there any time soon."

"No indeed." Laura's mother regarded Ford with a doting smile. "You have been gone far too long. We couldn't bear to part with you again now that we've got you back."

The butler cleared his throat. "Since all the family is gathered here, Mrs Penrose, shall I fetch tea?"

"An excellent suggestion! The tea Ford brought has such a delightful flavor. I feel quite invigorated when I drink it. And I caught a whiff of gingerbread when Laura opened the door. Could you bring us some of that, too?"

"Delighted, ma'am." Mr Pryce beamed with pleasure. Just that morning, Laura has overheard him whistling while he polished the silver.

No doubt the poor man was happy to have a proper staff working under him again. One of Ford's first tasks as master of Hawkesbourne had been to authorise the hiring of several new maids, footmen, gardeners and stable hands.

"Ford," said Belinda, "Cook is in raptures over the sugar, tea and spices you brought from the Indies."

Susannah nodded. "And I am in raptures over the bolts of silk and cotton. Did you mean it when you said we could have some to make up new gowns for the summer?"

"Of course I meant it." Though Ford kept his attention focused on her sisters, Laura sensed his words were aimed at her. "I have never been one to make promises I do not intend to keep."

Like her promise to wed him? She bristled at the thought. If he had not wanted her to break their engagement, why had he not lifted a finger to stop her?

"Besides," he continued in a lighter tone, "I don't believe peacock-blue silk or sprigged organdy would look at all flattering on *me*."

They all laughed at that, including Laura, though it gave her heart a wrench because he sounded so much like the Ford she remembered.

Mama's pale blue eyes sparkled with curiosity. "Tell us more about this new British trading post. Sing-a-song?"

"Singa-*pore*, ma'am. I must say I preferred it to India. Not nearly so hot, though often quite sultry during the monsoons. The settlement is still rather primitive at the moment. Everyone is too busy establishing their businesses and making money to worry about amenities. Besides, it is likely the Dutch will find a way to get rid of Singapore. It poses a threat to their control of the lucrative China and South Seas trade."

"It sounds like an exciting sort of place," said Laura's mother.

Ford nodded. "It is a crossroad of the world with so many races and cultures all mixed together—English, Spanish, French, Chinese, Indian, Arab, Malay. I have learned to curse fluently in a dozen different languages."

Laura fought to contain her amusement. She had survived the heartbreak of losing her first love, the shock of her father's death and the ordeal of her marriage by encasing her heart in a protective sheath of ice. Ford's coldness only hardened her defences. But the warmth of his wit and kindness toward her family threatened to chip a web of tiny but perilous cracks in her frozen ramparts, making them prone to shatter.

A few minutes later Mr Pryce returned, bearing a tray laden with tea things and a plate piled high with spicy-sweet nuggets of gingerbread. While Susannah and Belinda tucked into those with exuberant relish, Laura took a guarded sip of her tea. Pleasant as these small luxuries were after months of frugal living, they came at too high a price to suit her.

Despite Ford's assurance that her family was welcome to *visit* at Hawkesbourne, she knew he must want her gone as soon as possible. Every time they'd spoken in the past two days, she had braced for him to raise the subject. With any other gentleman, she'd have been confident he would never turn out an ailing widow and her penniless daughters. But Ford had boasted of his ruthlessness and she knew from bitter experience that he was not a man to let other people's problems stand in the way of his plans.

When the others had finished eating, Laura rose from her seat. "Enjoyable as this has been, we must not tire Mama."

"No indeed." Ford shot to his feet so quickly his arm brushed against hers, sending bewildering sensations rippling through her. "I have an appointment with Repton to look over the accounts and review his running of the estate in my absence."

His sharp tone and piercing look made Laura wonder what this meeting with his man of business had to do with her.

"Pray excuse me, ladies." After a stiff bow, he stalked away, leaving Laura feeling as if the breath had been knocked out of her.

As he marched toward the office of Hawkes-bourne's estate manager, the devilish hot ache in Ford's loins began to ease. The slightest accidental brush against Laura was all it had taken to set him on fire. Of course that had only struck a spark to the fuel, which had accumulated splinter by combustible splinter as he sat beside her. Hard as he'd tried to ignore her by focusing all his attention on her mother and sisters, he had failed.

The mellow lilt of her laughter had made him long to drink it from her lips like sweet wine. The sidelong glimpse of her dainty hands had made him yearn to feel her fingers running through his hair. But why?

Much as he'd loved Laura Penrose seven years ago, he had not burned for her with such fierce intensity. Was it the time he had spent trying to forget her? Had the blaze of his outrage kindled this unruly passion? Or was it some streak of perversity that made him crave her because she had spurned him?

He had no time to ponder such riddles now, Ford reminded himself. There were more practical questions to be answered first.

"Tell me straight, Repton." He dropped into a chair across the desk from the estate manager. "How bad is it?"

If the condition of the Hall was any indication, Hawkesbourne must be deep in debt. Ford recalled Laura's mention of economic hardship after the war.

Repton's brow furrowed at the question. He was a slight, balding man with ink stains on his thumb and forefinger. "I beg your pardon, my lord? How bad is *what*?"

"The debts, of course," snapped Ford. "How much do we owe and to whom? You needn't be afraid to tell me. I have the resources and the energy to set things right."

"I'm sure you do, sir." Repton pushed a large ledger book across the desk. "But I don't know where you got the idea that the estate is in debt. You can see for yourself—though there are improvements needed, Hawkesbourne is quite solvent."

Ford scanned the neat columns of figures. Seven years ago, he would not have been able to decipher them. Now he had no trouble. Rents minus expenses yielded a modest profit.

"Then why was so much of the house shut up?" he demanded. "And most of the servants gone? The larder nearly bare?"

Repton closed the ledger. "I told her ladyship the house was part of the estate and should be maintained in a suitable manner at the expense of the estate."

Ford nodded. "You were quite right."

"Thank you, my lord." A look of relief lightened Repton's stubby features. "Her ladyship did not agree. She refused to have any money spent on the house apart from a few urgent repairs, the coal bill and salaries for the cook and butler. Without your authority, I could not go against her wishes."

Ford mulled over this information, not certain what to make of it. In a similar situation, his stepmother would not have hesitated to maintain herself in luxury at someone else's expense. "Did her ladyship offer any reason for all this?"

Repton shrugged as if the explanations of women made no sense to him. "She said it was enough that her family should live under your roof without your permission. She did not wish to be any deeper in your debt."

Ford fancied he could hear Laura speaking those words in a haughty tone that grated on his pride. Had she assumed he would fail in the Indies and not be able to afford the expense of maintaining her family? Did she think he would be too mean to extend them decent hospitality? Or did she have some other motive for playing the poor but proud widow?

"I am surprised my cousin did not leave her better provided for." Leaning back in his chair, Ford strove to make the comment sound casual. "I thought he had a fair fortune of his own."

Repton grimaced. "A man can go through a deal of money if he isn't careful."

"Cousin Cyrus always preached frugality to me." The old fellow had kept him on a tight allowance. If Ford hadn't borrowed against his expectations, he never would have been able to live the way a gentleman was expected to. "But I suppose keeping a young wife and all her relations can be quite an expense."

"Lord Kingsfold made her ladyship a very generous settlement at the time of their marriage," said Repton. "I believe she provided for her family out of her own allowance. At least, I never received any bills for their support."

"That's right, you administered my cousin's personal accounts as well as the estate's." Ford pretended he had just recalled the fact.

"I hope you don't think I failed in my duty." Repton sounded defensive. "Or abused your cousin's trust in any way."

"Nothing like that, I assure—"

"Because you would be welcome to review the accounts," Repton rattled on. "Everything is perfectly in order."

The offer was too tempting for Ford to refuse, though not because he suspected *Repton* of any underhand dealings.

"I'm certain it is," he agreed in a reassuring tone. "But if it would ease your mind for me to see the figures, I am willing to take a look."

"I would consider it a service, my lord." Turning to a shelf behind his desk, Repton drew out another ledger. "Perhaps you could assure her ladyship everything is perfectly above board. I tried to go over the accounts with her after his lordship died, but she found it very distressing to see how little money was left."

Rather than passing the ledger across the desk, Repton brought it around to Ford, opening it to a page dated 1815. He pointed to a very large disbursement. "There is the sum he gave her ladyship upon their marriage."

Three thousand pounds? Ford's eyes widened. "Have you any idea what she did with the money?"

"She did not entrust the handling of it to me, my lord." Repton's tone bespoke offence over Laura's decision. "Perhaps she has her own man of business in London, though to my knowledge he has never called at Hawkesbourne."

What *had* become of that money? Ford wondered. Surely Laura would not be living in such straitened circumstances if she had an amount like that at her disposal.

"As you can see, my lord, all was well then." Repton turned the page. "By the next year, however, expenses had begun to exceed income. Your cousin was obliged to dip into his capital to make up the shortfall."

Ford did not need to be told what a dangerous downward spiral that created.

"I urged economy and retrenchment." With a sigh Repton turned to the accounts for Cyrus's final year. "My warnings fell on deaf ears."

His cousin's fortune was gone. Ford no longer doubted it. The evidence was there in black and white. But that evidence raised more questions than it answered.

"You have been most helpful." Ford rose abruptly and shook the man's hand. "I am relieved to discover the estate is not in debt. I shall return tomorrow to discuss what improvements are needed."

Repton tucked the ledger under his arm. "I should be happy to discuss them now if you wish, my lord."

Ford shook his head. He needed some time to collect his thoughts. "Other matters require my attention just now, if you will excuse me."

He took his leave in haste, heading back to the house

through the neglected gardens that had once been his grandmother's pride. Now several newly hired gardeners were busy digging and pruning. Ford paid them scant heed as he trod the overgrown paths, lost in thought.

It seemed Laura had told the truth when she'd claimed her inheritance was a paltry one. What she had failed to mention was the handsome settlement Cyrus had made her before her marriage. Had she squandered that, too? Or had she squirrelled it away somewhere while she played at poverty for some devious reason he could not fathom?

Rounding a boxwood hedge near the east wing of the house, Ford came to a sudden halt. Ahead, he spotted Laura talking to a slender young man with ginger hair. She was smiling at the young fool in a way Ford had not seen her smile since he'd returned to Hawkesbourne.

His heart began to hammer against his ribs as if trying to batter its way out of his chest. A bubbling cauldron of acid seethed in his belly. Could *this* be the reason Laura had remained at Hawkesbourne feigning penury? So she could stay close to her next conquest, engaging his sympathy and assistance on her way to winning his heart?

Ford wondered if that was the reason for her thinly disguised hostility toward him. Perhaps Laura feared he would spoil her plans to secure a new husband.

She would soon discover he had plans of his own for her remarriage.

Did Sidney Crawford suspect her plans for him? Laura wondered as she kept their handsome young neighbour engaged in conversation, hoping Belinda might happen by.

"We so enjoyed the fish you brought the other day. Mama ate with a better appetite than she has all winter. Then when Lord Kingsfold arrived so unexpectedly, we were able to offer him a much better dinner than we could have otherwise. So I must thank you once again for your kindness."

She treated him to a fond smile. Mr Crawford was one of the only neighbours who had shown her family any kindness. He was also one of the few men around whom she felt somewhat at ease.

Her praise brought a blush to the young man's fair features. "I am always delighted to be of service to your family. I hope the fish agreed with…your sisters."

His hazel eyes shimmered with particular interest. How could Belinda persist in ignoring Mr Crawford's shy fancy for her?

"Very much so. Belinda praised its flavour to the skies and said how fortunate we are to have so thoughtful a friend in you." It was not an outright falsehood, just a touch of well-meant exaggeration to reward his generosity.

"D-did she?" The poor fellow's face grew redder. "I hope she…er…you…that is…your family will always think of me as a friend. I would do anything in my power to assist…all of you!"

Where *were* the girls? It was a lovely afternoon for a stroll before dinner, especially since Ford had engaged the new servants, leaving her and her sisters more time for leisure. The sound of approaching footsteps made Laura turn with an expectant smile.

It froze on her lips when she spied Ford striding toward them, his stern visage dark as a thundercloud. The brooding power of his approach sent a chill of fear quivering through her, but she held her ground as she scrambled to rally her composure.

"Ford," she cried as if he were the person she most wanted to see, instead of precisely the opposite, "come and meet our kind neighbour I told you about. Mr Sidney Crawford, may I present Ford Barrett, the new Lord Kingsfold."

"Crawford." Ford thrust out his hand with the swift force of a combatant about to inflict a blow. "I must congratulate you on your fishing skill. I should try my hand at angling again. It cultivates patience and vigilant restraint—qualities a man needs to achieve his aims in life."

"It is an honor to meet you, my lord." Poor Mr Crawford winced at Ford's powerful grip. "If you would care to indulge in a day's fishing, I'd welcome the company. Lord Bramber sometimes hunts with me in the autumn, but angling is rather too leisurely a pursuit for his temperament."

Mr Crawford's tactful assessment of the impetuous Lord Bramber coaxed back a remnant of the smile Ford's arrival had dashed from Laura's face. The young marquis and his two sisters lived at nearby Bramberley, an estate much older and grander than Hawkesbourne, but even more neglected.

Ford drew back his hand. "I will let you know if I find myself with time on my hands. Between making improvements to the estate and setting up a London office for my trading company, I expect to be much occupied. Now, if you will excuse us, I have an important matter to discuss with her ladyship."

Important matter? Laura did not like the sound of that any more than she liked Ford's curt dismissal of Sidney

Crawford. What if he should feel unwelcome at Hawkesbourne, and stop dropping by? Any possibility of a romance between him and Belinda would wither on the vine. Laura had been willing to let love take its course, but now, with the threat that Ford might evict them from Hawkesbourne, she needed to hurry matters along.

"Of course, my lord." Mr Crawford looked torn between his unease with Ford and disappointment at leaving without a glimpse of Belinda. His candid features were as easy to read as Ford's were inscrutable. "I should be on my way."

He bowed to Laura. "My lady. Pray give my regards to your mother and sisters. Tell Miss Belinda I am most gratified to hear she enjoyed the trout."

"Indeed I shall. I am sorry you did not have the opportunity to tell her so yourself." Laura fixed her lips in the brittle imitation of a smile as she waved Sidney Crawford on his way.

As soon as he was safely out of sight, she rounded on Ford. "Are you always so rude to people who deserve your gratitude? I remembered you being more polite. Or perhaps I deceived myself."

Ford shrugged. "Memories can be deceptive. I seem to recall your character rather different than I find it now. As for your precious Mr Crawford, I was perfectly civil to the man."

Laura sensed an insult in his remark about her character. "If that was civility, heaven spare me your insolence!"

One corner of Ford's mouth arched ever so slightly, halfway between a gloating grin and contemptuous sneer. "Be assured, my dear, if I mean to offend, you will know it."

His frosty tone told Laura she was anything but *dear* to him. Had she ever been? Or were her misty memories of their courtship only the delusions of a foolish girl? If by finding her *different*, Ford meant that she was more guarded, no longer given to blind trust or reckless affection, then she would consider it a compliment.

"What is this important matter you wished to discuss with me? Or was that only an excuse to chase Mr Crawford away?"

Ford gave a hoarse, mocking chuckle. "What devious motives you credit me with. I certainly do have a matter of importance to discuss with you." He offered her his arm with exaggerated formality. "Shall we wander the bluebell path as we talk? The flowers should be in bloom now."

Was he being deliberately cruel? Laura wondered, though she took his arm without voicing any objection. Or had she meant so little to him that he could forget he'd once proposed to her in the bluebell wood?

Even with all the layers of garments between her hand and Ford's arm, Laura could not ignore her disturbing awareness of his hard, unyielding muscle as they walked.

"Well?" she prompted him, eager to distract herself from the perverse rush of heat that swept up her arm to kindle an unwelcome fever in her body.

"Yes…well…" By the sound of it, Ford's mind had been elsewhere too. "Now that I have been back for a few days and taken measure of the situation, I believe the time has come to discuss your family's continued residence at Hawkesbourne."

So he did mean to turn them out! Though that dread

had haunted her since long before his return, Ford's abrupt mention of it staggered Laura. Her knees went weak, obliging her to cling tighter to his arm when she would rather have pushed him away with all her strength.

By now they had entered a coppice of beech trees, green with the bright foliage of spring. Rays of golden sunlight pierced the canopy of leaves to shimmer upon a breathtaking carpet of bluebells below. Neither the beauty of her surroundings nor the sweet woodsy perfume of the wildflowers had sufficient power to ease Laura's desperation.

After all it had cost her to secure a home for her family, she could not let Ford snatch it away from them. But what could she possibly do to prevent him?

Chapter Four

So this poised, aloof woman *did* care deeply about something after all.

As Laura tightened her grip on his arm, a strange jolt of exhilaration rocked Ford. He told himself it was only the satisfaction of discovering a weakness he could exploit.

Laura sounded anything but weak when she replied, "What is there to discuss? I told you my family does not possess the means to go elsewhere."

How sincere she sounded. Almost as sincere as on the day she'd professed her love for him, on this very spot. If only he'd been able to see through her lies as easily then as he could now. She'd promised to wait for him until he could afford to marry her, when all the time she'd only meant to sustain the charade of their engagement until she could worm her way into the affections of his wealthy cousin.

"What a shame Cyrus left you so ill provided." Hard as he tried, Ford could not keep the nettle of sarcasm from his tone. "But wait! What about the three thousand pounds he settled on you before your marriage? It was quite some time ago. Perhaps you forgot about it."

Guilt had never been written so plain as on Laura's ghostly pale face. For a moment she seemed too morti-fied to speak. Or perhaps the accumulation of lies on her tongue had finally turned it to stone. Ford waited with anticipation to see how she would answer his charge.

Then, as suddenly as they had blanched, her features grew livid. She snatched her hand away from his arm. "What do you know of my personal finances and how did you find out?"

How dare she cast *him* in the wrong after all she'd done! "The subject came up during my meeting with Repton. Perhaps you should have warned him your set-tlement was meant to be kept secret."

"It was meant to be kept *private*!" Laura clamped her arms tight to her sides, her hands balled into fists. "You had no right—"

"I have every right." Ford rapped out each word, like flint striking flint. "You gave me the right when you pleaded poverty to impose upon my hospitality."

For an instant he thought she might strike him with one of her clenched fists. He pictured himself grabbing her wrists to restrain her, pulling her close so he could stare deep into her eyes, then…

Just as his blood was pounding in his ears, Laura deprived him of his expected sport by subduing the flicker of passion he had roused.

Expelling a quivering breath, she clasped her hands in front of her and answered in measured tone. "You make it sound as if I lied about that. I did not. The money Cyrus settled on me is long gone. Do you suppose I would have allowed my mother and sisters to live as we have these past months if I had three thousand pounds?"

A ring of sincerity in her voice tempted Ford to believe her. But the way her eyes darted as she spoke told a different story. Ford was about to observe that he would not put anything past her, when he suddenly recalled the reason he had brought her here. Satisfying though it might be to expose her lies, he did not want to risk making her angry enough to thwart his plans.

Before he could find a way to back down gracefully, Laura provided him with the diversion he needed. "Besides, money is only one of the reasons my family has stayed on at Hawkesbourne, and not the most pressing, either."

Ford cocked one eyebrow. "What is the most pressing reason, pray?"

"Mama's health, of course. She has been bedridden for the past few years. Her doctor warned me that a move of any distance could do her great harm."

Ford did not doubt that, for he had seen the truth with his own eyes. Though Mrs Penrose had put on a brave show, he could tell her time was running out. "I am sorry to hear it."

"Then you will let us stay?" For the first time since his return, a genuine smile lit Laura's face.

Its luminous magic bewitched Ford. For a wondrous instant, he relived a golden moment from his past, when he had stood on this very spot preparing to propose to his beloved Laura.

The beginning of a bemused smile was all the encouragement she needed to continue. "We take up very little room. I promise we will stay out of your way and not be any trouble. In such a large house, you need hardly know we are there."

Her eager rush of words shattered the spell that bound him. Heartbreak, betrayal and bitterness stung him again like a swarm of angry wasps, their venom all the more potent for the fleeting reminder of what he'd lost. Though he could never get that back again, he would get *something* to compensate him.

"I should like to assist your family, of course." He steeled himself against Laura's dangerously convincing look of gratitude. "Though, for the sake of propriety, if I am to provide you with a home, I must insist upon doing it as…your husband."

He watched her face with greedy relish as his words sank in. Her eyes grew wide and her lips fell open in a faint gasp that brought him an almost sensual thrill of satisfaction.

"H-husband?" she repeated as if the notion never would have occurred to her in a hundred years.

Once the idea sank in, Ford was certain she would seize this opportunity, pretending to accept only for the sake of her family. No doubt that was how she had justified her marriage to Cyrus—the little hypocrite!

"Does it not make admirable sense?" He took care to contain his eagerness in case it might make her suspicious. "We were once betrothed, but you required a husband of greater fortune to provide for your family. Now I am in a position to assist them and you are free to remarry. Shall we make a match of it at last?"

Laura flinched, as if from a sudden blow. It surprised and vexed Ford that her dismay brought him so little pleasure.

What surprised him more was her guarded response to his proposal. "Why should you want to marry me if you do not love me? You don't, do you?"

If she had drawn a loaded pistol and held it to his head, Ford could not have felt more threatened than by that one simple question.

Of course Ford did not love her! What on earth had made her ask such a daft, pathetic question?

It must be the place, Laura decided as she awaited his answer. The soft rustle of a breeze through the beech leaves, the melodic trill of birdsong, the woodsy fragrance of bluebells all revived long-buried memories and threatened to thaw long-frozen feelings. Ford had not forgotten the significance of the bluebell wood. He had brought her here on purpose to propose once again. But why?

"Love? I am quite cured of such nonsense, as I'm sure you must be." His scathing tone reminded Laura so much of his cousin's, it made her bilious. "That is precisely why we *should* marry. Neither of us is blinded by bothersome romantic delusions. You need a home for your family and I would like an heir to keep Hawkesbourne in mine. Would I not be wise to wed a practical woman who knows better than to seek other things from me that I cannot give?"

His question sent a clammy chill through Laura. Five years of loveless marriage to a domineering husband had been more than enough to last her a lifetime. But an even more urgent fear seized her by the throat and squeezed.

"An heir?" she whispered. Hard as she strove to keep her composure, her lower lip trembled.

"Naturally." Ford's predatory gaze fixed on her lips.

"What our marriage may lack in the warmth of love, I trust it will make up in the heat of physical desire."

He leaned toward her, as he had in the drawing room on the day of his return. This time Laura tried to retreat, only to stumble over a tree root. As she fell backward, Ford seized her, pulling her toward him. His lips bore down on hers and took possession of them, igniting a volatile brew of passion and panic within her.

How many nights of her marriage had begun with a kiss only to end in curses and blows? Those memories haunted her, as she feared they always would whenever a man tried to kiss or touch her. And yet, Ford's overwhelming desire kindled an unwelcome spark of arousal within her. Pulses of wicked heat coursed through her flesh, searing fiercest in her breasts and loins. Her husband's attentions had never provoked such sensations. If they had, perhaps her marriage would not have been such a wretched failure.

What dismayed Laura even more was that she'd never had such a wanton reaction to the tender kisses she'd shared with Ford during their long-ago betrothal. How could her traitorous body now burn for a man who so contemptuously proclaimed he cared nothing for her?

Ford's body sizzled with raw lust.

He hadn't meant to claim a kiss from Laura *before* she accepted his proposal. But when she'd backed away, he could no more resist the temptation to follow her than a questing hound could ignore the scent of a vixen.

He could tell his mention of an heir had shaken her poised detachment. Her tremulous whisper when she'd echoed his words, the ripe color that had flamed in her cheeks and the provocative parting of her lips had aroused him beyond prudence and far beyond propriety. When he caught her in his arms to keep her from falling, primal urges overwhelmed his reason.

The dewy fullness of her lips yielded beneath his fervid kiss. His tongue sought to plunder her soft mouth of all its sweet secrets. There had been an element of desire in the feelings he'd had for Laura once upon a time, but nothing so hot and reckless as the hunger that now possessed him.

The sound of approaching footsteps and voices jolted him back to his senses. He released his hold on Laura, but not soon enough. A gasp and a giggle told him her sisters had seen them.

"Don't stop on our account!" Susannah sounded delighted to catch her sister in such a compromising situation. "I was just telling Binny how much more interesting life has become at Hawkesbourne since Ford got home."

"I don't know what you're talking about, Sukie." Belinda's quavering voice belied her words. "Ford and Laura must come to pick a nosegay of bluebells for Mama."

Ford bit back a burst of derisive laughter. So Belinda meant to protect her sister's reputation by pretending not to have seen them kissing? He was not about to let Laura off so easily. "As admirable an endeavour as that would be, I must own I had more selfish intentions in bringing your sister here. I have just asked her to marry me."

He ventured a glance at Laura to find her glaring at him. Was it the kiss she resented or the fact that he'd informed her sisters of his proposal? Both, perhaps. And yet, he was certain she'd responded to his kiss.

He had no time to ponder that riddle for Laura's sisters let out piercing squeals of joy and flew toward them.

"Proposed?" Belinda threw her arms around Laura's shoulders. "How romantic!"

"Congratulations!" Susannah seized Ford's hand and shook it vigorously. "No wonder you made such a success in the Indies. You don't waste any time going after what you want. I so admire a decisive man."

"Save your congratulations." Laura's voice slashed through her sisters' hearty good wishes. "His lordship may have proposed, but I have not yet given him my answer."

Susannah refused to be cowed by her sister's stern tone. "Not in words, perhaps. But I saw what you were doing just now, even if Binny pretends to be blind. Are widows permitted to accept passionate kisses from gentlemen they *don't* mean to wed, without losing their reputations?"

The audacity of her sister's charge seemed to strike Laura dumb. Her lips parted in the very way that had compelled Ford to take liberties with her a few moments before. They were even more tempting now—infused with deeper color and slightly swollen from the intensity of his kiss. If her sisters had not been present, Ford might have seized her in his arms again to take up where he'd left off.

"Of course Laura means to accept him!" Belinda grabbed her sister by the hand and pulled her back down the path. "But you mustn't spoil it by speaking for her." She called to Ford and Laura, "Forgive us for interrupting. We didn't mean to, truly."

As Ford spun about to confront Laura, she rushed past him after her sisters.

Caught off guard, he barely had wit enough to seize

her wrist. "Hold on a moment. You did not answer my question. Will you marry me?"

It was a far cry from his first proposal to her, all those years ago. He's held her hands gently in his then, and looked deep into her eyes, sealing their pledge with a soft kiss once she accepted. How could he ever have been so blindly trusting and hopeful?

"You gave me no opportunity to answer." Laura tried to wrench her arm away, but Ford held fast. "Your proposal was quite unexpected. I need time to think it over."

Time to seek *dear Crawford's* advice, hoping he might make her a better matrimonial bargain?

"I will give you one day to weigh the advantages of my offer," said Ford. "Now that I have returned to England, I am anxious to settle my affairs and get on with my life."

"Very well then." She shook off his hand and retreated out of reach. "Tomorrow you shall have my answer."

One day to weigh the *advantages* of his offer? Laura spun away from Ford and fled down the wooded path after her sisters. That would not take one *hour*.

By marrying him, she would secure a home for her family. Her mother would be well cared for in the comfort of familiar surroundings. Belinda could remain near Sidney Crawford, giving him time to work up the nerve to court her. Susannah would be able to go about in local society and mix with gentlemen of good family.

But how long would her mother live? A year, perhaps two. And her sisters? Laura doubted it would take much longer for them to be happily settled. Meanwhile she would face many more years of unhappy wedlock to pay for their temporary comfort.

The girls looked surprised when Laura caught up with them.

Susannah broke into an impish grin. "You made quick work of accepting Ford. And you were so certain proposing would be the last thing on his mind. *I* knew better, though."

"I haven't accepted." Laura gasped for breath. "I only asked for time to decide. Until then, I want neither of you breathing a word of this to Mama."

"Why wait if you mean to say yes?" demanded Susannah, who seldom gave her own actions much forethought. "You'd better not take too long or some other lady may snap him up. I'm sure either of Lord Bramber's sisters would have him before you could bat an eye."

Despite all her confused, often hostile, feelings about Ford, a bewildering qualm of distress gripped Laura at the thought of him married to someone else.

"It was because we interrupted you, wasn't it?" Belinda reached for Laura's hand and gave her fingers a gentle squeeze. "We spoiled the magical moment, so you want to recapture it later in private. How romantic that Ford proposed to you so soon. He's probably been yearning for you these past seven years. The moment he heard you were free, he flew to reclaim his first and only love!"

Her sister's cloying flight of fancy made Laura's gorge rise. She knew better than to indulge in such starry-eyed delusions about Ford's proposal. Not only did he no longer love her, if he ever had, the man now proclaimed love an absurdity he was incapable of feeling for any woman.

"Don't talk such nonsense, Binny." What she meant

to be an impatient demand came out sounding more like a desperate plea. "This isn't a fairy story and seven years is a very long time. A great deal has happened to both of us since we parted. We have changed and our feelings have changed—it is only natural."

Susannah scowled. "Ford's feelings cannot have changed a great deal if he still wants to marry you. Whatever your feelings, he's a vast improvement over your first husband. I think you'd be a fool to turn him down."

Before Laura could box her ears for her impertinence, Susannah flounced off toward the house.

"I do not care what you think!" Laura cried after her. "After this, kindly keep your opinions on the subject to yourself!"

"Don't mind her." Belinda's arms stole around Laura from behind. "She was too young to understand why you married Lord Kingsfold. I'm sorry if what I said before upset you. I'm certain Ford still loves you. A man cannot kiss a woman that way unless he feels something for her."

"Don't say that, Binny, please!" With a massive effort, Laura shored up her flagging self-control. Her sister was too innocent to understand that what Ford felt for her had nothing to do with love.

"Very well, if you don't want me to." Belinda sounded bewildered and a little hurt. "But whyever not?"

Laura refused to answer. Indeed, she refused to enquire too closely into her reasons. She feared if she did, she might discover some tiny, very foolish part of her wanted to believe it could be true.

Chapter Five

What was Laura playing at? Ford wondered as he watched her hurry down the wooded path away from him. Much as he hated to admit it, some part of him found perverse enjoyment in the challenge of guessing her motives and anticipating her next move. So far, she had defied his expectations at every turn.

Despite her barely concealed antagonism, he'd been certain she would seize the opportunity to secure another wealthy, titled husband. Especially when the plum landed in her lap with so little effort and an admirable excuse to accept. Yet in spite of her surprising response to his kiss, she seemed reluctant to wed him.

How could that be? Ford asked himself as he strode away through the beech coppice. After all, she'd married Cyrus—a full generation older and never a favorite with the ladies. But perhaps that did not signify. Cyrus was not his rival for Laura's hand. Young Mr Crawford, however…

That thought sent Ford in search of information from the one person at Hawkesbourne he dared ask. He found

Pryce, the butler, in the drawing room, supervising a troop of new maids and footmen as they swept, scoured, dusted and polished every visible surface.

Catching sight of Ford, the butler bowed. "May I be of service, my lord?"

"I have a few questions about our neighbour, Crawford." Ford made it sound like a trifling matter. "Does he call here often?"

"Not in a formal way, my lord. He does stop by now and then to pay his respects to Mrs Penrose."

Using the ailing mother as an excuse to get closer to the daughter. Ford's lip began to curl. "Have you any idea of his fortune? Does his family still own that brewery in Southwark?"

"Mr Crawford takes no active part in running it, but I believe the family maintains a share of the profits." Pryce mentioned a figure he'd heard bandied about in connection with Crawford's income.

Ford's brows shot up. No wonder Laura liked the fellow so well.

"What do you make of his temperament?" Ford thought the young fellow rather insipid. Not the type of man capable of making his fortune in distant, forbidding lands.

"Mr Crawford has been very kind to Mrs Penrose and the young ladies since the master died," replied the butler. "He often sends presents of game or fish. Sometimes fruit from his hothouse."

No question the fellow knew how to ingratiate himself. Him and his miserable fish! Laura had gone on as if they were the greatest delicacy in the world, procured by the most extraordinary effort. Meanwhile,

Ford's offerings of spices, silks and all the treasures of the Orient had scarcely merited an acknowledgement.

Pryce seemed to sense that his praise of their neighbor did not please Ford. "I have observed the young gentleman is rather backward in the social graces. Her ladyship is one of the few people with whom he converses freely."

Ford lowered his voice so the other servants would not hear over the scrape of scrub brushes and the slosh of water. "Do you reckon Crawford has any interest in her ladyship? Interest of a romantic nature, I mean."

"Oh, no, my lord," the butler answered, swiftly and emphatically.

But before the tension in Ford's body could ease, Pryce added, "Though now that you mention it, I often see them talking together. Her ladyship speaks highly of him and he goes out of his way to make himself agreeable to her."

The butler's observation prodded Ford's conscience. Since returning to Hawkesbourne, he had been rather severe with Laura. No more severe than she deserved, his embittered heart protested. Besides, she provoked him at every turn with her quiet defiance, her flagrant lies and her damned icy allure! His mouth tingled with the memory of their kiss, as if he'd just eaten a highly spiced curry.

Reviewing Crawford's attractions as a prospective husband, Ford found the list weighted far too heavily in the young man's favor. He feared if Laura told their neighbour that she was being forced into marriage, it might spur the young fool to make her a better offer.

He must give her no opportunity to go running to

Crawford. And, much as it irked him, he must put aside his gnawing resentment and make an effort to be more agreeable.

The person most likely to prevent her from accepting Ford's proposal was…Ford, himself. Laura pondered that bit of irony as she hurried to check on her mother. She was determined never to endure another marriage as wretched as her first, and Ford's manner toward her suggested she would be no less miserable as his wife than she had as his cousin's.

But what choice did she have if she wanted to protect her family? No more than when she'd been forced to accept Cyrus's proposal. She doubted Ford would turn them out of Hawkesbourne, if he were convinced they had no other resources. But it was obvious he did not believe that nothing remained of her marriage settlement. She might have persuaded him if she could have told him where the money had gone, but he was the last person she would dare trust with that terrible secret.

Long-suppressed memories stirred, threatening to torment her. When she eased open the door to her mother's room and discovered Mama's bed empty for the first time in years, her emotions overwhelmed her.

"Mama!" Laura rushed toward the bed, darting glances around the deserted room. Her stomach churned with panic and her heart raced like a runaway horse.

The muted sound of voices wafting up from the garden outside sent her flying to the window. She sank against it, faint with relief at the sight of her mother sitting in a wheeled garden chair, swathed in shawls and blankets. Ford was pushing it down a gravel path between the flowerbeds.

What was he trying to do—kill poor Mama? Laura marched out of the room and down the back staircase. Wrenching open a side door, she stormed out into the garden. Her footsteps crunched over the gravel path as she followed the indented tracks left by the wheels of the garden chair. Up ahead, she heard her mother cough.

Breaking into a run, she rounded the hedge so quickly she barrelled into Ford. The sudden, violent contact between them assaulted her with intense, unwelcome sensations. All her churning anger burst forth.

"What do you think you are doing?" She leapt back from him like a cat tossed into a water trough. "Bring my mother back inside at once! You had no right to drag her out here where she might catch a chill."

"A chill? Rubbish!" A glint of venom flashed in Ford's green eyes. "It is a mild day and I made certain your mother was well wrapped. Sunshine, fresh air and a change of scene will do her far more good than wasting away in that dark, stuffy room."

After all she had suffered to secure her mother's comfort, this arrogant man had the gall to imply that Mama was ill cared for? "How dare you say such a thing? What makes you think you know what my mother needs after being here less than a week?"

"Don't be cross with Ford, dearest." Her mother's frail protest halted the bitter torrent of words Laura had been about to unleash. "He asked me if I felt…strong enough for a walk in the garden. I thought how pleasant…it would be to smell things growing."

Laura's insides twisted in a knot of shame. No matter

how much Ford vexed her, it was no excuse to distress her mother. The fact that he had provoked her outburst made her resent him more. The possibility that he might be in the right was simply intolerable.

"Forgive me, Mama!" She flew to her mother's side, giving Ford as wide a berth as possible on the narrow path. "I was so alarmed to find you gone from your room that I lost my head. Of course you should come out and enjoy the flowers if you feel up to it. I only wish I'd been told so I would not have worried. Are you quite certain you're warm enough and not too tired?"

Before Mrs Penrose could answer, Ford did. "We have not been out more than ten minutes. I told your mother to let me know the moment she feels chilled or fatigued and I will take her back inside at once."

Though he spoke in a calm tone, Laura sensed answering hostility behind his composed features. In his level gaze she detected a hint of something unexpected. If she hadn't known better, she might have fancied his feeling slighted.

Refusing to acknowledge his words, she fixed her attention on her mother. "If you are quite comfortable, then I will leave you to your walk."

Mrs Penrose laid one delicate hand upon Laura's. "I should enjoy my outing so much more…if you accompanied us. I'm certain Ford would, too." She twisted about in the chair to offer him a wan smile. "He tells me you are considering a rather special request he made of you."

"Did he?" For her mother's sake, Laura strove to mask her exasperation. "I thought it was customary to keep such matters private until a decision had been reached. Perhaps Ford is used to different customs from the Indies."

"I am." Ford began to push the garden chair forwards at a leisurely pace. "In the East, a girl's parents negotiate all the details of her marriage before she is informed of it."

"And the bride has no say in the matter?" Almost against her will, Laura began to walk along beside. "Infamous!"

She caught Ford in a fleeting grin. He enjoyed goading her, the beast!

"Do not be so quick to condemn a tradition that has endured for centuries. Perhaps it is we English who are misguided in our willingness to base the commitment of a lifetime upon the passing romantic fancies of callow youth."

So that was all he'd felt for her—a passing romantic fancy? Though Laura fought to stifle her emotions, her eyes stung and her throat tightened. Cyrus had used almost those exact words seven years ago, when he'd insisted his cousin had no deeper feelings for her. For the longest time, in spite of mounting evidence, a stubborn corner of her heart had refused to believe it. Now she felt as if Ford had reached into her chest and ripped out that last sliver of dogged faith.

"I am surprised," he added, with callous disregard for her feelings, "that a woman of your admirable prudence should not perceive the merits of arranged marriages."

"My dear Ford," Mrs Penrose chided him with gently, "you sound so severe one might believe you were in earnest. You men take such delight in teasing your sweethearts. Laura's father was just the same when we were courting."

Ford gave a rich, rustling chuckle that seemed to

confirm her mother's charge. Laura thought it more likely he was mocking Mama's naïveté. "If I must not tease my sweetheart, what should I talk about, ma'am?"

"Why not tell us about your plans for improving the estate. I'm certain my daughter will be as interested in hearing about them as I am."

Ford glanced toward Laura. "Would you?"

By now she had regained sufficient composure to look him in the eye. But she still did not trust her voice. Instead she replied with a curt nod.

"Very well then." Ford launched into a discourse on animal pasturage, fruit cultivation and drainage, which Laura hated to admit she found fascinating.

From the time she'd come to Hawkesbourne, the tenants had always treated her with respect and kindness. She'd watched with helpless dismay as Cyrus had neglected the estate. If Ford's ideas helped put more acreage under cultivation, or increased crop yields, those hardworking people she'd come to know and admire would prosper.

Several questions slipped out before she could contain them. To her surprise, Ford answered readily, with no hint of condescension.

"How did you come to know all this?" she asked at last, grudgingly impressed by the breadth of his information.

He shrugged. "I had to do something with my time on the long voyage home. I bought every book I could find on the subject of agriculture and studied them. When I found out one of the other passengers had been the overseer of a plantation in India, I quizzed the poor fellow until he was heartily tired of my company."

For the first time since his return, Laura compared

the *new* Ford to the old and conceded an improvement. The old Ford would have rather spent the long voyage playing cards or drinking with his fellow passengers than pouring over books about agriculture. But what would his tenants make of Ford's innovations?

She was about to observe that Mama had been outdoors long enough when Ford suddenly turned the garden chair down a side path that led back to the house. "Time to take you back inside, Mrs Penrose. I do not wish to exhaust you on your first excursion, or your daughter might forbid us going out again."

A sharp retort rose to Laura's lips, but she bit it back, not wanting to upset her mother or to give Ford the satisfaction of baiting her again.

When they reached the house, Ford scooped Mrs Penrose out of the chair and carried her to her room while Laura ran ahead to open doors. Hard as she tried, she could not deny her intense awareness of his strength and vitality. Neither could she ignore the unexpected gentleness with which he treated her mother.

"There." Ford set Mrs Penrose on her bed. "Your face has a bit more color. The next fine day, I shall take you out again. In fact, I believe we should move you to rooms on the ground floor to make it easier for you to get out. I shall arrange it at once."

When he had gone, Laura removed her mother's bonnet and shawls and tucked her in. "I hope the outing did not weary you."

"Only a trifle, dearest." Mrs Penrose seemed to wilt once Ford had gone. "But what does that signify? I would rather spend my strength enjoying a pleasant time once in a while than let it ebb away doing nothing."

That was the closest her mother had ever come to voicing a complaint or admitting the gravity of her condition. It sank Laura's spirits. Could Ford be right about what was best for Mama?

She drew the window curtains closed. "I will leave you to rest, then."

"In a moment." Mrs Penrose patted the bed beside her. "First come and sit with me. Have you made up your mind about Ford's proposal?"

"I still have a few more hours to decide." A feeling of futility welled up in Laura, as if she were being pushed toward the edge of a high cliff. The harder she struggled to escape, the more pressure Ford brought to bear upon her.

"What is there to decide, dearest? It sounds like the answer to a prayer."

Answer to a prayer? Of course her mother would see it that way. But then, she had said the same thing about Laura's marriage to Cyrus. Instead it had proven to be a devil's bargain.

There was no help for it, though. She had no choice but to accept Ford's offer. That did not mean she would tolerate the kind of abuse from him that she'd endured from his cousin. Cyrus knew things that had given him a terrible power over her. But she knew something about Ford that would give her a weapon to resist him if he ever tried to hurt her. She only hoped he would never force her to use it.

Laura was about to cut him down to size—Ford sensed it as surely as an impending summer storm.

She lingered at the dining-room door after her sisters had excused themselves and the servants cleared the last few dishes. No doubt she intended to tell him all the things her mother's presence had prevented her from saying that afternoon. Well, let her! He did not care how she insulted or raged at him. It amused him to bait her into losing control of her emotions while maintaining a firm hold on his.

Though, truth to tell, he had not meant to provoke her by taking her mother for a walk in the garden. He pitied poor Mrs Penrose, being slowly suffocated by her daughters' concern.

Steeling himself against Laura's hostility, he raised his brandy. "Have you decided to join me in a drink?"

"No. I have two things to tell you." Laura pushed the door shut and stood with her back to it. "I want to beg your pardon for the way I spoke to you this afternoon. Mama enjoyed her outing, which seems to have done her no harm. Her color is better than I have seen it in a great while."

Prepared for criticism, Ford found it hard to hide his surprise at Laura's frank, sincere apology. "I…never meant to alarm you."

He could not bring himself to say he was sorry. That would be an admission he'd done something wrong, which he had not. Neither would he promise to consult her in future. That would seem to be asking her permission. Unlike Cousin Cyrus, who might have indulged his young wife, Ford was determined to be master of his house.

"What is the other thing you wish to tell me?" The moment the words left his lips, he knew. Laura was about to give him her answer. His gut tightened. What if she refused?

Inhaling a deep breath, Laura tilted her chin to a

resolute angle. "After considering your proposal, I have decided to accept. As you say, it will be a most…convenient arrangement."

"Very good." A gust of elation swelled Ford's chest. "I shall set out tomorrow for Lambeth to procure a special licence. We can be wed before the week is out."

"No!" Laura's hand flew to her bosom, fingers spread protectively. "That is, I see no need for such a rush. My first wedding was a rather…hasty event. This time I want banns read and our neighbours invited to the wedding."

Banns? That would require the vicar to announce their impending marriage on each of the next three Sundays. "Do you think it appropriate to make such a public fuss over a marriage of convenience?"

"Why not? You said we should get married *for the sake of propriety*. What could be more proper than having banns read in the local church and all the neighbours witnessing our nuptials?"

She had him there. Ford acknowledged it with a rueful nod. He had waited seven years already. What would a few more weeks matter? It would give him time to anticipate and savour his approaching victory.

Rising from his chair, he walked slowly toward Laura. "Shall we seal our betrothal with a kiss?"

A flicker of alarm leapt in her eyes. For an instant Ford thought she might turn and flee. But why? In every other situation, she had stood up to him, refusing to be intimidated. Why did the prospect of physical contact between them unsettle her so? Did she find him repulsive? She hadn't used to.

"A kiss?" she repeated in a tremulous whisper. Then in a firmer voice she added, "Of course…if you wish."

"If I *desire*," Ford murmured. "And I do."

An arm's length away from her, he stopped. "Since our last kiss was a rather hasty event, I believe we deserve a proper one this time."

Their kiss in the bluebell wood had taken him unawares—shaken him out of his accustomed restraint. This time he was determined to maintain control no matter how powerful the provocation.

His gaze riveted on Laura's lips, he reached up to cradle her chin with his fingers. Then he moved closer and lowered his face to hers, tilting her head to meet his approach. She resisted the firm pressure of his touch just enough to stoke the heat of his desire. And when his lips hovered over hers, ready to claim them, the rapid gust of her breath whispered against his skin. He raised his other hand to stroke her neck, relishing the mad flutter of her pulse beneath his fingertips.

With a sigh of anticipation, he played his lips across hers, barely making contact, savouring the silky friction when he did. Half a dozen times he brushed her mouth, increasing the pressure of each one by a minute degree. On the final pass, he felt her lips part slightly. A bolt of searing satisfaction ripped through him, igniting a fire in his loins.

His control threatened to slip away, but he clung to it with grim determination. Extending his tongue, he eased the hot, wet tip into the narrow fissure between her lips and slowly pried them open. When at last he gained entry to the sultry cavern of her mouth, he explored, caressed and tasted Laura to her delicious depths.

The wicked hum of lust in his veins urged him to tug up her skirts, fumble open the buttons of his breeches and take her there, up against the door. All that stopped him was his fierce resolve not to lose control and a troublesome remnant of tenderness he had thought long since purged from his heart.

An even more troubling thought slithered into Ford's mind, piercing his triumph with sharp fangs and injecting noxious venom. Laura might have promised to marry him, but that was no guarantee she would. Perhaps she only wanted this month-long betrothal to give her time to secure a husband more to her liking. And what if her true motive for wanting such a public wedding was so she could humiliate him before all his neighbours?

Breaking abruptly from their kiss, he wrenched open the door behind her and growled, "Away with you. Go!"

Chapter Six

Did Ford want her or not? Laura asked herself as they drove to church on Sunday morning with her sisters. A few days after their bewildering betrothal kiss, the only question that perplexed her more was whether she wanted him. After the other night, it seemed the answer might be…yes.

Buried beneath stifling ashes of fear and mistrust, nearly quenched by shame, an ember of desire smouldered within her. Whenever she remembered Ford's deep, brandied kiss or the restrained intensity of his touch, that ember threatened to set her on fire.

How had Ford felt about their kiss? She stole a sidelong glance at him as her sisters chattered on about some harmless bit of local gossip. As usual, his harshly handsome features betrayed nothing of what he might be thinking or feeling.

What had made him push her away when his passion had reached at its sizzling peak? Could her reluctance have repelled him as it had Cyrus? She felt like a fool, understanding so little about men after five years of marriage.

Without any warning, Ford spoke. "I have decided to host a ball to celebrate our engagement."

"A ball?" Susannah squealed, clapping her hands. "How splendid! Laura never breathed a hint of it to us, the sly minx."

"That is because I knew nothing of it until this moment." Laura tried to stifle her annoyance. Would it have been too great an inconvenience for Ford to ask her wishes in the matter?

She appreciated his kindness to her mother and admired the effort he was making to improve the estate. But when he arranged matters to suit himself without consulting her, it made her feel as controlled and powerless as she had been with Cyrus.

"I expect Ford wanted to surprise you," suggested Belinda, putting a pleasant face on the situation, as was her habit. "I should enjoy a ball, though we haven't any ball gowns that aren't years out of fashion, nor proper dancing slippers. I fear our shabbiness would disgrace him."

"That would never do." Ford's firm mouth tightened in a frown of mock-gravity. "I can abide anything but disgrace."

Though Laura knew he meant nothing by the quip, his mention of *disgrace* still gave her a qualm. If he ever guessed the disgrace she could unleash upon him if she chose, he would treat her with far more consideration.

"I reckon I have no alternative," he continued, "but to bring the three of you along to London when I go there on business this week. While I look for suitable premises and hunt up the brother of my partner, you ladies can shop for ball gowns, wedding wear and my bride's trousseau."

There he went again, arranging *her* life without the slightest regard for her wishes.

"We cannot all go away and leave Mama," Laura protested. "And how are we to pay for all these new clothes?"

Perhaps with the three thousand pounds he refused to believe she no longer had?

"I have already discussed the idea with your mother," replied Ford with vexing good humour. "She thinks it will do you all good to get up to London for a few frivolous days. As for the bills, have them sent to Hawkesbourne. By the time they arrive, we will be married and I will pay them gladly."

He had discussed it with her mother, but not mentioned it to her? Laura wished she could believe Belinda's explanation, that Ford had planned the ball and the trip to London as surprises he hoped would please her. But it felt more like he was forcing her every move. Wasn't it enough that he was compelling her to wed him? How much worse would it be when he gained a husband's power over her?

Before she could raise any further objections, their carriage came to a halt in front of the old parish church, St Botolph's. The solid sanctuary of ivy-covered Horsham stone dated from Norman times.

Laura sensed many eyes upon her and Ford as they took their seats in the right-hand front pew, which generations of Barretts had occupied before them. Across the aisle sat the other noble family of the parish, the Dearings. The young Marquis of Bramber was not in attendance, but his great-uncles, Lord Edward and Lord

Henry, were there along with his sisters, Lady Artemis and Lady Daphne. The latter, a vivacious little beauty with wide blue eyes and golden curls was a particular friend of Susannah's.

Laura had never managed to strike up a close acquaintance with the proud, reserved Lady Artemis. Though the two sisters shared a certain similarity in their fine features, their overall looks were as opposite as a glittering ray of sunshine and a cool, shimmering moonbeam. Lady Artemis was tall and slender, with raven hair, alabaster skin and striking violet eyes.

This morning she looked across the aisle and acknowledged Laura with a polite nod. Or had that been meant for Ford?

Susannah's warning echoed in Laura's mind. *I'm sure either of Lord Bramber's sisters would have him before you could bat an eye.* Despite her conflicting feelings about Ford and her reservations about marrying him, jealousy wrung Laura in its tight, possessive grip.

Following the Second Lesson, the curate mounted the lectern and spoke in a loud voice. "I publish the Banns of Marriage between Ford, Lord Kingsfold of Hawkesbourne, and Laura, Dowager Lady Kingsfold of Hawkesbourne. If any of you know cause, or just impediment, why these two persons should not be joined together in holy Matrimony, ye are to declare it. This is the first time of asking."

A furtive murmur stole through the sanctuary after the banns were read. Though Laura pretended not to hear, her ears tingled furiously. She could imagine what was being said. Censorious whispers had dogged her ever since she'd come to Hawkesbourne, as Cyrus Barrett's hastily wed young bride, with her dependent family in tow. She'd hoped her decorous conduct over the years might improve their neighbours' opinion of her. Now she wondered if that had been wishful thinking.

Once the service concluded, a throng of neighbours surrounded Ford at the church door to welcome him home and offer congratulations on his betrothal. Shunted aside by the crush of people jostling to speak to him, Laura drifted into the churchyard where she found Sidney Crawford standing off by himself.

She could not help notice the longing looks he cast in Belinda's direction as her sisters engaged in animated conversation with Lady Daphne. "I think my sister looks especially pretty this morning, don't you?"

"I have never seen her anything less than beautiful." The words seemed to burst out before he could stop them. "I beg your pardon, my lady! I meant no offense."

"None was taken, I assure you." Laura edged a little closer to him, lowering her voice so as not to be overheard. "I am certain Belinda would be delighted to hear of your admiration."

Before he had a chance to respond, Ford's voice rumbled behind them. "Congratulating my fiancée, are you, Crawford?"

It was a perfectly civil question, but the tone held a sharp edge of menace. Drat the man! Did he have to discourage the one neighbour willing to offer her a kind word?

Mr Crawford turned pale. "J-just so, my lord. I must congratulate you, as well, on your fine choice of a wife."

Bobbing a hasty bow, he fled.

Ford gave a most infuriating chuckle. "A nervous fellow, your Mr Crawford. I get the feeling he doesn't much like my company."

He offered Laura his arm, but she ignored it, marching back toward the carriage. Not caring whether Ford heard her, she muttered, "He is not the only one."

So Laura did not care for his company? Ford fumed as his carriage rolled north over the High Weald toward London. She flattered herself if she thought it mattered to him! The only reason he'd brought her along to London was to keep her away from Sidney Crawford while he was absent from Hawkesbourne.

The way the two of them had stolen off for a secretive tête-à-tête in the churchyard the moment his back was turned had put him on his guard. Crawford's nervous behaviour and abrupt exit were clear signs of a guilty conscience. Laura's reluctance to come to London and her undisguised irritation at having her chat with Crawford interrupted were clear evidence she was up to something.

Not that any one would suspect it, seeing her now. Ford cast a sidelong glance at his betrothed, dozing peacefully with her head lolled against his arm. Her scent made him fancy he was sitting in the midst of an orange grove on a sultry night with all the trees in bloom. She looked a picture of angelic innocence with a single golden curl tumbled over her brow. How deceiving appearances could be.

If she planned to deceive him again, as she had seven years ago, she would not find him as easy a mark as she had then. He was no longer a love-blinded young fool without influence or resources. He *would* get her to the altar this time and he *would* get her into his bed, if it meant spending a fortnight shadowing her every move.

Gradually the muffled clatter of horses' hooves and the rolling of the carriage wheels lulled Ford to sleep.

A while later, he woke with a start, uncertain how long he'd been dozing. Quite a while, it seemed, for the view out the carriage window showed them to be on the outskirts of Southwark.

Laura was still asleep, her head resting against his shoulder, the way it never would have if she'd been awake. On the opposite seat, Susannah slept, slumped against Belinda, who stared out the window, a tear sliding down her cheek. When she heaved a muted sob, Ford realised that was what had woken him.

"What's the matter, Belinda?" He kept his voice low so as not to rouse her sisters. "Are you ill?"

She shook her head slowly. "I just saw h-home…I mean, the house where we grew up…for the first time since we left. A cousin of Papa's lives there now. His horrid wife could hardly wait to get her hands on it."

Ford craned his neck to catch a glimpse of the Penrose house. He recalled a long-ago day and a sour-faced woman answering his frantic enquiries about Laura.

"I'm sure I don't know where they've gone. She's made a fine match to some rich, old lordship. Perhaps she had him take her on a bridal tour to Paris to spend all his money." The woman had sounded frankly envious of Laura's good fortune. Every word from her sneering lips had struck a blow to Ford's fragile hope that Laura's tersely worded letter breaking their engagement was some preposterous mistake.

Those wrenching memories hardened his bitterness, shoring up the weak spots Laura had begun to sap in his defences.

He continued to gaze out the window as the carriage turned on to a familiar stretch of Harleyford Street. But something looked different.

"What became of your father's place of business?" he asked Belinda. "There is a new building where it used to be."

"It was destroyed." Belinda wiped the tear from her cheek. "By the fire that killed Papa."

"I didn't know. I'm sorry."

"Of course, you were abroad then." Belinda lower lip quivered. "It was a terrible time. We were afraid the shock would kill Mama. Then having to give up our house so quickly. I don't know what would have become of us if Laura had not married Lord Kingsfold and offered us a home with them."

Ford reeled as if she'd just struck him in the face. Before he could collect his scattered wits, the carriage hit a deep rut in the road, jarring the two sleepers awake. Laura abruptly pulled herself upright.

Susannah stretched and rubbed her eyes. "Where are we?"

"Newington," said Belinda. "Near Elephant and Castle."

"I can't wait to see the city again!" Susannah peered out the carriage window at one of the busiest intersections south of the Thames. "I can scarcely remember the last time I was here. Is anyone else hungry? I hope they give us a good supper at Osborne's."

Ford scarcely heard her; his mind was spinning with

questions that his brief conversation with Belinda had raised. He watched Laura out of the corner of his eye as the carriage made its way up London Road, past the obelisk in the middle of St George's Circus, then across the Thames over Waterloo Bridge.

By the time they reached Osborne's Hotel, nestled in the elegant Adelphi Terraces, Ford's curiosity had intensified to a burning itch.

Scarcely able to master his impatience, he secured accommodation for their party, then turned from the front desk, offering Laura his arm. "I could do with a breath of air and a chance to stretch my legs. While our luggage is being unloaded, let us take a stroll along the promenade in front of Royal Terrace. It has a fine view of the river."

Susannah eagerly endorsed the idea and Belinda pronounced herself willing to go along with whatever the rest decided. They were soon walking along the wrought-iron-fenced terrace overlooking the Thames.

It was a fine spring day with a fresh breeze blowing from the west. The great river bustled with watercraft of every size and kind. Susannah flitted about the promenade, towing Belinda by the hand, first pointing east toward the great dome of St Paul's, then west toward the austere dignity of Whitehall, exclaiming over them as if she had never seen either before. Ford suspected her show of vivacity might be for the benefit of two swaggering young bucks who were also enjoying the view.

Ford and Laura stood at the eastern end of the promenade, peering out over the line of slender, spiked railings that enclosed the Adelphi's lofty terrace. Down on the river, spritsail barges ferried bumpers of coal and barrels of wine to the wharf below for storage in the great arched vaults. The bustle reminded Ford of Singapore when the great junk fleet arrived from Amoy. It made him unaccountably nostalgic for the place.

Though he had not appreciated it at the time, he now realised his life there had been enviably straightforward with nothing to do but work hard and make his fortune. He'd been fired with such righteous certainty then, not nagged by doubts and taunted by conflicting needs, as he'd been from the moment he arrived back at Hawkesbourne and seen Laura again.

He stared across the Thames at the Southwark bankside. "Why did you not send word to me of your family's plight when your father died?"

That was almost as much a betrayal of him as her hasty marriage to his cousin. He wanted answers from her. He deserved them and he *would* get them.

"Who told you about that?" Laura's arm fell slack in Ford's, as if all the bones had melted out of it. "And what makes you bring it up now?"

"I noticed a new building where your father once had his office. Belinda told me he died in a fire there. Why did I have to wait seven years to get that information from your sister?"

"I see no sense in dredging up the past." She'd spent seven years doing her best to forget. She had no intention of exhuming those horrible memories just to satisfy Ford's tardy curiosity. "What happened cannot be changed. The reasons no longer matter, if they ever did."

"You are wrong." He clung tighter to her arm. "The past lays a foundation for the present and the future.

How can one hope to build anything solid and lasting without knowing what sort of groundwork it rests upon?"

"Then perhaps you should have made the effort to ask your questions seven years ago. If you start digging now, everything you have built on those foundations may come tumbling down." She tried to walk away from him, to avoid further questions by taking refuge with her sisters.

Ford refused to release her. "Is that some kind of threat?"

"I threaten you?" Laura stared pointedly at his large, brown hand clenched around her slender, gloved wrist. "That would be a fine turnabout."

Ford released her arm. "No threats, then, just plain answers. Tell me what happened. How did the fire start? Was your father killed trying to fight the blaze? Why was your family left with no resources?"

Laura struggled to master the turbulent feelings his questions roused. She had once longed to tell him everything he now demanded to know in such a peremptory manner, and a great deal more besides. But his questions were seven years too late.

The last thing she wanted now was to relive those wretched days.

"Please," she begged him as she had once begged Cyrus for his help, "I cannot bear to talk about what happened. It is too painful."

Besides, she could not risk letting something slip that might expose long-buried secrets. Secrets that would destroy her family. Secrets that had already cost her a high price to keep hidden.

"Was what happened so painful it made you jilt me

to marry my rich cousin?" Though Ford had released her arm, his fierce gaze bored into her.

"Why does it matter to you now, if it did not then?" Laura demanded. "Were you so relieved to be rid of the burden I'd become that you did not care why I had such a sudden change of heart? If you did not want me to marry Cyrus, you might have tried to prevent it. But you didn't. Explain that to my satisfaction and I might answer *your* questions."

She stared into his face, frozen into a stern mask of chiselled dusky marble. It did not give her the slightest indication of what he might be feeling.

"You were the one who broke your promise, remember? I owe you nothing. Least of all an explanation for my behaviour, which was perfectly correct." With that, he turned his back on her and walked away…just as he had done seven years ago.

The next evening, as Ford, Laura and her sisters walked the short distance to the Adelphi Theatre, his thoughts churned with questions and doubts. He'd scarcely slept a wink the previous night for thinking about the few things Laura had told him and the many things she hadn't. After what she'd done to him, he was entitled to an explanation at the very least. Why would she not give him one? Were the events of seven years ago truly so painful that she could not bear to recall them? Or was she hiding something? All the instincts he had honed in the cut-throat world of Indies trading assured him she was.

But recent events had presented a possible explanation. Much as Ford wished to dismiss it, he could not.

"Were you able to find suitable premises for your business, Ford?" Belinda's question roused him from his restless brooding.

"I…looked at quite a few." His mind had not been on the task, though. "But none satisfied all my requirements. Some had wharf and warehouse, but no proper counting house or office. Others had office and warehouse, but no wharf to unload goods. In a busy port city, dock space is at a premium."

"Then wouldn't it be cheaper to unload your goods at some other port?" asked Laura. "Southampton or Portsmouth or Dover, then bring them overland to London?"

Her remark caught him by surprise until he recalled the interest she'd taken in his improvements to the estate. Perhaps now that she'd agreed to wed him, she wanted to make certain he continued to prosper, unlike his cousin. "The trouble is, all those ports are a good seventy miles away from London. Cartage costs money, too."

Thinking she might be offended by the tone of his reply, he added, "It might still be worth making enquiries. There could be more savings to using a port other than London. Labour and such."

"Must we talk about tiresome business?" Susannah complained as they entered the theater. "Did you find that young man you were looking for, the brother of your business partner? Is he handsome? Agreeable?"

"I did locate Julian Northmore at his lodgings in the Inns of Temple." Ford paid for the best box available and collected playbills for the ladies. "He invited me for a glass of wine at the Grecian Coffeehouse. He's well enough looking and seems tolerably agreeable."

"Then why didn't you invite him to the theater with

us tonight?" Susannah demanded as if his stupidity confounded her.

"Mind your manners, Sukie!" Laura snapped. "Is it not enough Ford has brought us up to London to have new gowns made and take us to the theater? Must he spend his business hours recruiting beaux for you as well?"

For once Susannah looked duly chastened. "I beg your pardon, Ford. I do appreciate all your kindness. It's just that I don't get to meet many young gentlemen out in the country. Lord Bramber hardly ever comes down from London and I know better than to suppose a marquis would look twice at me. Even if Mr Crawford did pay attention to anyone but Laura, he's so backward."

Susannah's mention of his kindness and Sidney Crawford in the same speech stung Ford's conscience. It was not kindness that had compelled him to bring the ladies with him, but mistrust and suspicion. "I did invite young Northmore to our engagement ball. I thought the presence of an extra gentleman might not go amiss."

"Splendid!" Laura's sister squealed. "I can hardly wait to meet him!"

By now they had reached their box. Belinda and Susannah were about to settle into the two back seats, but Ford waved them forwards. He wished to speak with their sister while their attention was focus elsewhere.

The minute they were seated, she forestalled his questions with one of her own. "Did you find young Mr Northmore very much like his brother?"

Ford shook his head. "About as much as you and Susannah. They both still have a trace of the Durham dales in their speech and there is a certain resemblance of feature. The brother is a fine-looking fellow, but there's something bland about his looks. Hadrian Northmore is anything but bland."

"And in character?" said Laura. "That is where Susannah and I differ more than in our looks."

"It is the same with the Northmores." Ford had thought so often as he talked with Hadrian's brother. "The young fellow seems to think of nothing but his own amusement. He would not let me in until I told him his brother had sent me with money. *Then* he could not have been more cordial. Hadrian makes him a liberal allowance, yet he has managed to run up debts—gambling, drinking and wenching. I'd wager ten guineas he hasn't read a brief or attended a session of court in months. It disgusted me, to think of him squandering the opportunities his brother has worked so hard to provide him. The young whelp isn't even grateful. He went on and on about Hadrian controlling his life."

"He does not sound like the sort of fellow I would want courting Susannah." Laura glanced toward her sisters, who were busy peering around at the rest of the audience. "Why did you invite him down to Hawkesbourne for the ball?"

"Because I promised his brother I would do my best to help him get on. I will not go back on my word just because the task is more difficult than I expected." The way her father's death had made Laura break her promise to wed him. "Besides, people can change. I did and perhaps Julian Northmore will, too, with proper encouragement."

He hoped the young man would not need to lose everything that mattered to him before he reformed his habits. And what had happened to Laura to bring about such an alteration in her?

More to himself than to Laura, he murmured, "I don't know why Hadrian is so set on making his brother into a great man when he has already achieved such success himself. But it is all he thinks about and works for. I would hate to see him thwarted because young Julian prefers to waste his life in dissipation."

His voice trailed off as the curtain opened and the first play of the evening began.

"They sound like interesting men, these partners of yours," said Laura. "You must tell me more about them some day."

Loath to admit he did not know a great deal more about his partners, Ford gave a vague nod. Hadrian and Simon had seldom talked about their pasts, and were always quick to deflect any questions. Of course, they might say the same about him.

For so many years, he had brooded over his past, sharing his feelings with no one, not even those closest to him. Now an irresistible urge compelled him to broach the subject with Laura.

Leaning toward her, he whispered, "Julian Northmore is not much like his brother, but he reminds me of someone else I used to know."

She turned toward him, her dainty brows raised in a mute question. *Who?*

"On his own in London," said Ford. "Answerable to nobody. Blessed with unlimited credit and the society of questionable companions. Julian Northmore is far too much like *I* was at that age." It was not an easy thing to admit with her unsettling gaze upon him.

But he had an even more difficult admission to make. "I know why you did not turn to me for help when your father died and your family was forced from their home."

"You do?" A glint of alarm flashed in her eyes and there was an edge of bewilderment in her whisper.

"You thought I was too feckless to be of any assistance and perhaps too selfish to care." Ford struggled to maintain control of his features and his voice, so that nothing would betray the bitter sting that realisation inflicted.

Laura wrenched her gaze away from his, to stare down at the stage as if entranced by the ridiculous capering of the actors. That confirmed his belief more clearly than any words. He should let the matter rest, discretion warned Ford. His emotions were running too high. If he persisted, they might flare out of his control, revealing the depth of his bitterness. But he could not let it go, any more than he had been able to let go of her all these years, even when the memory of what he'd lost had driven him to the brink of despair.

Ford leaned close to whisper in her ear, "You were wrong, you know. I could have borrowed more money or taken work. I would have found some way to help your family if I'd known."

"Would you?" Laura kept her eyes fixed ahead and her voice pitched so low, Ford could barely make out her words above the dialogue of the play and the laughter of the audience. "How was I to believe that when I heard you'd gone off to gamble at Spa? Should I have pinned my family's survival on the hope that you'd won a great deal at the tables? Besides, I was afraid if I saddled you with all my family's problems you would soon grow to hate me."

"I was not at Spa to gamble!" Ford protested in a fierce whisper. "I promised you I would stop and I did. You should have believed that."

As his lips puckered and parted to pronounce the word *believed*, they grazed Laura's ear. That feather-light brush made her flinch as if stung by a bee.

She did not hesitate to sting back. "Perhaps I should. But you should not have been so quick to assume I wed your cousin to enrich myself. If you had sought me out to ask for an explanation seven years ago, you would have learned the truth. Instead, you sailed away to the Indies without a word."

Again, she swung about to fix him with her accusing gaze. "Admit it, you were relieved to be free of me."

Part of Ford yearned to bellow an adamant denial of that ludicrous charge at the top of his lungs, for the whole theater to hear. But that would be as good as admitting how deep her actions had wounded him. And he could not do that.

So he averted his face before she could catch a traitorous glimmer of the truth in his eyes.

Chapter Seven

An awkward chill still hung between Laura and Ford two nights later when she and her sisters dined with him at the hotel. Much as their whispered confrontation at the theater had stirred unwelcome memories and bewildering feelings, it had also brought Laura a vital sense of release and a hope of peace. Now that Ford knew she'd had a compelling, unselfish reason to marry his cousin and since he'd as good as admitted his secret relief at being rid of her, perhaps he would let the matter rest.

"Any luck today, finding premises for your company?" Belinda asked Ford as the waiter arrived with their dinner plates. "Or shall you have to come back another time to look again?"

Susannah greeted that possibility with an eager grin, which Ford's answer quenched. "I found something I believe will suit Vindicara. Two things, actually. Laura's suggestions about shipping into some other port gave me an idea. I was able to secure a fine wharf and large warehouse downriver at a very good price. Then I found a smaller warehouse with office space just a little way down the Strand. East Indies ships can offload cargo downriver, then goods can be brought to the West End by barge in smaller quantities."

Ford had acted on a suggestion of hers? Laura could scarcely believe it.

"Not a moment too soon." Susannah paused with her fork halfway to her mouth. "We've been drumming up business for you…at least Laura has."

"You have?" Ford appeared as surprised by her behaviour as she was by his.

"It was nothing." Laura concentrated on cutting her chine of beef to keep from meeting his gaze. "The mantua-maker went on and on about the silks we brought to have made up, what fine quality they were and how bright the colors. She asked if we'd bought it from any of the local mercers. Finally, to keep her quiet more than anything, I told her they were East Indian, imported by the Vindicara Company."

"That's not all," said Susannah. "She told the lady Vindicara would soon be opening for business in London and she would hear much more about the company then."

"Nothing like a bit of shopkeepers' tattle to attract customers." Ford reached for his wine glass and took a deep draft.

"You haven't heard the best part yet, Ford," said Belinda.

"There's more?"

Susannah gave a vigorous nod. "While we were talking about you to the mantua-maker, one of the other customers overheard and introduced herself. You'll never guess who it was."

One corner of Ford's mouth arched upwards. "I have no intention of trying, since you are clearly bursting to tell me."

"Mrs Paget!" cried Susannah. "At least I think that's the name she gave."

Ford shook his head. "The lady must be mistaken. I never heard of—"

"Your stepmother!" Susannah fairly glowed with satisfaction at revealing the surprise.

Ford looked as if he'd just had a heavy dinner plate broken over his head. Mrs Paget's announcement had staggered Laura, too. She knew Ford's mother had died when he was quite young, but never once had he mentioned his father's second marriage. She felt cheated out of information she had a right to know. Could that be how Ford felt, not knowing about her father's death?

Belinda hastened to fill the gaping silence that greeted Susannah's announcement. "Mrs Paget told us the two of you lost touch after your father died. But she remembered you very fondly and was so pleased to hear what a success you'd made in the Indies."

"I'm sure she was," replied Ford.

Laura thought she detected an edge of hostility in his tone. Clearly he had not cared for his stepmother. Mrs Paget spoke as if she'd doted on him even though he'd done nothing to assist her after his father's death. He had cut her out of his life, leaving the poor woman to fend for herself. Why, Laura wondered, should she believe Ford would have done any more for her family if she *had* appealed to him?

"Mrs Paget bade us give you her warmest regards," said Susannah. "She said if you would care to call on her, she'd be delighted to receive you. She gave us her address in Mayfair."

When Ford did not reply, Belinda added, "When we told her you and Laura were engaged, Mrs Paget said she would be honoured to attend your wedding to such a charming bride."

"Your stepmother seemed very cordial," said Susannah. "Are you going to invite her to the wedding, Ford?"

While the girls were speaking, Ford rose from the table, though he'd hardly touched his supper. Now he threw down his napkin. "Invite her to the wedding? Only if we lock up all the silver first!"

As he strode away from the table, Laura sat with her mouth half-open, exchanging bewildered glances with her sisters. It amazed her to discover there was someone Ford detested even more than her.

"Why do you hate your stepmother?" Laura's softly murmured query seemed to roll through the carriage box like a clap of thunder.

Ford half-expected it to rouse her sisters, but they continued to doze on the opposite seat. How he envied them! His fingers clutched a sheaf of lease documents so tightly, he feared they might never unclench again. He stared at the top paper, pretending to read, pretending he had not heard Laura.

"I am at a loss to guess the reason," she continued, undeterred by his silence. "Mrs Paget seemed pleasant, though rather...excessively cordial. She certainly seemed devoted to you, in spite of everything."

"That woman can *seem* any number of things," Ford growled before he could stop himself. "And what do you mean *in spite of everything*? What rubbish did that woman tell you about me?"

"Only what Susannah mentioned at supper last night—that the two of you lost touch after your father died, because she was obliged to make her own way in the world."

Outrage blazed through Ford. Despite his resolve to say nothing more on the subject, he could not hold his tongue. "That is surprisingly close to the truth, for her. We lost touch *before* my father died. She ran off with another man as soon as she'd spent all Father's money. Faced with losing her on top of financial ruin, he could not go on, the poor fool."

Ford clenched his teeth to keep from saying more. He had never spoken to anyone about all this and he had no wish to start now. Especially not with a woman he had reason to suspect of similar treachery. Though that suspicion had eroded in the past few days, memories of his stepmother threatened to revive it again, which was probably a good thing.

Laura lifted a trembling hand to her lips. "You mean your father...did away with himself?"

"No!" The denial burst out of Ford in an emphatic whisper. "Nothing that terrible, thank God. He just gave up. Began drinking more than was good for him, didn't eat properly, stayed out all hours. When he fell ill, he didn't even *try* to rally."

"I'm so sorry." Laura radiated a mixture of dismay and sympathy that made Ford wish he'd held his tongue, even as it invited him to unburden himself further. "How old were you?"

Though her question tempted him as powerfully as

her ripe beauty, he would not yield. "Ten when my father married Helena. Fourteen when he died."

"How hard it must have been for you having to witness all that while being too young to help. I wish I'd known."

Laura reached for his hand, but Ford jerked away, shuffling the lease papers he was determined to resume reading. He did not want her pity! Neither did he want to give up more of his secrets to her. How dare she pry into *his* past while being so guarded about hers?

Yet hard as he tried to hold back, he could not. "She used me, that grasping baggage! Father never would have married her if he had not been convinced I needed a mother. So Helena proceeded to ingratiate herself with me. I was too young and stupid to see through her deluge of attention."

That painful admission rung from him, Ford vowed it would be his last word on the subject. "There. I have answered your question. Now, I will thank you to let me get on with my reading."

"Very well," said Laura. "Only do not blame yourself for what happened. Your father was a grown man. He may have acted out of love for you, but you did not force him to marry Helena. Besides, it *is* possible that in spite of her fortune-hunting schemes, your stepmother truly cared for you."

Harsh laughter scoured Ford's throat. "I assure you, I have learned a thing or two since my gullible youth. Now I view all protestations of affection with a healthy dose of scepticism."

He made the mistake of glancing over at Laura, only to find he could not look away.

"I suppose you could never forgive what she did,"

Laura's eyes searched his. "No matter what the circumstances?"

Was she asking about Helena or herself? During the past few days, Ford had been forced to consider the circumstances that had led Laura to forsake him in favor of his cousin. By times, a flicker of sympathy had kindled in his heart as he'd imagined what it must have been like for her. But this moment, with the memories of his despised stepmother so painfully fresh in his mind, was not one of those times.

Forcing himself to ignore the wistful plea in Laura's eyes, he kept his features immobile as he shook his head. "I cannot imagine *any* conditions under which I would be willing to forgive her."

Ford's damning words ran over and over in Laura's mind as she walked briskly along a wooded path toward one of Hawkesbourne's tenant farms. Though he'd been speaking of his stepmother, she had no doubt his implacable resentment extended to her as well.

Ever since they'd returned from London, he had been more distant than ever. She would have given a great deal to know what he was thinking. Was he still brooding about the past? Or was he having second thoughts about marrying her? That possibility unsettled her more than she expected.

Laura slowed her pace as she approached the spot where her path cut across a drove road that had been trampled into the ground by centuries of hogs heading to market in London. The packed earth was nice and dry as she crossed over it and scrambled up the opposite bank. But troubling thoughts dogged her footsteps.

How would she feel if Ford jilted *her*?

He couldn't, of course. For a man to break an engagement was a *breach of promise*—a complete loss of honour and grounds for legal action. But if he had been able to change his mind and marry some other woman...? One younger and prettier, perhaps. More agreeable, less apt to take offence at everything he said or did. One without a dependent family.

She would be humiliated, of course, angry and resentful, even though she had not wanted to marry him in the first place. Even though she would be relieved to regain her freedom. Could that be how Ford had felt seven years ago, when he'd received her letter?

She asked herself that uncomfortable question as she glimpsed Appleshaw Farm through the budding orchard for which it was named. Spotting the farmer's wife taking laundry from the line, Laura welcomed the distraction from her disquieting thoughts.

"Good afternoon, Mrs Cooper!" she called. "I hope I have not come at a bad time."

"Never, my lady." The neat, capable little woman shook her head emphatically. "I just wanted to fetch this lot in before it gets washed a second time."

"Do you think it will rain?" Laura glanced up at the threatening sky with a grimace. "Then I had better keep my visit brief. I came to bring you a little token of thanks for your kindness to Mama this winter. Your chest poultice did wonders for her congestion and I fear she would still be coughing without your horehound tea."

It had been a blessing to find someone so skilled and caring near at hand when they could no longer afford the doctor's fees.

"It was no bother, my lady." Mrs Cooper hefted her brimming clothes basket and headed into the cottage. "Only sharing what I do for my own. Come in, rest your feet and wet your throat with a drop of cider."

A few moments later, Laura was seated in the Coopers' snug parlour sipping cider while the farmer's wife exclaimed over her parcel of sugar, tea and spices.

"Come see, Richard!" she called to her husband when he entered the cottage. "Isn't this a boon? These things cost so dear at the shops in Horsham."

When Mrs Cooper protested that the gift was far more than she deserved in exchange for a few home remedies, Laura shook her head. "I assure you, your assistance was priceless. Lord Kingsfold brought a whole shipload of such goods from the Indies. He says they are quite cheap there."

Mr Cooper gave a gruff chuckle. "I wish some of the ideas his lordship brought home with him were as sweet to swallow as this lot."

"Now, Richard—" Mrs Cooper shot her husband a warning look "—I'm sure Lord Kingsfold means well with all his plans for improvements."

The farmer looked doubtful. "No respect for the old ways. I run this place the way my father did and his father before him. We've always managed."

"I'm sure you have, Mr Cooper," said Laura. "I must admit I have been resistant to some of the changes his lordship has made up at the house. It is not always easy to accept a little well-meant interference when we have become accustomed to neglect."

Mrs Cooper nodded. "Remember, Richard, how you used to grumble about old Lord Kingsfold letting everything slide." She clapped a hand to her mouth. "Begging your pardon, my lady. I meant no offence to your late husband."

"Of course you didn't," Laura assured her, "and I took none. Please, Mr Cooper, will you try some of his lordship's new ideas? I know he can be rather...forceful at times. But I truly believe he wants to help his tenants prosper, as he has done."

What had come over her, Laura wondered, defending Ford and making excuses for his overbearing ways? Whatever their differences, she could not deny he was a better master and landlord than Cyrus had ever been. Since returning to Hawkesbourne, he'd worked tirelessly to reverse the damage done by years of his cousin's neglect.

But did he have the necessary qualities to be a better husband than her first? Laura was far less certain about that.

The farmer mulled over her words. "When you put it that way, ma'am, I reckon it never hurts to try. I'll say one thing for his lordship, the man has more energy than a steam-engine. Not much wonder he made such a success abroad. I'd be daft not to want a bit of that to rub off on my farm."

Seven years ago Ford had been full of energy and high spirits. Looking back, Laura had to admit that energy had not been well harnessed, but dissipated in idle amusement, like the young man he'd visited in London. Now it was channelled in productive ways that would benefit others.

After chatting a few more minutes with the Coopers, she glanced toward the window. "I wish I could visit longer, but I must be on my way if I am to reach home before it rains."

"My husband can harness the cart and drive you back to Hawkesbourne," Mrs Cooper offered.

"That won't be necessary." Laura tucked her basket back under her arm. "The way by road is much longer and I would not want Mr Cooper to be caught in the rain on his return. Good day to you."

Before she had walked a mile from Appleshaw Farm, Laura regretted refusing Mrs Cooper's offer. The angry clouds began to hurl fat drops of rain at the ground—a few at first, then faster and harder, until she was caught in a drenching downpour. It was no use going back, for her clothes were already soaked through. She would just have to press on and make the best of it, the way she'd done with so many other unpleasant experiences life had dealt her.

"A pox on all poets who wax lyrical about springtime in England!" she muttered, trudging over the soggy turf as rain dripped from the brim of her bonnet.

She had even more cause for dismay when she reached the drove road. The sunken track had now become a swift-flowing stream that cut across her path, far too wide to jump. The rain showed no sign of easing, but pelted down with a force that made Laura's flesh sting where it hit her.

Vexed with herself for not staying at the Coopers, she shrieked a curse that would have shocked her mother speechless. Having eased her feelings with that outburst, she decided to wade across the muddy torrent, though it would ruin her old walking shoes.

Then Ford's voice rang out over the tumult of wind

and rain. "If you must swear like that, you should do it in a foreign language."

He sounded almost cheerful. Did he find her predicament amusing? She looked up to see him sitting astride his horse on the opposite bank of the drove road.

"I could teach you a few in Malay," he offered. "Only I would be too embarrassed to tell you what they mean. Stay where you are. I'll fetch you."

His imperious command made Laura want to leap straight into the rushing water, but she managed to restrain herself. "What are you doing out here? Paying calls to antagonise your tenants?"

Ford did not heed her question as he urged his horse down the slippery bank and through the swirling muddy water, which came up past its fetlocks.

"Climb on." Ford held out his arm to her. "Quick, now, before the water gets any deeper!"

Bristling at his peremptory tone, Laura seized his hand and hurled herself into his waiting arms. As Ford caught her and swung her up in front of him, his left hand brushed against the bodice of her spencer. Beneath the light fabric, her nipples were puckered from the chill of the rain, keenly sensitive to his touch. Suddenly aware of how her light muslin dress clung to her body, nearly transparent, she tensed and focused her gaze straight ahead.

Once she was securely seated in front of him, Ford swept up the reins in his right hand, using his left to circle Laura's waist. With a jog and a tug, he urged the horse back up the opposite bank to higher ground. For an instant, the animal lost its footing, its hooves slithering on the slippery mud. Ford tightened his hold on

Laura, pulling her firmly against his chest. The sudden forced nearness made her tremble.

"You're cold," said Ford as the horse regained its balance and scrambled on to solid ground. Before Laura could protest, he removed his coat and wrapped it around her.

Then he pointed his mount back toward Hawkesbourne and urged it to a brisk canter. "Belinda told me you'd gone out to pay a call. I thought you might be caught in the rain. Tell me, what did you mean about antagonising my tenants?"

Though his coat was wet through in places, Laura found it surprisingly warm. The smell of damp wool mingled with the aroma of sandalwood and the distinctive masculine scent of Ford himself. With every hastening breath, Laura drew his essence deeper and deeper inside her.

To distract herself from his vital, enveloping presence, she concentrated on answering his question. "All your new ideas for improvements are as good as telling them they and their ancestors have been doing it wrong for hundreds of years. How would you like it if they told you a better way to run your trading company? Especially if they had the power to enforce their plans."

She felt Ford's muscles tense. "All I want is for this estate to prosper. That will not happen if everyone ambles along, doing everything the way their grandfathers did. People must embrace change if they mean to succeed."

Was he talking about his tenants, Laura wondered, or himself? He had changed and prospered, but at what cost?

"Not all change brings improvement," she muttered.

"What would you have me do then?" demanded Ford. "Neglect the estate, like Cyrus did?"

"Of course not. And I told Mr Cooper so. But you might use a bit of your old charm. I know you haven't lost it entirely for you lavish it upon my mother and sisters. Try asking your tenants what sorts of changes *they* would like to make. Find out what you can do to help them instead of barking orders and putting plans into effect without consulting them."

"I don't bark orders," Ford protested.

"You do." Laura parroted his earlier words back at him. *"Stay where you are. Climb on. Quick now."*

"I didn't say them like that. Well, perhaps I did, but what does that matter? Would you rather I'd left you there to get soaked…more soaked? Or fall down wading through that wretched ditch? You might have been swept away."

Was that a note of concern she detected in his voice? Or was her maddening awareness of him confusing her hearing as much as her other senses?

"It was good of you to ride out in the rain to fetch me home." Though the admission did not come easily, Laura meant it. "And take Mama out for walks in that garden chair. And bring my sisters and me to London. And host a ball to celebrate our engagement. I do not mean to be ungrateful, but it is not pleasant to be tyrannised—having no power over anything that happens to you, always dancing to someone else's tune. Perhaps you do not know what that feels like. But I do and so do your tenants. It may be that young Mr Northmore feels the same way about his brother."

Ford did not reply. Had he even listened to a word she'd said?

As the rain began to ease, Laura could see the turrets of Hawkesbourne Hall rearing above the trees ahead.

When they reached the stables, Ford lowered her to the ground. Then he swiftly dismounted and offered her his arm. Water dripped off the wide brim of his hat and his shirt was drenched—plastered to his chest in a way that made him appear naked from the waist up.

Laura struggled to catch her breath. A man with such a powerful physique could do her far worse harm than his ageing cousin ever had. Why had she risked antagonising him just now? Yet, mixed with her alarm came an ache of something like hunger…only it gnawed much lower than her stomach.

Ford seemed unaware of her reaction. Or was he? It was always so hard to tell with him. "We must get you out of those wet clothes before you catch a chill."

He did not mean it in a wanton way. At least Laura did not think so, judging by his brusque movements and curt tone of voice. Yet her fevered imagination conjured visions of falling into a swoon while Ford swept her off to her bedchamber where he proceeded to undress her. Much as she hated to admit it, there was a strangely arousing aspect to his masterful nature

Ford's voice crashed in on her wicked thoughts, sending them flying to hide in shame. "That was a suggestion, by the way, not an order. If you *wish* to catch a chill and drip water all over the house, be my guest."

His quip was so unexpected and her agitated emotions so urgently in need of release, Laura could not suppress a sputter of laughter. "No, indeed. It is a sound suggestion, which I mean to follow at once."

Suddenly aware that she was still wearing his coat, she removed it with a puzzling tug of reluctance. "I would be even wetter and colder without this. Thank you."

She held the sodden garment out to Ford, who looked rather thoughtful as he took it. "I do not mean to tyrannize over anyone, you know. I only want to do what is best and do it quickly, without wasting time over *by your leave* and *if you don't mind*. I never would have made my fortune if I had not learned to act decisively."

"There is a time for decisive action." Laura removed her bonnet and pushed a damp lock of hair off her forehead. "But surely there are other times when the exercise of a little consideration would not be wasted. People work harder and faster when they understand and agree with the reasons for what they are doing. You might find people have helpful suggestions, if you are willing to ask them and listen to their ideas."

"Like yours about finding a wharf outside London?"

Ford might not have asked for her idea, but he had listened and acted on it. Perhaps there was hope for him, after all. "I have one about how you could help your tenants and perhaps win their co-operation with your improvement plans."

After a moment's hesitation, Ford replied, "Very well, what is it?"

Before he had a chance to change his mind, Laura ploughed ahead, repeating what Mrs Cooper had said about the expense of goods from the Indies. "I thought, since your company imports such items, perhaps you could provide them directly to your tenants at a reduced price."

She braced for him to reject her idea, perhaps ridicule it. Instead he gave a cautious nod. "There might be something to that. I will consider it. But for the moment, we had both better get into dry clothes."

As he strode away, Laura followed him with her eyes, admiring the lithe grace of his gait. Then, abruptly, he stopped and spun about. She gave a guilty start as if he'd caught her doing something shameful.

But Ford seemed too much occupied with his own thoughts to notice she'd been staring after him. "I *do* know how it feels, to be at the mercy of someone else's actions and powerless to prevent it." His voice had a forced quality, as if the words were being pulled out of him against his will. "That is why I have worked so hard to make certain it never happens to me again."

Chapter Eight

What in blazes had come over him?

After a night spent tossing and turning, Ford still had no satisfactory answer. For a man who hated to reveal his feelings, he'd been appallingly quick and candid about disclosing some of his deepest to Laura. So deep, in fact, that he had scarcely been aware of them before the words burst out of his mouth.

It was true, though, he admitted to himself as he sat alone in the dining room absently munching toast. For most of his life he'd been at the mercy of Fate and the actions of others, which had often seemed equally cruel and arbitrary. From his mother's death to Helena's schemes and his father's downfall—all lost beyond recovery and nothing he could do to prevent them.

But he was no longer a helpless child when Laura's betrayal had brought his whole world crashing down around him. It had been a struggle, but he'd learned to take control of his emotions and his destiny. If it meant other people must dance to *his* tune for a change, was that such a bad thing?

Ford directed his unspoken question at the portrait of his cousin Cyrus that hung above the mantelpiece. The face in the painting stared down at him, its stony features devoid of expression, the eyes betraying no emotion. What sort of husband had his cousin been to Laura? The besotted fool, indulgent of a pretty young wife…or something else? The portrait taunted Ford with its secrets.

If what he'd learned in London was true, Laura had not lured Cyrus to the altar to get her hands on his fortune. She'd only turned to him for help after her father's sudden death, desperate to secure a home for her mother and sisters. Perhaps she, too, had learned something about the tyranny of Fate that demanded wrenching choices.

His thoughts strayed back to the day before, when he'd ridden home with her in his arms. He'd only gone looking for her because he feared she might be meeting her *Crawford*. He had been surprised to find her out visiting his tenants and quite confounded when she took him to task over his improvement plans. Though he'd been reluctant to admit it, her suggestion about selling East Indian goods directly to his tenants had merit.

A soft gasp drew his startled gaze toward the door where Laura stood frozen in her tracks. "I beg your pardon! I did not mean to disturb your breakfast. I thought you would be away by now."

"Don't go!" Ford called, as she turned to rush off. "I mean…do not feel obliged to leave on my account. I was just finishing."

Laura glanced back at him. "You looked deep in thought. I did not wish to interrupt."

"It was nothing important," Ford assured her, not entirely certain that was true. He did welcome the diversion of her sudden arrival. Delving too deeply into his past and the reasons for his actions was an uncomfortable occupation at best. One he was not eager to prolong. "I hope you are feeling well this morning. No ill effects from your drenching yesterday?"

She did not look ill. Indeed, she seemed to have put on a little much-needed weight since his return. Her face had filled out, making her look younger. The bust of her gown fit more snugly over breasts. Remembering the feel of her in his arms the day before and way her wet skirts had clung to her legs, Ford looked forward to their wedding night with growing anticipation.

"I am feeling quite well, thank you." Laura edged back into the room. "It would take more than a little rain to hurt me. And you?"

Ford gave a careless shrug. "Never better. I believe a bracing ride in the rain agrees with me."

Something about the experience had brought him a heady rush of vitality. The lingering contact of her body against his, perhaps?

"I am glad to hear it." Laura eased on to her usual chair at the opposite end of the table. "I would hate for you to suffer any harm on my account."

Her words took him so much by surprise that Ford could barely contain a gust of harsh laughter. Had she truly managed to convince herself she'd done him no harm by marrying Cyrus? If so, he was not about to disabuse her. Those feelings of humiliation, betrayal and heartbreak were ones he guarded most heavily of all.

"Never fear. I have learned to thrive on adversity." He rose from the table. "Now I must go check how much damage yesterday's rain did to the drainage work over at Den Marsh. I doubt it escaped as unscathed as you and I."

On his way to the door, something compelled him to stop a few feet from Laura. "By the way, I expect my time to be much occupied with estate business for the next few days. Pryce has been pestering me about plans for the ball—who to invite, what kind of punch to serve, how many musicians to hire? What do I know about any of that? I should like you to take charge of the arrangements...if you are willing?"

For a moment, Laura looked bewildered by his request. Then a strange warm light kindled deep in her eyes. Ford steeled himself to resist its enchantment and almost succeeded. "I would be pleased to. I have never planned a ball before, but I have attended a few. No doubt Mama and the girls would be happy to advise me."

"I will leave it in your hands, then." Ford headed for the door, fighting a strong urge to linger in Laura's company. "Don't trouble yourself about money. Spend whatever you need to make it an evening our guests will remember."

He had almost reached the door when she called his name.

Her tone had a ring of winsome sweetness he had not heard in seven empty, arid years.

He stopped in mid-stride and swung about. "Yes?"

Laura turned to look at him. Her lips were spread in a luminous smile that sent golden sunbeams shimmering through him. "Thank you."

"For what?"

"For asking my help. For giving me some say about what happens in this house."

It had brought him a measure of mordant amusement to bait Laura, a perverse satisfaction to vex and thwart her. But they were pale, sour sensations compared to the heady gratification of pleasing her.

Caution warned him it could be addictive. "It was nothing, I assure you."

Her smile faltered a little. "To you, perhaps, but not to me. I will do my best to make this ball a memorable one."

"I have every confidence in you." With a hasty bow, Ford took his leave. He managed to get safely out the door before he broke into a damned idiotic grin.

Perhaps it had meant nothing to Ford, letting her make arrangements for the ball, Laura reflected as she supervised the final preparations. But to her it was a tangible sign that he might be a better husband than his cousin had been. While their marriage would not be the kind of romantic idyll of which she once dreamed, it might be bearable—if Ford could learn to curb his arrogance and not treat her like a possession with no will or feelings to consider.

She glanced up from a floral arrangement she'd been admiring to spot Mr Pryce crossing the ballroom toward her. "Do the arrangements meet with your approval, my lady?"

"Indeed they do." Laura rewarded the butler with a grateful smile. "I hardly recognise the place."

From the time she'd first come to Hawkesbourne, the ballroom had been a vast, dark cavern she'd avoided. Now, glass, marble and fine wood gleamed in the soft radiance cast by scores of wax candles. Lighter paint and wallpaper gave the room an open, airy quality. New curtains and more modern furnishings helped, too, as did the garlands of greenery and flowers draped over the mantelpieces.

"You wanted it to look like an indoor garden, my lady." Pryce glanced around the room, his face glowing with satisfaction. "And I believe we have granted your wish."

"I hope his lordship and our guests will like it as much as I do." That thought gave Laura qualms. What if this was some kind of test Ford had set to decide whether he could depend upon her? Would their neighbours be the judges? She could think of several who might be eager to find fault.

If that were the case, there was nothing she could do about it now. Laura inhaled a deep breath and squared her shoulders. She must concentrate on making this an entertaining evening for those who came with open minds. "What is still left to do? I see the musicians have arrived. Do they have everything they need?"

Pryce grimaced at the screech of discordant notes coming from the platform where the quartet was tuning up their fiddles and pipes. "So they tell me, my lady. Cook reports that preparations for supper are going well. I was about to begin compounding the punch unless you need me for something else."

"Not at the moment." Laura's confidence rose. She might be a novice at entertaining on this scale, but Mr Pryce had had plenty of experience. If he assured her everything was well in hand, then it must be. "But could I prevail upon you to fetch my mother once the guests have arrived?"

Pryce bowed. "Consider it done, my lady."

"I'm not certain how long Mama will feel well enough to stay," Laura continued. "But she is so eager to see everyone and watch the dancing. Perhaps if you could watch over *her* and persuade her to return to her room before she tires herself out. She is more likely to listen to you than to me or my sister."

"You may rely on me, my lady." The butler seemed moved by her trust in him. "I will make certain Mrs Penrose does not overtax herself."

"Of course, I rely on you. We all do and have ever since we came to Hawkesbourne. I cannot imagine what we would have done without you."

"Hawkesbourne without Mr Pryce?" Susannah's merry voice rang out behind them. "It doesn't bear thinking of!"

"No, it does not," echoed Belinda, her tone not as lively as her sister's, but no less sincere.

Laura cast a critical glance over them both, relieved to see how lovely they looked. Susannah sparkled in a gown of buttercup yellow while Belinda's lace-trimmed lavender silk flattered her gentle beauty. They might grace even the most exalted company.

The butler regarded them with almost paternal pride. Perhaps he was remembering them when they had first come to Hawkesbourne, little more than children.

It took him a moment to summon his voice, which came out a trifle husky. "It has been an honour to serve such excellent ladies. Now, if you will excuse me, I must see to the punch before your guests arrive."

"The dear man," Belinda whispered when Mr Pryce was out of earshot. "He is so happy to have Ford home. Now he has the resources to run the house properly."

With a bubbly giggle, Susannah nudged her sisters. "Speaking of Ford, there he is now. How handsome he looks—even better than Lord Bramber, and you know I partial I am to him!"

Laura's gaze flew to the doorway where Ford stood, framed like one of the many fine portraits of his ancestors that hung throughout the house. But none of them had been nearly as attractive. His dress clothes fit so well on his tall, straight frame. He had let his hair grow out from the harsh cropped stubble to crisp dark curls. The stark contours of his face gave it a striking intensity that made commonplace words like *handsome* quite inadequate.

A deep, insistent hum began to pulse beneath Laura's skin, as if she were a taut string on the musicians' bass fiddle.

"He's seen us!" cried Susannah.

Laura did not need to be told. Ford's gaze ran over her like the gliding caress of a skilled bow stroke.

"We should all curtsy to him," suggested Belinda. "After he was kind enough to take us all the way to London to get these gowns made up."

"Yes, let's!" Susannah prodded Laura. "Come on. You as well."

Roused from her admiring contemplation, Laura took her sisters' cue and sank into a deep curtsy.

Susannah was the first to bounce up again, brimming with high spirits. "What do you think of our fine feathers, Ford? Precious little fear of us putting you to shame tonight."

"Not in appearance, perhaps." Laura tried to sound severe, but it was not easy when an unaccustomed froth of elation bubbled inside her. "But you should curb your spirits a little so you do not expose yourself to ridicule. That would reflect worse on Ford than a shabby gown."

"I swear I shall be on my best behaviour." Susannah placed her hand over her heart. "Only don't expect me to be all prim and pruney at my first proper ball."

Ford laughed. And for the first time since his return, it did not sound forced or mocking. "I don't believe you could if you tried. And I for one would not want you to—especially not tonight. This is meant to be a festive occasion."

He offered Laura his arm. For a change, his smile did not disappear when he turned his attention to her. "You have done a marvellous job. This old barn of a ballroom has never looked so fine. And all the preparations seem to be running like clockwork."

A rush of tingling warmth suffused Laura's cheeks. She was not certain what provoked it—Ford's unexpected praise or the intensity of his nearness. She cautioned herself not to set too much store by his kind words. He was only surprised by how well she'd managed the challenge he had set her. Perhaps he thought she might be an asset in his future business dealings.

She raised her fan and fluttered up a little breeze to cool her face. "The proof of the pudding will be in the eating. I hope our guests will enjoy themselves this evening."

"Of course they will." Ford's hearty tone dared them not to. "And speaking of guests—" he gestured toward her sisters "—will you ladies join us in receiving them? You know our neighbours better than I do."

"We'd be glad to help," replied Belinda. "Wouldn't we, Sukie?"

"Very well, only please don't call me that once the guests arrive—especially the handsome, young gentleman guests. You have invited a few of those, I hope, Ford."

"Every one we could recruit for miles around," he assured her. "Along with Julian Northmore, who is coming all the way from London."

"Your partner's brother, of course!" Susannah clapped her hands. "I'd almost forgotten."

The musicians had finished their strident tuning and now began to play a sweet, lively melody. Ford's reassurance quieted the discord within Laura, replacing it with buoyant rhythm and delightful harmonies. It had been so very long since she'd experienced such pleasant feelings, they threatened to intoxicate her more than the most potent punch.

Music seemed to vibrate under Ford's skin and in his chest. He savoured the subtle warmth of Laura's hand on his arm. Pretty as her sisters looked in their new gowns, she outshone them in a soft, warm shade of pink that put him in mind of a tropical flower. His nostrils flared to inhale the sweet tang of her scent. Nectar-starved desire swarmed his loins.

He hadn't felt like himself since returning from London. Busy implementing improvements to the estate and plans for the expansion of Vindicara, he'd been too preoccupied with the present and the future to brood upon the past. Laura seemed different, too—more relaxed and talkative at mealtimes, sometimes joining in her sisters' ready laughter. Tonight she seemed to have recaptured the sparkle of her younger years, only better.

Their time in London had forced him to realise the events of seven years ago were more complicated than he'd believed. That did not excuse the hell she'd put him through, but it did ease the crushing grip of resentment.

Perhaps that was the first step toward loosening her hold upon him. Though tonight, Ford had to admit, it did not feel any looser.

Shortly after they reached the entry hall, the first of their guests began to arrive and they were swept up in a round of greetings and congratulations.

Among the first arrivals were Mr Crawford, his mother and sister.

"Lord Kingsfold, how delightful to have you back in the neighbourhood!" Mrs Crawford gushed. "You will be such excellent company for my son. He and Lord Bramber get on well, but the marquis is obliged to spend so much time in London, while Sidney prefers the country."

The lady and her daughter were dressed in what Ford presumed must be the height of fashion, their gowns heavily trimmed and their hair tortured into towering topknots and stiff ringlets. Mrs Crawford reminded him so much of his stepmother, he felt an unexpected qualm of sympathy for her son. Little wonder the young man wanted to escape his house as often as possible to spend time with pleasant, unaffected women.

Perhaps Laura sensed his distaste for Mrs Crawford. Or perhaps she was alarmed at the speed with which the receiving line was backing up. "Lady Daphne assured us the marquis will be here tonight. If you go straight through to the ballroom, you can secure a good seat from which to spot him when he arrives."

Without another word, Mrs Crawford seized her daughter by the wrist and charged toward the ballroom.

A chuckle of mingled amusement and relief welled up in Ford's throat. "I have seen fillies at Newmarket slower off the start. Well done."

He and Laura exchanged a fleeting grin of fellow conspirators. Then she gestured toward the next guests in line, two long-faced gentlemen who looked like a pair of effigies in the crypt of St Botolph's. "I expect you remember Lord Henry and Lord Edward Dearing of Bramberley?"

"I do indeed." Ford bowed. "My lords, it is an honour to welcome you to Hawkesbourne."

The senior of the two men cast a critical glance around the entrance hall. "The first ball I ever attended was here, back in your grandfather's day. There was a man who knew how to entertain. Not certain what he would have made of his grandson dabbling in trade."

Ford was surprised how much Lord Henry's remark offended him. As a child he had often spent holidays with his grandparents, who'd doted on him. His grandfather had been proud of the estate and his ancient title. Would he have been ashamed of Ford's commercial activities, no matter how successful?

While he searched for a civil reply, Laura chuckled, as if Lord Henry had spoken in jest. "Lord Kingsfold has done a good deal more than dabble, sir. He has made an honest fortune, which he is using to restore this house and the estate. I cannot imagine his grandfather would object to that."

"Lady Kingsfold has you, Uncle Henry!" cried the cherubic girl behind him, whom Ford had seen gossiping with Susannah after church. "This is the *nineteenth* century, remember."

As her uncles huffed off, Lady Daphne seized Laura in an eager embrace, bobbed Ford a quick curtsy, then fell squealing upon Susannah.

Leaning toward Laura, Ford murmured, "That is the second time you've come to my rescue this evening."

She cast him a teasing glance. "Would you rather I minded my own business?"

"I think not. Your efforts so far have been most amusing."

Laura had no opportunity to reply, for she was obliged to exchange very proper curtsies with their next guest.

"Lady Artemis." Ford bowed. "Thank you for coming this evening. The Dearings are always welcome at Hawkesbourne."

"My sister would have made us pay dearly if we had even considered refusing your kind invitation." A hint of a smile crossed the lady's face, which was as solemn as Lady Daphne's was animated.

She was rather attractive, in an understated way. Compared to the Crawford women's elaborate style, Ford preferred the austere simplicity of Lady Artemis.

As she moved on, Laura greeted the Marquis of Bramber. "Welcome, my lord. Have you come all the way from London at Lady Daphne's behest?"

"Not entirely." The marquis bowed over Laura's hand. Silver flecks in his blue eyes sparkled with admiration. "I was coming as far as Epsom for the Derby, so what was another twenty miles?"

"Be on your guard," Ford warned Lord Bramber, "I believe Mrs Crawford is anxious to get you in her sights this evening."

"Relentless, that woman. Three years she's been stalking me for her daughter." The marquis leaned toward Ford. "If I don't win at Epsom, I may *have* to marry the tiresome chit or watch Bramberley fall down around our ears. You are fortunate that you can afford to marry for love."

The marquis's words hit Ford square in the conscience. Possessing both title and a fortune, he *could* afford to marry for love. Unlike Lord Bramber...and unlike Laura.

Chapter Nine

For one weak, fleeting moment, Laura wished what she'd overheard Lord Bramber tell Ford could be true. If only he wanted to marry her for love rather than convenience or lust or some other inscrutable reason.

She wasn't certain what had come over him this evening. He was not the same aloof, intimidating man who had confronted her in Hawkesbourne's drawing room a few short weeks ago. In some ways, he seemed more like the man she'd once loved…yet better, somehow. The old Ford had been a charming, amiable boy, but looking back, Laura now realised there had been little substance behind those superficial qualities. The new Ford was a responsible, determined and generous man. When those sterling virtues were warmed with a dash of good humour, the combination was very hard to resist.

Once all their guests had been welcomed, Laura and Ford led off the first dance. Laura feared her rusty skills would provoke unfavorable comment from some of their guests. But once the music began she could not keep her mind on anything but Ford, how he moved with such dignified, manly grace. Every time he grasped her hand, the warmth of his touch set a delicious thrill coursing up her arm toward her bosom, where it made her heart beat faster and the tips of her breasts tingle.

The intensity of his dark, brooding gaze stirred her even more. She had been its object many times before, but tonight she sensed a different intent behind it. That difference made her blush and look away, but not for long. Such was its power that she felt compelled to glance back. She had trouble keeping her mind on the dance steps.

"Why do you stare at me so?" she asked. "Am I too awkward? Do my gown and hair look too much behind the fashion?"

"You move with such grace, no one would notice if you made a misstep," he assured her as they joined hands to dance a circle with the couple beside them. "As for the other, I was thinking how well this elegant simplicity suits you and how many gentlemen here tonight must envy me."

The low volume of his voice, together with its usual husky timbre, made Ford's words sound like an intimate endearment. It sent a shiver through Laura that was part-delight and part-dismay. In her experience, intimacy had a dark, disturbing side. Was he was only playing the part of an attentive fiancé for the benefit of their guests?

Those doubts tied her tongue. Fortunately, the dance concluded before her silence became too embarrassing.

If Ford noticed anything untoward, he gave no indication. "Tempted as I am to be selfish and monopolise your company, I must make some effort to be a good host by dancing with the other ladies."

"Of course." Laura found she could not let go of his arm. "Though I hope you will not forsake me entirely."

Dear heaven, where had that come from? She sounded like an infatuated little chit flirting with her beau, rather than a widow with one loveless marriage in her past and another in her future.

"I can assure you, there is no fear of that." Ford lifted her hand from his arm and raised it to his lips.

Even through the fabric of her glove, the heat of his kiss seared. A glint of something deliciously wicked flashed in his dangerous green eyes. It made her breath catch and her heart skip in a fast, erratic rhythm. A moment later he turned from her and approached one of their guests to request the honour of the next dance. Only when Laura realised his new partner was the vicar's sister did the watchful tightness inside her ease.

It alarmed her to be in the grip of such intense, volatile feelings. But when she tried to summon her old icy self-possession, it failed her. Since his return, Ford had tested her composure far too often, provoking fiery rage, searing shame or fevered yearning. The heat of those emotions had thawed her heart, leaving it tender and all too vulnerable. Much as that unsettled her, she could not deny the tremulous joy of feeling truly alive again after seven cold, dormant years.

Hoping a cup of punch might help settle her nerves, she headed for the refreshment table, casting a glance around the ballroom to see how her guests were enjoying themselves. Her mother was sitting with the vicar's mother and another older lady. She watched the dancers with a wistful smile, perhaps remembering the balls of her youth. Nearby, Susannah and Lady Daphne were engaged in vivacious conversation with Julian Northmore. On the dance floor, Sidney Crawford was partnered with Lady Artemis, neither of whom looked to be enjoying it much. Sidney scarcely took his eyes off Belinda, who was dancing with the marquis.

Though Sidney was a dear, kind fellow, Laura's patience with him was rapidly wearing thin. Ford would never moon about like that if there were something he wanted. He would act swiftly and decisively, sweeping aside any obstacles in his way. A bit too forcefully, perhaps, but surely that was better than hanging back, doing nothing, while the desired object slipped through his fingers.

When the dance concluded and Sidney drifted toward her, Laura decided the time had come to give him a nudge. "Mr Crawford, I hope you are enjoying the evening."

He started at the sight of her, casting a furtive glance over his shoulder. "Very much, Lady Kingsfold. Everything looks…beautiful."

Her sister most of all, no doubt.

Laura seized two cups of punch from the table and thrust them into his hands. "I was just about to fetch my sister a drink, but I see Mama requires my attention. Could I prevail upon you to deliver this to Miss Belinda?"

Before he could refuse, she pretended to take his agreement for granted. "I knew I could depend upon you. And I would consider it a great favor if you would ask her to dance."

Laura did not stay to parry his excuses, but hurried off to check on her mother. The next time she glanced toward the dance floor, she spotted Sidney and Belinda dancing a lively quadrille. Her satisfaction soured a little when she spied Ford partnered with the lovely Lady Artemis. She told herself not to be so foolish. Ford was merely continuing his duties as a good host.

"What a shame," remarked Mrs Crawford, who suddenly appeared by her side, "for such an accomplished lady of fine family to be on the shelf. When I heard Lord Kingsfold had returned from India, I immediately thought of him for Lady Artemis."

Laura could not believe the incivility of the woman to say such a thing to Ford's fiancée. "Is matchmaking a pet pursuit of yours, Mrs Crawford?"

"You could say so." The woman gave a brittle laugh. "I take a warm interest in seeing eligible ladies and gentleman of my acquaintance paired to their best advantage. I pity Lady Artemis and Lady Daphne with all my heart. Never brought out properly, either of them. I suppose it would not occur to their brother or uncles, even if they had the means. If only they had the right sort of sister-in-law to take them in hand."

Laura wondered what proud Lady Artemis Dearing would think if she knew Mrs Crawford had the effrontery to pity her?

"You might consider, ma'am," she replied with icy politeness, "the greatest advantage a person can gain from marriage is someone to love and be loved by in return."

"Why, Lady Kingsfold—" Mrs Crawford sounded highly amused as she tapped Laura's arm with her fan "—you are the last woman I would have expected to entertain such sentimental notions about matrimony!"

A slimy wave of humiliation broke over Laura. Was

that what all their guests thought of her, behind their polite smiles and lively banter? Did they see her as a calculating creature who had snared one well-fixed husband, more than twice her age, then wasted no time securing his heir? Much as she hated to admit it or tried to excuse it, she could not deny that her actions contradicted her beliefs about love and marriage.

She wished Ford would come and sweep her back on to the dance floor, banishing her shame and regrets with his potent, rousing presence.

Laura had roused him to such a pitch of desire, Ford could not bear it much longer. As he bid farewell to departing guests, he fought the urge to heave the last few out the door and slam it behind them. He wanted them gone so he could retreat to his bedchamber and douse himself with cold water!

He must have been mad to agree to a three-week delay in their marriage. How could he have persuaded himself he would savour the anticipation of claiming Laura, the way he might anticipate and savour the taste of sweet pudding at the end of a satisfying meal? Instead, he'd been like a starving beggar, tormented with a succulent dish waved under his nose. Once or twice he'd been driven to snatch a bite, but never enough to satisfy him. Only enough to fuel his hunger.

Early on, her barely concealed hostility had not blunted his yearning. But since their trip to London and their ride in the rain, he'd sensed Laura gradually warming to him, and felt an answering spark of desire. Tonight, her ripe, fragrant beauty and subtle flirtation had ambushed him. Whenever they danced, the space between them had seemed charged with passionate possibilities. When her skirts rustled against his leg, it gave the impression of a deliberate, intimate caress. When he grasped her delicate hands to perform a turn, it had taken every scrap of self-control to keep from pulling her into his arms for a scorching kiss that would have scandalised their guests.

Past experience warned Ford to be wary of such reckless passions that threatened his self-control. Hadn't the whole point of wedding Laura been to purge her from his system? Instead, she had made him a captive of his desire, tormented by yearning that intensified every hour. If he wasn't careful, she might sink her claws into his heart so deeply that he would only be able to wrest it away in bloody pieces.

For the first time in many years, Ford turned a deaf ear to the urgings of caution.

He chafed under the tyranny of self-restraint, though it was of his own making and for his own good. He had never felt so fiercely alive as these past weeks, with his passions stirred dangerously close to the surface. The torment of his yearning for Laura eclipsed the vague pleasure he'd found in the effortless conquest of other women. Perhaps his fascination with her was like an illness of the body that must rise to a blistering fever before it broke.

At last the guests were all gone and good riddance to them.

Thoughts of Laura writhed and whirled in Ford's thoughts, like as enticing Eastern dance, as he mounted the stairs two at a time and strode down the wide corridor toward his quarters. But as he passed her door, the scent of orange blossoms ambushed him with its luscious invitation.

He must have one last glimpse of Laura. One word from her. One breath of her. One touch. One taste. And if one would not suffice…

He eased the door open and slipped into Laura's bedchamber.

A single candle flickered from her dressing table. Her bewitching pink ball gown hung over the back of a chair in wanton neglect. Laura stood by her bed wearing nothing but a chemise. The lacy edge of its low-cut bodice nestled over her breasts, while a breath-taking span of her willowy legs showed beneath the garment's knee-length hem. Through the fine-woven linen, flickering candlelight silhouetted her ripe body.

A blaze of tropical heat swept through Ford. Passion stormed the ramparts of his self-control and pounded it to rubble.

His sudden entrance made Laura recoil with a soft gasp. "Ford, you startled me! What are you doing here? Is something wrong? Is Mama…?"

The question and her alarm dampened Ford's ardour a little. "Your mother is perfectly well. She seemed to enjoy the ball—stayed later than I thought she might. Nothing is wrong."

Except that he could not bear to wait one more day to make Laura his.

His reassurance seemed to ease most of the tension in her body, but some lingered. "Then…what are you doing here?"

He took a step toward her, then another. "This is my house, remember. I have a right to go where I please, when I please. Just now it would please me very much to kiss you goodnight."

"Are you certain that is a good idea?" Laura retreated a step, the back of her legs pressed against the bed.

"One of the best I ever had." A smile of anticipation rippled across Ford's lips. How obliging of her to move nearer the bed.

"But...propriety..."

He gave a husky chuckle. "To hell with propriety. We have been living under the same roof for weeks."

He pulled her into his arms. "We are going to be married the day after tomorrow."

He nuzzled his cheek against her hair. "In fact, if I had not agreed to your demand for banns, we would have been married over a fortnight by now."

"And all you want is a kiss?" The breathless quality of her voice would have been sufficient to provoke him all by itself. But in the shadowy intimacy of her bed-chamber, with the outline of her tantalising curves visible beneath her chemise and passion fairly crackling between them, it all proved impossible to resist.

"To begin with." He lowered his lips to hers and kissed her hungrily.

Oh, the taste of her kiss—so tangy-sweet and intoxicating! Of course he knew that was only the rack punch she'd been drinking at the ball—a mixture of lemon, sugar, brandy and Batavia arrack. But the soft, luscious warmth of her mouth had fermented it into an even more potent brew. One he could imbibe again and again without ever slaking his thirst. Instead, like a fine *aperitif*, it stimulated his appetite for other tantalising delicacies.

As he continued to kiss her, nibbling the ripe fullness

of her lower lip then plunging between her parted lips to caress her tongue with his, one hand strayed down her back to cup a soft, rounded lobe of her bottom

Laura twitched at his touch, thrusting her breasts against his chest. He could hardly wait to feast his eyes, his hands and his lips upon them. In the same instant, she gave a muted gasp, a sultry gush of breath that whetted Ford's desire sharper still. He slid his knee between hers, nudging her thighs apart. Then he tugged up the hem of her chemise, the better to fondle her tempting body.

His passionate attentions seemed to stir an answering desire in Laura. Where she had been gently complaisant before, she began to engage him with fevered eagerness—grappling with him, wriggling against him, tearing at his clothes, tugging at his hair. If he could not rally a little control, she would push him over the edge before he had the opportunity to satisfy her.

That would never do.

She could not let Ford do this to her! That conviction spurred Laura even as her traitorous body responded to him. Two nights from now, she would be his wife and she would have to submit to his attentions. But for the moment, her body was still her own—not his to possess on a whim.

While watching Ford advance upon her, his mesmerising green eyes aglitter with feral lust, Laura had frozen, caught in a web of haunting memories. She'd permitted him to kiss her with only a token protest, in part out of harshly conditioned habit. Another part of her hoped if she let him have his way in that, he might be content to go no further. A final part that she could scarcely bear to acknowledge *wanted* his kiss.

And afterward? When his lips grew more demanding, when his hands began to rove and plunder, as if to say she would soon be his property to do with whatever he wished, whenever he wished, did she want that too?

She could not deny some perverse part of her took wanton pleasure in the strange, hot sensations he provoked. But she must not allow such wayward passion to ride roughshod over her self-respect. Nor could she let him treat her as Cyrus had!

She began to struggle against Ford and against her own unruly desires. Her heart pounded a swift, violent tattoo and her breath hissed furiously in a desperate struggle for air. She clutched at Ford's clothes, at his flesh. At times she scarcely knew whether she was trying to fight him off, or hurl herself upon him. Her writhing forced one of his thighs high between hers, igniting a blaze of torrid yearning. Before she could prevent it, her hips gave a convulsive thrust, striking sparks of savage pleasure through her whole body.

Their fiery tussle churned up the rug beneath their feet. Laura stumbled over it, lost her balance and tumbled back on to the bed. An instant later, Ford landed on top of her. The impact forced the breath out of her, stunning her for a moment.

As she lay beneath him, Ford's hands continued to range over her body, making it devilishly difficult to think. Still she managed to recall that she'd had no choice but to submit to Cyrus in order to protect her family. With Ford, she had another means of recourse—

one she'd hoped he would never compel her to use. But he had left her no alternative.

Once she caught her breath, Laura mustered her strength, planted her hands on Ford's chest and pushed him away with all her might.

"Let me go!" she gasped. "If you take me now, against my will, I swear I will destroy you! I have the means and I will use it if you force me to."

"Take you? Force you?" Ford flew back, as if propelled by her desperate words as much as her actual push. "I have never taken a woman against her will and I am not about to start. I thought you wanted this as much as I do."

The moment she was no longer pinned beneath him, Laura scrambled on to the bed. She grabbed a pillow and held it in front of her to batter Ford with if he tried to approach her again. "I did not ask you to barge into my bedroom at this hour of the night. Demanding a kiss. Throwing yourself at me. Did you expect me to be flattered by such attentions? Well, you could not be worse mistaken!"

Ford flinched as if she had just slapped him very hard. "Are you saying all that flirting at the ball was just for show? You find me repulsive and only agreed to marry me for the sake of your family?"

Repulsive? If anything, she found him far too attractive. Dangerously so. What if she should fall into the trap of mistaking that intense attraction for something more? Something it could never be.

That fear and her roused passion spurred her to lash out. "What choice did you give me? Storming back into Hawkesbourne after seven years abroad. Taking advantage of my family's situation to coerce me into marriage, just like—"

Just like your cousin, she meant to say. But Ford interrupted before she could finish. "How is it you propose to destroy me? Been planning it all along, have you?"

His questions were like a garrotte, slipping around her throat and pulling tight. She barely recalled making that desperate threat and ached to take it back. Her family had every bit as much to fear from the exposure of that scandalous secret as Ford did. Perhaps more.

"I didn't mean it." Laura prayed he would believe her. "I thought you were going to force me and I said the only thing I could think of to stop you."

Ford's lip curled in a contemptuous sneer, but Laura thought she glimpsed a shadow of anguish in his green eyes. "You expect me to believe that? I am not a complete fool, you know. I have learned a thing or two in the past seven years."

What did he mean by that? Did he guess the secret she had paid so dearly to keep? "I never thought you were a fool."

"But you were ready to make a fool of me, weren't you?" Ford lashed out. "By running off to marry Crawford. You meant to leave me standing at the altar this time—the laughingstock of all my neighbours."

Marry Sidney Crawford? The accusation left Laura speechless. What on earth was Ford talking about? Had he gone mad…or had she? Everything that had happened since he walked through her door felt like a nightmare.

"I am offended that you should assume something so trivial would be capable of destroying me." Those words seemed to unleash something terrible from deep inside

Ford. His eye flashed with bolts of wrath, but his features contorted as if in agony. "I did not allow it to destroy me seven years ago, when I actually *cared* about you. When your marriage to my cousin broke my heart, robbed me of my expectations and set my creditors after me like a pack of wolves baying for blood. When I was forced to slink away from England like a criminal and begin a new life in a strange land where I had not a single friend or a penny to my name!"

The thunder of his fury struck Laura with such force, she would not have been surprised if it left bruises. It stormed into her heart, seizing her cherished perceptions of the past and smashing them into jagged shards. It was every bit as brutal a violation as if Ford had forced himself upon her a few moments ago.

Was it only *moments*? It seemed so distant already. And the early hours of this evening, when they had danced and laughed and flirted, felt lost beyond recall.

Something between a gasp and a sob burst from her lips. "I never knew."

Never knew, her conscience protested, *or did not want to know for fear it would overburden her with guilt and make it impossible to do what she must?*

"Are you saying it did not occur to you that marrying Cyrus would mean the death of my expectations? Perhaps I ought to thank you for failing to bear him a son, who would have robbed me of the title and an estate that have been in my family for centuries!"

Laura sought to shield herself with the justification she had clung to seven years ago. "That might have happened with any other lady Cyrus married. Would you have nursed such a grudge against *her*? Did your cousin not have a right to marry and beget children if he chose, just because they would stand in the way of *your* inheritance?"

For an instant, she feared Ford might seize the first thing that came to hand and hurl it at her. Instead, he made a visible effort to master the fiery rage that had possessed him. He jammed his eyes shut, perhaps to block out the infuriating sight of her, or perhaps to hide the true, raw emotions he feared they might betray. His whole body went rigid, hands clenched at his sides. He drew several shuddering breaths, so deep they seemed to suck all the air from the room.

When he looked at Laura again and spoke, his feelings were back under cold, scornful, exasperating control. "My cousin did not marry some other lady. He wed *you* and you knew how much my inheritance meant to me. You betrayed me once and you intended to do it again. But you seem to have forgotten, I now possess a fortune you cannot steal. I have my lands and my title. The gossip might be rather humiliating, having you throw me over for a second-rate bumbler like Crawford. But it would pass quickly enough, I expect, as such things do."

All the harsh lessons of her marriage urged Laura to hold her tongue and not risk provoking an enraged man further. Yet, in spite of everything that had just happened, some part of her refused to believe Ford was capable of harming her as Cyrus had. She could not deny the ring of truth in his voice when he'd claimed to believe she wanted him in her bed. Given her conflicted desires, she could not swear he was entirely mistaken.

Hard as it might be, Laura was willing to take responsibility for her past actions. That did not mean she would allow false accusations to go unchallenged. Especially when they tainted the reputation of an innocent person. "You know why I married Cyrus. It was not to hurt you, but to save my family. I did not know you went abroad to escape your creditors. I thought you wanted to be free of me so you could sail off to the Indies to pursue your fortune. And if I ever intended to run away with another man, which I assure you I *do not*, Sidney Crawford would be the very last I would consider."

She was about to explain why, vexed that Ford could not see what was so obvious to her, when he cut her off. "Save your breath. I refuse to believe another deceitful word out of your mouth."

He turned and stalked toward the door, then paused to fling down a final challenge. "Go ahead. Do your worst."

Chapter Ten

Do her worst—what had possessed him to taunt Laura with such a challenge?

Hours after leaving her bedchamber, Ford prowled his like a trapped beast. Only this trap was one he had set and sprung on himself.

Bad enough he had dared Laura to do the one thing he most dreaded. But to do it after providing her with the perfect means to secure Crawford's sympathy was nothing short of madness. She would only have to go to their neighbour with a tearful tale of how Ford had sought to force himself upon her before their wedding. Whatever scruples had previously kept him from stealing Ford's fiancée, Crawford surely would leap at the opportunity to *rescue* Laura from such a licentious brute.

Ford ploughed his fingers through his hair with violent force, as if he wanted to tear it out. The prospect of Laura jilting him yet again made his heart bound into his throat and needles of sweat break out on his brow. He tried to convince himself it was because he might lose the chance to break her hold over him at last. But deep down he suspected it was more than that.

Part of him wanted to marry her for no other reason than to have her in his life. That part was growing stronger by the day, threatening to overthrow his caution and his self-control, as it had this evening.

This evening… Shame gnawed at Ford as he recalled what he'd done. He struggled to justify his behaviour, a task that proved more difficult than he'd expected. He could see now that entering Laura's bedchamber had been a fatal lapse in self-control. But he'd been consumed with desire and certain she wanted him. How could he have been so badly wrong?

He'd bedded enough women to recognise when his attentions were welcome. Never had he found them so urgently sought as in Laura's arms…or so he'd believed. Then, at the peak of his desire, he'd been suddenly and viciously rejected. Accused of base dishonour. Threatened with the worst humiliation he could imagine. It demolished the restraint Laura had already breached. His old hurt and bitterness had come pouring out.

Though he knew such an outburst would only seal his fate, it had been such a blessed relief to vent the resentment that had been eating away at him for so long. Even now, though his plans lay in ruins, he felt strangely lightened and freed. Free enough to acknowledge the truth of what Laura had said. Even if she'd borne Cyrus a dozen sons, destroying any hope of Ford inheriting, she would not have stolen anything to which he'd been truly entitled.

Part of him longed to tell her that—make a clean breast of everything, including his original reason for wanting to marry her. But pride and his finely honed sense of self-preservation would not permit it. She had threatened to destroy him, after all, and he had given her plenty of ammunition. Damned if he would give her any more.

Fearing his resolve might weaken if he encountered her again, he rode out at first light, telling Pryce he intended to check on the progress of improvements he had ordered around the estate.

Ignoring the butler's look of puzzled concern, he added, "If anyone asks, tell them I do not expect to be back for dinner."

He spent a wretched day riding from one far-flung part of the estate to another, an activity that left him entirely too much opportunity for brooding. At each site, he found the work proceeding at a satisfactory pace, which was gratifying but provided little of the distraction he craved.

Late in the afternoon, when he arrived to inspect a drainage project near the boundary between Hawkesbourne and Lyndhurst, he spotted Sidney Crawford riding toward him.

"Lord Kingsfold! A word if I may." The younger man looked pale and a little intimidated, as usual. Yet his mouth was set in a resolute line and his gaze did not waver when Ford tried to stare him down.

"Very well." Ford mustered his self-control to hear the worst without flinching. "What is it?"

His horse must have sensed his tightly wound emotions, for it grew restive, tossing its mane and pawing the ground. The same might be true of Crawford's mount, for its ears flicked and its nostrils quivered.

"I must warn you, sir, what I have to relate might be unpleasant to you."

Might be unpleasant? Ford's fingers tightened around his riding crop. He longed to thrash the young bounder for his impudence. At the same time, he could not quell a grudging flicker of respect for Crawford. At least he had the civility to confront Ford face-to-face. That was more than Cyrus has done.

"Perhaps more than unpleasant," Crawford amended. "But you must realise much of that is due to your own disagreeable conduct."

That bit of understatement made Ford flinch, in spite of his resolve not to. Hard as he tried to excuse last night's behaviour, he could not.

Ford's persistent silence seemed to rattle Crawford, but he forged ahead. "It was my sincere hope that we might be on cordial terms. However, from the moment we met, you have made your dislike for me quite plain. I am accustomed to this prejudice against the source of my family's fortune from others of our acquaintance. But I had hoped you would not share their contempt for honest trade."

"What are you blathering about?" Ford demanded the instant Crawford paused to draw breath. "I don't dislike you on account of your damned brewery. I might have tolerated your company, if you'd kept your distance from my fiancée."

"I protest, sir!" Crawford bridled. "I have never had the slightest dishonourable intention toward her ladyship. It was she who sought me out to encourage my feelings for her sister."

"Sister?" Ford wondered if he'd heard right.

Or were his wits addled after a sleepless night?

"Lady Kingsfold's sister—Miss Belinda." The moment her name crossed his lips, Crawford sat taller in his saddle. "I have admired her for a great while and was working up the spirit to court her when you returned to Hawkesbourne and made me so unwelcome. The more I experienced of your arrogance and ill humour, the more I detested the notion of that dear lady having to reside in your household. I have resolved to make her an offer of marriage this very day, before you have any authority to prevent her accepting."

With that, Crawford wheeled his horse and headed toward Hawkesbourne. He had only gone a few strides when he reined his mount and called back, "If Miss Belinda accepts my proposal, I mean to offer her family a home at Lyndhurst as well. That includes Lady Kingsfold, if she ever has need of sanctuary."

Crawford and *Belinda*? As Ford sat watching his young neighbour ride away, he struggled to make sense of what he'd just heard. The longer he reflected upon the past several weeks, the clearer it became that Crawford's version of events must be the correct one, while his was a distorted fiction, spun out of jealousy and suspicion.

No wonder Laura had been so resentful of his incivility to their neighbour. No doubt she would have dispelled his assumptions about Crawford long ago, if he'd told her straight out what he suspected. Last night, when feral jealousy had broken through the iron cage of his self-restraint, she'd been swift and emphatic in assuring him Crawford was the last man she would ever consider running away with. And how had he responded? By refusing to believe her or even listen to a single word of explanation.

At last Ford roused from his brooding enough to turn his horse toward Hawkesbourne and give the reins a half-hearted jog.

He no longer had to worry that Laura would jilt him to wed Sidney Crawford. But that was no consolation. After what he'd said and done last night, Laura would surely accept Crawford's kind offer of sanctuary. She would leave Ford standing at the altar, the laughingstock of all his neighbours.

And he had driven her to it.

Laura sank into her bed on the eve of her wedding, craving the peaceful oblivion of sleep. She'd got no real rest the night before, with so many powerful, conflicting emotions swirling inside her.

She wanted to hate Ford for the way he'd burst in upon her, terrifying her with his wild, perilous passion, and rousing similar dangerous urges within her. Then, when she'd made a desperate bid to defend herself, he had turned on her with scathing recriminations and cruel accusations. More painful than any of those was a glimpse of the deep hurt and betrayal he had suffered as a result of her actions.

All these years she'd blamed Ford for abandoning her in her time of need, only to discover he had been forced into unwilling exile as a result of *her* actions. Worse than that, she had broken his heart.

Through the long bleak hours of the night, Laura sought to ease her conscience by reminding herself she'd had no choice but to do what she'd done. She'd been forced to accept a devil's bargain to protect her family and to protect Ford, even though she believed he'd forsaken her. She had paid a far higher price for that protection than she could have foreseen. Somehow, none of that mattered when she recalled the look on Ford's face—like a wounded beast, baring its fangs in the hope of frightening off a fresh attack. Much as she disliked and even feared some of the ways he had changed in the past seven years, she now faced the wrenching likelihood that she was responsible for turning him into the man he had become.

At last she'd fallen into a fitful doze, haunted by elusive dreams of Ford that left her with a hot, hungry ache in her loins and a wretched, rueful ache in her heart. When she woke the next morning, she'd forced herself to go in search of Ford, hoping that in the cool light of day, he might be willing to hear her out and recognise the truth when he heard it.

Instead Mr Pryce informed her the master had ridden off to inspect the improvements being carried out around the estate and did not expect to return for dinner. After going through the motions of the day in a daze of regrets, painful memories and questions about her future, she'd retired for the night, only to have sleep elude her again.

A faint trace of Ford's scent still lingered in her bed—sandalwood, arrack and dangerous, seething passion.

How could she wed a man who provoked such dangerously intense feelings in her and she in him? But what choice did she have with her family still dependent on her? Even if Ford did not turn them out of his house, the upset of Laura calling off the wedding would put a strain on her mother's frail health. And the scandal would taint her family's reputation, making it even harder for her sisters to find good husbands. All she'd endured during her first marriage would have served no purpose but to postpone her family's ruin.

A light, rapid tap on her door made Laura's heart race. Could Ford have returned to continue their confrontation where he'd left off last night?

Bounding out of bed, she pulled on her dressing gown.

"Who is it?" she called, taking up a position near the hearth where the fire irons were within easy reach.

The words had scarcely left her mouth when the door flew open and Belinda burst in.

"Lolly, I'm so glad you're still awake!" Belinda threw her arms around her sister and twirled them both in a dizzy circle. "I'd have hated to wake you when I know you need your sleep before the wedding. But I couldn't keep this wonderful news until morning or I might burst with happiness!"

"N-news?" Laura struggled to collect her badly ruffled composure.

"I'm surprised you haven't guessed by now since you had a hand in it." Belinda pulled her over to sit on the bed. "Mr Crawford—dearest Sidney—has asked me to marry him!"

"That *is* wonderful!" Laura seized her sister in a joyful embrace. "And so quick. Mr Crawford only danced with you for the first time last night. When did he propose? What did he say? Tell me everything."

"It was just after you went to bed," Belinda began, clearly bursting to relate every detail, "since it was such a lovely evening, I decided to take a walk in the garden. When Sidney appeared, I thought he must be looking for you, so I told him I was sorry but you'd retired for the night. He said I must not be sorry because he had come to speak to me."

"It was always you he hoped to see, whenever he called at Hawkesbourne." Laura squeezed her sister's hand.

"That's what he told me." Belinda blushed. "But why did you never say a word to me if you guessed his feelings?"

"I did not want to raise your hopes in case I was wrong or Mr Crawford could not work up the courage to speak to you himself. I'm delighted he did at last."

"He said he has admired me for a very long time." Belinda's eyes sparkled with the pure joy. "But he could not bring himself to tell me, in case I might not be able to care for him. There was also his mother, who had her heart set on him making an advantageous marriage."

Laura grimaced. "Mrs Crawford gave me quite a lecture about that at the ball. I hope she will not make trouble for you."

Belinda did not look the least bothered by the prospect of having Mrs Crawford for a mother-in-law. "I'm certain I can win her over. I may not have your strength of character or Sukie's high spirits, but I do know how to make myself agreeable. Besides, Sidney told me he would not tolerate any interference from our families. After he found the courage to stand up to Ford, he said managing his mother should be the easiest thing in the world."

"How did he stand up to Ford?" Laura found it hard to believe Sidney Crawford had survived such a confrontation.

"It really is the silliest thing." Belinda gave an indulgent chuckle. "But I suppose I must not be vexed since it provoked Sidney to act on his feelings for me at last. Somehow Sidney conceived the bizarre notion that Ford was a cruel tyrant who would make all our lives miserable. So he resolved to rescue me."

Laura shook her head in amazement at the strange way things had worked out. After all her worry that Ford's rudeness would drive Sidney Crawford away, it had driven the young man straight into Belinda's arms instead.

"Men do get the strangest notions in their heads, poor things," Belinda continued. "You will never guess what a daft idea Ford had. He thought Sidney was in love with you! I suppose that explains why he wasn't as pleasant to Sidney as he might have been."

Laura tried to look amused though it sickened her that Ford could have harboured such suspicions.

"Now that I think of it," said Belinda, "perhaps it was not so farfetched a mistake for Ford to make. You and Sidney did talk together very often and you always spoke well of him. I know you were only trying to encourage his interest in me, but men do see rivals everywhere when they are in love, don't they?"

Part of Laura wanted to believe Ford's irrational jealousy of Sidney Crawford was a sign that he might still care for her, in spite of his denials. But reason and past experience suggested otherwise. It was Ford's distrust of her that had spawned the suspicion she was plotting to betray him with their innocent neighbour.

"Now I must leave you to get a good night's sleep for your wedding." Belinda pressed a kiss on Laura's cheek then headed off with such a light step, she seemed to be floating on air. "I wish Sidney had proposed sooner so we could have a double wedding tomorrow."

Laura quailed at the thought of Ford and Mr Crawford sharing altar space at St Botolph's.

"I almost forgot." Belinda paused with her hand on the knob of Laura's bedroom door. "Sidney said to tell you he would be delighted to have any of my family come and live with us at Lyndhurst, including you. Nothing I could say would persuade him Ford will be a very kind husband to you. Once we're all settled down and they get better acquainted, I'm sure the two of them will become great friends and laugh over this foolish prejudice against one another."

After Belinda had departed, humming the tune to which she and Sidney had danced at the ball, Laura sat frozen, mulling over Mr Crawford's generous offer. Half an hour ago, she'd had no choice about marrying Ford. Now she did.

To her dismay, she realised that choice did not make her situation the least bit easier. For it meant she would have no one else to blame for her future misery if she made the wrong decision.

Standing at the altar of St Botolph's, Ford pretended to ignore the escalating chorus of whispers from the pews as he consulted the gold pocket watch that had once belonged to his grandfather. In two more minutes the guests should be all assembled. He wanted to be certain everyone was there to hear his announcement. The last thing he wanted was to be obliged to repeat it.

Anger thundered through him, demanding all his self-control to hold it in. All his plans had been thwarted. Laura had eluded him once again, but only after deepening her hold upon him.

How far would he have to go and how long would he have to wait for those memories to fade? His longing for her had already pursued him to the other side of the world and held him in bondage for more than seven years. At this rate, he would *never* be free.

Though he was not in danger of losing his fortune, title or estate, he felt even worse than the first time Laura had jilted him. Then, he'd been able to slip quickly out of the country without facing anyone who knew what had happened. And he'd had the comfort of his unshaken belief that he'd been wronged. This time, Ford could not escape the bitter knowledge that he had only himself to blame.

There now. His two minutes were up. The pews were full and the guests were growing restless, casting frequent, expectant glances toward the back of the sanctuary. Watching for the bride who would not come.

Ford mustered his composure, determined that no one should suspect his true feelings. He would speak with brisk detachment, as if the loss of his bride were a trifling inconvenience and he could find a suitable substitute at a moment's notice if he wished to bother.

But before he could get the words out, he heard soft footsteps and faint rustling from the back of the church. Surely it could not be…

Ford's heart began to pound so hard that he feared it would tear a hole in the breast of his coat.

Belinda and Susannah appeared at the head of the aisle, clutching nosegays of early summer flowers. The organ wheezed to life with the opening chords of a stirring processional. The wedding guests rose and a moment later Laura swept toward the altar on the arm of Sidney Crawford.

Her beauty staggered Ford anew. For her second wedding she had forgone a white gown in favor of a warm apricot color. Her hair was gathered up in a mass of loose golden curls, crowned with a halo of orange blossoms.

What in heaven had brought her here this morning, after he'd lost the means to compel her and after the way he'd treated her?

Upon reaching the foot of the altar, Laura suddenly raised her downcast eyes to meet his. Her captivating blue gaze held a glow of vulnerable hope clouded by wary uncertainty.

The organ fell silent and the guests resumed their seats.

"Dearly beloved," intoned the vicar, "we are gathered together here in the sight of God, and in the face of this congregation, to join together this Man and this Woman in holy Matrimony, which is an honourable estate, instituted of God…and therefore is not by any to be enterprised, nor taken in hand, unadvisedly, lightly, or wantonly, to satisfy men's carnal lusts and appetites, like brute beasts that have no understanding, but reverently, discreetly, advisedly, soberly, and in the fear of God."

The vicar's warning stung Ford, for that was precisely the type of marriage he had offered Laura. One to satisfy his carnal lusts without any bothersome complications such as love.

"Therefore," continued the vicar, "if any man can show any just cause, why they may not lawfully be joined together, let him now speak, or else hereafter for ever hold his peace."

Ford braced for Sidney Crawford to raise an objection, but the awkward pause passed without a word from anyone.

Ford had no time to savour a sense of relief, for the vicar now looked from him to Laura. "I require and charge you both, as ye will answer at the dreadful day of judgement when the secrets of all hearts shall be disclosed, that if either of you know any impediment, why ye may not be lawfully joined together in Matrimony, ye do now confess it."

A mad compulsion seized him to confess his true reason for wedding Laura, but he clenched his teeth tight, imprisoning the words. Noticing her lower lip tremble, he wondered what secret motive quivered, unspoken, on *her* tongue.

Once again the perilous moment passed.

"Anthony Ford," said the vicar, "wilt thou have this woman to thy wedded wife, to live together after God's ordinance in the holy estate of Matrimony? Wilt thou love her, comfort her, honour, and keep her in sickness and in health, and, forsaking all other, keep thee only unto her, so long as ye both shall live?"

When Ford tried to answer, he found his jaw still clamped tight. After a self-conscious hesitation, he managed to make the proper response.

The vicar turned to Laura with a reassuring smile, "Laura Eleanor, wilt thou have this man to thy wedded husband, to live together after God's ordinance in the holy estate of Matrimony? Wilt thou obey him, and serve him, love, honour, and keep him in sickness and in health, and, forsaking all other, keep thee only unto him, so long as ye both shall live?"

The vicar's solemn question evoked a memory of Laura, sodden but defiant, challenging Ford's treatment of his tenants…and her. *"It is not pleasant to be tyran-*

nised—having no power over anything that happens to you, always dancing to someone else's tune. Perhaps you do not know what that feels like, but I do."

After all that had happened, feeling as she did, would Laura dare place herself in his power with vows to serve and obey him?

"I will." Her tremulous whisper told Ford she had asked herself the same question.

"Who giveth this woman to be married to this man?" asked the vicar.

After a brief hesitation, Sidney Crawford answered, "I do."

The vicar placed Laura's right hand in Ford's, bidding Ford to speak his wedding vows. Despite his most strenuous efforts, Ford stumbled over his promise *to love and to cherish*. A moment later, Laura's voice caught on her vow *to love, cherish, and to obey*.

The vicar did not seem to notice. Perhaps he mistook their faltering for ordinary wedding nerves. Beaming benignly, he signalled Ford to place the wedding ring upon the open pages of his prayer book. After he had blessed it, he returned it to Ford to place on Laura's finger, then led him in the final portion of his vows. Kneeling beside Laura on the steps of the chancel, Ford scarcely heard the hopeful prayers spoken over them.

The next thing he knew, the vicar had clasped their right hands together, saying, "Those whom God hath joined together let no man put asunder."

Several emotions warred inside him as the vicar pronounced them man and wife. Elation was one of the strongest. After all, the moment he had yearned for so long had finally arrived. His flesh hummed with anticipation of their wedding night. Yet he could not escape the haunting suspicion that he had just made a terrible mistake.

Had she made a huge mistake by marrying Ford?

Laura toyed with the helping of creamed oysters on her plate as she swept a glance down the dining table, crowded with guests for the wedding breakfast. Everyone looked so happy and festive, tucking into an ample repast washed down with cups of tea or chocolate. The air bubbled with spirited gossip and laughter.

A host of toothsome smells wafted up and down the table: roast quail, grilled trout, veal pie. Two months ago, any of them would have set Laura's mouth watering. Today, they made her queasy. Or was that the prospect of her wedding night? How shocked her bridegroom and their guests would be to know a widow of her age was as nervous as any maiden bride of eighteen.

In fact, she had far more reason to be anxious than an innocent girl, for whom the event held only fear of the unknown. Her first marriage had given her enough disagreeable experience to justify her qualms. Ford's recent behaviour gave her further cause for alarm. What on earth had induced her to go ahead with the wedding when necessity no longer dictated it and caution urged strongly against it?

Guilt? Hope? Madness?

Of one thing she was quite certain. Love had not prompted her decision. If anything, she shrank from the possibility that she *might* grow to love her husband. Such feelings would only provide Ford with more power over her—a kind of power with which she dared not trust him.

"Where you are going for your bridal tour?" asked Lady Daphne. "Up to London, perhaps? Or to the Continent? Paris? Italy?" Her voice lingered longingly over the names of foreign destinations.

"Er...actually..." Laura searched for a way to avoid the embarrassing admission that she had no idea where they were going.

Ford came to her rescue, "I meant to surprise my bride, Lady Daphne. But since you ask, we will only be venturing as far as Brighton. Perhaps some day I will make it up to her with a voyage to a tropical island."

"Brighton would be exotic enough for me." Lady Daphne sighed. "I've never been anywhere."

In Laura's opinion, Brighton was a most satisfactory destination for their wedding tour. It was only twenty miles from Hawkesbourne, by good road, in case Mama's health should take a bad turn in their absence.

Had Ford considered that when making his choice? Laura wished she could believe he had. She dreaded the prospect of spending three hours alone in a carriage with him almost as much as the approaching ordeal of their wedding night.

The wedding breakfast had passed far too quickly for Laura's liking. She soon found herself back in her bedchamber, changing into a travelling gown and pelisse. When she had finished dressing, she dismissed her maid. Then she sat for a few minutes, struggling to compose herself so she could bid her mother a cheerful farewell. But her fears beset her worse than ever.

Would her aversion quench Ford's desire as it had

done with Cyrus? If so, would he lash out at her as his cousin had, with harsh hands or cruel words?

That thought sent Laura rummaging in the drawer of her night table for her Bible. It occurred to her that she might seek comfort or strength in the stories of women like Ruth or Queen Esther, though Ford might think she had more in common with Delilah or Jezebel. It was not the scriptures from which she sought to shore up her courage, but something she had hidden in the pages of her Bible seven years ago.

She leafed through them—Genesis…Deuteronomy… Samuel…Psalms…The Gospels. Where was it?

A folded piece of paper fell out into her lap. Laura's hand trembled as she picked up the marriage certificate and examined it. This was the instrument of destruction, with which she'd threatened Ford. She had kept it all these years as a kind of insurance, a bargaining tool she'd hoped never to use. She wished to heaven she had never mentioned the beastly thing the other night. But how was she to know he would let her alone simply because she *asked* him to?

There was one small mercy for which she felt vastly grateful. At least Ford's irrational suspicion of Sidney Crawford had made him jump to the wrong conclusion about her threat. If he ever guessed otherwise, Laura feared he would not rest until he discovered the scandalous secret buried in his past. Knowing how badly she had hurt him seven years ago, her conscience shrank from the harm it would inflict upon him.

Her fingers itched to tear the paper into a thousand pieces and release them on a gusting east wind. But she could not afford to…yet. Perhaps when Belinda was safely married to Sidney Crawford. Then she might be able to tear up this paper or burn it to ashes and try to forget she had ever laid eyes on it.

But for today, it must go back in her Bible in case of future need.

Chapter Eleven

Her signature was on the marriage certificate beneath his. Laura belonged to him at last.

As their carriage rolled away from Hawkesbourne on its way to Brighton, Ford leaned back in his seat and contemplated his bride. She looked exquisite in a dark green pelisse and a wide-brimmed straw bonnet trimmed with matching green ribbons—the kind of woman any man would be proud to squire around the fashionable seaside resort of Brighton. Yet somehow she looked younger than her years—inexperienced and uncertain.

Peering out the carriage window toward Hawkesbourne, Laura waved to her sisters long after they must be out of sight. No doubt it was an excuse to keep her attention directed away from him. Ford could have understood her aversion if she'd been compelled to wed him as he'd planned. But she'd had a choice, damn it, and she'd chosen to see the thing through.

Seeking to break the tense silence between them, he

remarked, "That was a fine wedding breakfast. Cook outdid herself."

Laura started at the sound of his voice, but quickly regained her composure. "I hope you told her so. She has been in her glory all week, preparing refreshments for the ball and then the wedding breakfast. She was eager to prove her skills were still equal to such grand occasions."

"Was that why you went through with the wedding?" The words flew out of his mouth before Ford could stop them. "So Cook would not have prepared all that food for nothing?"

Why? That question had burned inside him from the moment Laura glided down the aisle at St Botolph's. Now that they were married, he was in a position to obtain some answers.

Her wavering gaze betrayed her uneasiness with his question, but she managed a poised reply. "I must confess I did not give Cook's wedding breakfast a thought. Why do you ask? Did you truly expect me to leave you standing at the altar this morning?"

Vexed that she had so deftly put him on the defensive, Ford shrugged. "It would not be the first time you jilted me."

Laura flinched.

Not long ago, that might have brought Ford a sense of grim satisfaction. Now it stung him with shame, forcing a regretful admission from his lips. "Besides, I gave you ample cause this time. Though I swear I would never have behaved as I did had I known my...advances would be so...repugnant to you."

His confession brought Ford a disarming sense of

relief, even as male pride chided him for exposing such treacherous weakness. He braced for Laura to exploit it.

Her reply caught him off guard. "Not repugnant. Unexpected. Rather…alarming in their intensity."

The provocative dance of her gaze—catching his for a tantalising instant, then flitting away—rekindled Ford's desire.

He stretched out his legs just enough to bring the foot of his boot in glancing contact with her slipper. Then he grazed her delicate kidskin with his sturdy dark leather, and was rewarded by her sudden, soft intake of breath.

"Does that mean," he asked in a low, caressing voice, "if you were better prepared and I exercised greater restraint, my attentions might not be unwelcome?"

The flesh of her throat rippled as she swallowed before answering. But she met and held his gaze. "I would not have wed you if I were not prepared to undertake my marital duty."

It rankled, hearing her refer to the experience of passion and pleasure he anticipated as an irksome obligation. "Which brings us back to my original question—what made you go through with the wedding, if not for Cook's sake?"

"Is it so hard to believe I did it for *your* sake?" Laura's defiant challenge sounded strangely wistful, too. "Whatever you may have thought at the time, I did not *want* to jilt you seven years ago. I had no choice. Today I did and I chose to keep my promise."

"So you married me out of pity?" Ford cursed himself for revealing she'd once broken his heart. He wanted to reclaim her, but not on such mortifying terms.

"No! Well…perhaps a little. Not for the man you are

now, but for the one you once were and for what he suffered on my account. But mostly so I could reclaim a little of my self-respect."

To Ford's surprise, her answer soothed an old corrupted wound.

But before he had a chance to fully savour the unexpected relief, Laura turned the tables on him again. "I have given you an honest answer, now you owe me one. If, all these years, you believed I was a heartless fortune hunter who'd wronged you so badly, and if you thought I was capable of scheming to jilt you for Sidney Crawford, why on earth did *you* wed me?"

His motives were not nearly as admirable as hers, and he dared not confess them. "I thought I explained my reasons quite clearly when I proposed."

"Because you are cured of such nonsense as love?" Her eyes seemed to search inside him far deeper than he could bear. "Because you want a practical wife who will be content with your fortune and not long for your heart?"

Those words sounded blasphemous coming from Laura's lips. Ford wanted to renounce them, for he sensed they might no longer be true…if they ever had been. But if he denied those reasons, what others could he give her? Definitely not the truth—that he'd wanted to possess her long enough to break her hold upon him once and for all.

Laura seemed to take his silence for agreement. "Perhaps you are right. After all that happened to us, we have both been stripped of our romantic delusions. Better for you to be married to me and know where we stand than risk hurting others who might want more than we can give."

It seemed perfectly sensible, as it should, for Laura had only parroted his own arguments back at him. Yet something about it sounded wrong to Ford.

"There is a difference in what happened to *us*, seven years ago, remember." He did not hurl his words as an enraged accusation, but put them forth calmly, as a judicious statement of fact. "I was not responsible for whatever harm came to you. I was not aware of your father's death or the consequences it would have for your family. I could not possibly foresee those misfortunes occurring while I was abroad. Whatever we suffered was a result of events beyond our control and the decisions you made. I will grant that you did not mean me any harm. But, intended or not, I did suffer as a consequence of your actions."

A weight lifted from Ford's chest as he spoke. What a blessed relief to get such thoughts out in the open, rather than keeping them trapped inside him, smouldering and ready to explode at unguarded moments into hostile recriminations.

Laura's face paled and her luscious lips compressed into a stubborn line. "How magnanimous to concede that I might *not* be a heartless jade who intentionally abused your trust and tried to rob you of your inheritance."

"That was not what I meant." Ford wished he'd held his tongue after subtly caressing Laura's foot. A spiteful exchange now would not put them in a favorable mood for their wedding night.

"But you do blame me for the choices I made and the consequences they had for you?" Laura's gloved hands clenched in her lap. "Perhaps you ought to consider the possible consequences if I'd acted as you believe I should. What if I had written to you after my father died, begging for help instead of giving you your freedom?"

Her question dealt his righteous indignation a bewildering blow, but it rallied to his defence. "I would have returned to England at once, of course, married you and done everything in my power to assist your family."

Laura's gaze searched his and for once Ford was not afraid of the scrutiny. After a highly charged moment, the tension eased from her face. "Yes, I believe you would. But think what a burden that would have placed upon you. Your accomplishments in the Indies prove you had the cleverness and ambition to succeed. But your situation there was not what it would have been if you'd stayed in England. There you started with nothing, but at least your creditors were half a world away, with no means to harass you and seize every scrap of capital you accumulated. And you only had one mouth to feed instead of five...or more."

Ford's righteous indignation collapsed, battered and bloody. Leaning forwards, he reached across the carriage and took one of her hands in his. Then he voiced an idea he had never dared consider. "You were trying to spare me?"

When Ford asked that question in a hesitant, hopeful murmur, his green eyes shone with a light quite different from any Laura had seen in them before. Not the merry sparkle of sunrise on a dew-kissed meadow. Not the emerald glitter of jealous rage. Not even the cool impenetrable patina of a jade carving. It was the quiet radiance of fresh moss growing over old stonework.

She longed to respond to that light, and to the firm

warmth of his touch, with a nod or a whispered *yes*. But that would simplify the truth beyond recognition. Besides, it was the eager expectancy of his question that unnerved her. Despite all Ford's declarations to the contrary, she feared if she gave him that response, it might encourage him to want something she might not be able to give.

Beginning tonight…in their marriage bed.

Her fear of suffering any physical harm at Ford's hands had eased. But other kinds of hurt ran far deeper and left scars that remained long after cuts and bruises healed. Ford had inflicted one just now by pointing out a painful truth about the events of seven years ago. Her actions were to blame for what they'd suffered then and since.

"I wish I could claim I acted out of kindness. But the truth is I thought you were eager to be free of me. I was hurt and angry, grieving for my father and the life I'd hoped to have with you. If my letter sounded unfeeling, even cruel, that is why."

A shadow of disappointment dimmed the faint stirring of hope in Ford's eyes, but he was quick to conceal both. "Enough talk of the past. On their wedding day, a couple should look to the future—even when they are not giddy with rose-colored romantic dreams. I am looking forward to a pleasant stay in Brighton, with no estate improvements or Vindicara business to occupy my energies."

Relieved as she was not to dwell on the painful memories, Laura could not look to the immediate future with any eagerness either. With no estate or company matters to distract him, all Ford's attention would be focused upon her, as it was at this moment.

He had not released her hand but cradled it in his. Memories of every time he'd touched her flooded Laura's mind, igniting a fierce blaze in her cheeks. That blaze grew hotter still when Ford pressed the pad of his thumb against the palm of her glove and began to move it in a slow, rhythmic caress. There could be no mistaking what part of their stay in Brighton he was looking forward to.

How would he react when he discovered her deficiencies as a wife? He'd been quite frank that passion was one thing he wanted from marriage. She had spoiled so many things for him in the past. Could she bear to spoil that too?

Both her forebodings and her physical awareness of her new husband intensified as the day wore on. When Ford helped her out of their carriage in front of the Old Ship Inn, she was more conscious than ever of his size and air of overpowering masculinity. Yet, while they were eating dinner in the inn's elegant dining room, she could not fail to notice his deft touch with the cutlery and glassware.

After dinner, they took a stroll on the Steyne where Brighton's fashionable visitors gathered to promenade.

"As bad as Rotten Row," Ford muttered to her out of the corner of his mouth, "only without the horses."

Laura could not help noticing how many female gazes followed Ford's every move with predatory stares. It was not much wonder, she supposed after looking about, for he was by far the most attractive gentleman she spied. Would he soon consider those attractions wasted on a wife so ill equipped to appreciate them?

When Ford suggested they return to the inn, Laura gave a silent nod of agreement. She feared her voice would tremble if she tried to speak. As she climbed the wide, luxuriously carpeted stairs, her heart seemed to sink deeper with every step.

At last they entered their spacious, elegantly appointed room. A huge four-poster bed, hung with brown and gold curtains, dominated the chamber while a matching screen hid a dressing area in the far corner. Beside the screen stood a mirrored table, with Laura's hairbrush and toiletries already arranged upon it

Ford closed the door behind them with solid finality. "I hope you will find everything to your satisfaction."

He removed his coat, then set about untying his neckcloth. Did he intend to disrobe entirely, right there before her? When he began to unbutton his waistcoat, Laura dived behind the screen. There she removed her bonnet and pelisse, acutely aware of every sound as Ford dispatched the rest of his clothes and climbed into bed.

Slowly and deliberately she peeled off her gown, stockings and shift. Then she donned her white linen nightgown and dressing gown. Having no further excuse to delay, she slipped out from behind the screen and took a seat in front of the dressing table. As she pulled the pins from her hair, she could see the bed behind her reflected in the looking glass.

There sat Ford, propped up against the pillows. The sheets covered him below the waist, but his lean-muscled chest was bare to her startled gaze. His arms were raised, hands tucked behind his head in a pose of insolent power, the way she imagined some eastern emperor might look.

For an instant, their eyes met in the glass. He flashed her a wicked grin that set her pulse galloping. Laura seized her brush and began to rake it through her hair. Though she tried to avoid looking at Ford again, she could not keep herself from stealing repeated glances. Each one sent a billow of heat rippling through her.

A devilish chuckle rumbled from the bed. "If you are hoping I will fall asleep before you finish your *toilette*, I fear I must disappoint you."

Once again Laura could not resist glancing toward his reflection.

Ford twitched down the covers beside him and patted the bottom sheet. "Come to bed, now. I have waited more than seven years for this night and I mean to savour it to the fullest."

"As soon as I plait my hair."

"To hell with plaits!" Ford surged out of bed, throwing on a dressing gown of rich wine-red. "I will only pull them out again."

For a fleeting instant, Laura glimpsed him completely naked—hard muscled thighs shadowed by dark hair, a proudly rampant sceptre rising between. She gasped for air. She gasped again, when he strode up behind her chair and hoisted her into his arms. He buried his face in her hair, drawing in deep draughts of her scent.

"If you are only dallying to fuel my desire," he suggested in a husky whisper, "it is working very well."

Dallying to fuel his desire? Laura struggled to catch her breath again. Did he reckon she was some sort of wanton temptress? When he discovered she was quite the opposite, would he feel betrayed by her again, in the most intimate way?

Ford carried her to the bed and laid her upon it. Then he reclined beside her and leaned over to kiss her.

"We must not be derelict," he whispered between exploratory applications of his lips, "in undertaking our marital duties."

Anxious as she was, Laura could not resist the sensual invitation of his kiss. His lips moved over hers, the subtle friction striking sparks of delicious sensation through her whole body. Then he captured her lower lip between his and began a languorous, velvety suckle, fuelling those tentative sparks to burn hotter. Her nipples puckered against the fine linen of her nightgown and a dewy fever kindled between her thighs.

Lulled by the sweet, wanton urges that possessed her, she responded to Ford with some long-suppressed instinct. Her lips parted, releasing a tremulous sigh. As if it were a sign he'd been waiting for, Ford pressed his kiss deeper. His hand found the sash of her dressing gown and untied it with a single deft tug.

That first breach of her cover, flimsy as it might be, let loose a swarm of sordid, distressing memories that she had locked away deep in her mind. She froze, haunted by visions of Cyrus's cold, possessive hands pillaging her unwilling body.

Ford pulled back. "Good Lord, you're trembling. What is the matter?"

Reluctantly, she opened her eyes, dreading the disappointment she might see in his. She could not admit the truth. "I f-felt a draught."

"Nonsense." Ford spoke in a tone of tender concern, which Laura saw reflected in his eyes. "This room is an inferno. Or perhaps that's just me. If you are cold, it is my duty to warm you up. Wasn't that one of our vows—for better for worse, for richer for poorer...for hotter for colder?"

Despite the bewildering whirl of emotions in her heart, Laura could not suppress a shaky smile at his jest.

Leaning in closer, Ford tilted his head until she could not avoid looking into his eyes. "If this is because of the way I behaved the other night, I swear you need have no fear of me. I cannot pretend it will be an easy task to curb the passion you provoke, but you have my word I will do everything in my power to bring you pleasure."

Ford sealed his pledge with an insistent but tender kiss that somehow banished thoughts of Cyrus and held them at bay. Instinctively Laura sought refuge in that kiss and found it. The fires in her flesh rekindled, raising a protective barrier of flame between her and those skulking memories. When Ford's hand closed over her bosom, she did not shrink from his touch.

It was not the first time a man had touched her breast, not even the first time Ford had. Yet it seemed that way, for his present attentions provoked very different sensations in her. Always before, it had felt as if something was being taken from her. This leisurely, stimulating caress seemed intent upon *giving*. It offered reassurance, bestowed admiration and lavished sweet, unexpected pleasure. When Ford lifted his hand away, Laura arched her body in an effort to maintain contact. A soft but urgent note of protest droned deep in her throat.

But Ford's hand strayed only as far as her shoulder to ease down the sleeves of her nightgown. As soon as her breasts were bare, he disengaged his lips from hers to strew tantalising, feathery kisses over her chin and throat. Once again he began to grace her breasts with his most ardent favors.

He grazed his cheek back and forth over them several times, a provocative variation of smooth and rough textures. Then he dusted kisses over them, working inward toward her straining nipples. Just when she could scarcely bear the sweet torment an instant longer, Ford rewarded her patience with a long slow stroke of his tongue. Laura let out a gasp of pleasure at the sensation of hot, liquid velvet. Then his lips closed over the exquisitely sensitive flesh to provide the offering she craved instinctively.

As he continued to suckle her breasts so pleasurably, Ford stretched his hand down and caught the lace hem of her nightgown. He tugged it up over her knees, then slid his fingers beneath to caress her thighs.

Deeply ensnared in this delectable labyrinth of sensation, Laura found a welcome escape from all her old fears and failures. The past and all its regrets were lost to her as if they had never been. The future stretched no further than the fulfilment of her body's escalating desire. Within passion's crucible, the shards of her shattered trust melted and reformed, forging a sweet certainty that Ford would sate this baffling hunger he had stirred in her.

He continued to rouse it hotter and deeper with every touch of his hand. The enticing patter of his fingertips. The deliciously wicked friction of his nails. The firm, masterful stroke of his palm. Higher and higher they ventured, tormenting her with the captivating promise of bliss. Hardly conscious of what she was doing, Laura parted her legs in a beseeching invitation, her hips straining toward the irresistible lure of his touch.

At last came the searing bliss of contact. Ford cupped his palm over the crest of her thighs, then his wanton fingers delved into the slick, sultry crevice below. At the same instant he raised his mouth from her breast to press a kiss of thrilling intensity upon her lips. As his tongue flicked in and out of her mouth, his fingers slipped and glided, fluttered and stroked below. He roused her to a perilous pinnacle of sensation, then launched her over the edge into a bottomless cauldron of molten delight. She writhed beneath him, keening her rapture in cries his ravenous mouth devoured with greedy zest.

While she was still drowning in pleasure, he eased himself over her, kneeling between her splayed legs. With one reckless, rending thrust, he plunged deep into her. A cry of mingled pain and rapture rose in her throat to collide with a growl of predatory passion from Ford's.

Before she could entirely take in what was happening, he began to move inside her. Slow at first, the rhythmic thrusting of his hips rapidly gathered momentum to a wild gallop. His hot, ragged breath hissed against her cheek. At last, a fierce frenzy jolted his body and a hoarse, exultant roar broke from his lips. Panting and spent, he crashed down upon her

As Laura lay beneath him, a sense of warm, weightless peace flowed through her. So this was what it meant to be a proper wife to her husband. And she had done nothing different…except to want him. Could it be the burden of failure she'd borne so long was not hers alone?

"I'm sorry," Ford whispered, his lips pressed against

her ear. "I didn't mean to coax you over the edge too soon and for it all to be over so quickly. Give me a little while to recover and I promise you better the next time."

Laura's lips spread into a slow-blooming smile of long-denied fulfilment. Her husband must be well satisfied to propose having her again so soon. And to think *he* had begged *her* pardon for his fancied failings.

She reached up to stroke his hair, the first time she had touched him that night. "I cannot imagine any better."

They made love twice more before morning.

After the most restful sleep Laura had enjoyed in a very long time, she woke to find Ford watching her with an expression of tender curiosity.

"You look like an angel when you're sleeping." He pressed a gentle kiss on her forehead. "Now tell me, what shall we do today? Take a tour of his Majesty's Pavilion? Go for a donkey ride along the cliffs?"

"Sea bathing?" suggested Laura. Her body was feeling deliciously tender after last night. The prospect of soaking in cold, salty water appealed to her.

"Sea bathing it shall be." Ford rolled out of bed, giving his bride a splendid view of his firm, lean body. "But the first order of the day must be an enormous breakfast. I am famished!"

"No wonder." Laura reached for her dressing gown, which had found its way to the floor along with her nightgown. "After all your exertions."

Ford turned to answer her quip, but no words came out. Instead he stood frozen with his mouth half-open, staring at the bed. Laura followed his gaze to a smear of blood upon the sheets.

A bright blushed seared her cheeks. "Please, Ford, I can explain…"

She could explain, but would he understand? The shocked expression on his face made her fear he would not.

Chapter Twelve

The sight of those bloodstained sheets made Ford's stomach twist.

He waved away Laura's efforts to explain. "You should have told me you were having your courses. I would have waited."

With a sharp pang of shame, he recalled her reluctance to come to bed and his insistence. Had he given her cause to believe he would brook no delay in consummating their marriage? Reflecting on his behaviour the past few weeks, Ford feared so.

Before he could heap any more blame upon himself, Laura shook her head. "I am not having my courses."

An even worse possibility clouted him. "Did I use you too roughly? I swear I did not mean—"

"No," Laura snapped, as if angry to deny it.

"Then what…?" An impossible explanation knocked the legs out from under him. He sank on to the bed. "Do you mean to tell me you are still…*were* still a…?"

"A virgin? Yes." Laura clutched her dressing gown

around her. "I know I should have told you, but I wasn't sure you'd believe me. Now I suppose you must for there is the proof."

A virgin and he hadn't taken the least care, certain she was well used to the attentions of a husband. Not once, but three times—it was a wonder the poor woman could move after such handling.

"How?" Ford raked his fingers through his hair. All his old certainties turned on their heads again. "Why?"

"Does it matter now?" Laura gnawed her lower lip. "We are married. Our marriage is consummated. Can we not forget the past seven years? Yesterday in the carriage, you said we should look to the future."

"Can we forget?" Ford slid back on to the bed and beckoned her to join him.

It was a seductive thought, but there was a world of difference between *forgetting* and *not knowing*. The latter he could not bear. What a man did not know could very well hurt him, and probably would. There were so many things he wished he'd known seven years ago.

As Laura edged on to the bed beside him, Ford offered an alternative. "Perhaps if we make a clean breast of things we can lay the past to rest and start afresh. I wish you'd told me your marriage to Cousin Cyrus was only in name."

"It was more than name." Laura averted her eyes and spoke in a subdued murmur. "At least Cyrus wanted it to be. He tried to…be a husband to me but he… couldn't."

"Cyrus was impotent?" Ford wasn't sure why that came as such a shock to him—perhaps because he'd been so bedevilled by desire for Laura that he found it hard to imagine a man incapable of being roused by her.

"Is that what it's called?" She twisted her wedding ring around and around her finger. "I only know he couldn't do…what you did last night. He tried quite often at first, but less and less as time went on. Mostly when he'd had too much to drink."

"That would not have aided his performance," Ford muttered. It must have driven Cyrus mad to have a beautiful, desirable young wife in his bed and not be able to avail himself of her charms. "Have you any idea what ailed him, that he couldn't be a proper husband to you?"

"Must we talk about this now?" Laura scrambled from the bed and bolted behind the dressing screen. "I thought you were hungry. We should go get something to eat."

Her voice had the high, tight pitch of barely controlled panic.

"Laura, what's wrong?" Ford surged to his feet, threw on his dressing gown and followed her. "I know this is not a very pleasant topic of conversation, but—"

Ducking behind the screen, he found her pulling on a gown. A tear trickled down her cheek, leaving a faint moist trail behind it.

"My dear!" He tried to take her in his arms, but she backed away, wiping her face with her sleeve. "I am sorry to distress you with my questions, but this all came as such a shock."

For a moment he feared more tears might follow the first one, but Laura inhaled a deep, quivering breath and composed herself. "Don't you see? *I* was what ailed Cyrus. It was my fault for not doing my duty, not being a proper wife. I tried to be. But when he tried to make love to me, I felt as if I was going to retch."

Her confession affected Ford the same way. "Was that how you felt last night with me?"

To his vast relief, Laura shook her head. "Surely you do not need to ask that. You made me feel things I never imagined—as if I was on fire or pounded by the surf. I must have done what I was supposed to, mustn't I? Because you had no difficulty...with your part."

Though she held herself back from him in a wary stance, her anxious expression begged for reassurance. Some instinct warned Ford he could hurt her very badly if he was not careful. There was a time he would not have hesitated to press his advantage, eager to repay all the pain she had caused him. None of that entered his head now.

"No difficulty at all." Sensing she might feel cornered, he backed away. "Quite the contrary, in fact. Though I must confess, that had only a little to do with your reaction. I hope I would have behaved like a gentleman and not persisted if I thought my attentions were offensive to you." Memories of his *ungentlemanly* conduct a few nights ago reproached him. "But that would not have hindered my ability to take my pleasure, if I'd chosen to."

"It wouldn't? But Cyrus said..."

Ford took a few more steps back and sat on the foot of the bed. "What did he say? That *you* were to blame because he could not perform?"

Laura gave a hesitant nod.

A grunt of bitter laughter burst out of Ford. "That is the biggest load of rubbish I have ever heard. If every man in England was rendered impotent by his wife's aversion, most titled families would have gone extinct long ago."

His wry quip brought the ghost of a smile to Laura's

face, but it vanished as quickly as it came. Ford sensed there was more she had not told him about her marriage to his cousin. Perhaps because he'd never bothered to ask. That was about to change, but for now he had heard as much as his peace of mind could bear.

Was this what peace of mind felt like? Laura wondered as she bobbed about in the bracing, briny waves off the Brighton coast.

As far back as she could remember, there had been some worry nagging at her—her mother's health, her father's business, whether Ford would ever be in a position to marry her. Then her world had been rocked by tragedy that made all her past cares seem like nothing. In its wake had come a host of new worries about Cyrus's advances and his temper, the effort to conceal her misery from her family. In recent years the old spectre of poverty had returned to haunt her along with the fear of Ford's return and the trouble it might bring.

Now her mind felt as lightened and invigorated as her body, buoyed by the cold, salty seawater. There were still a few clouds on the horizon, but why spoil her enjoyment of the moment brooding about them? Hadn't she worried herself sick about her wedding night, all for nothing? Ford had given her a taste of pleasure beyond anything she'd imagined. But his passionate lovemaking had helped her begin to see the failure of her first marriage in a new light.

"Begging your pardon, ma'am," called the brawny *dipper* woman who had plunged Laura into the water a few minutes earlier. "You look to be enjoying yourself, but you'll take a chill if you stay in much longer. Back into the bathing machine, if you please."

Shivering in her sodden bathing costume, Laura climbed into the back of the small wooden shed on wheels. As the horses towed it back toward the shore, she stripped off the long-sleeved flannel shift and groped around in the dark to dress in her own clothes.

She found Ford waiting for her up on the promenade. "Survived the dipping, did you? You are braver than I. Give me a Turkish bath any day."

"It felt beastly cold at first—" Laura took his arm and they began walking back toward the inn "—but once I got used to it, I found it very refreshing."

"It seems to have agreed with you." Ford looked as if he was trying to suppress a smile, but not succeeding. "Your face has excellent color and your eyes are sparkling."

"Are they?" After an instant's futile resistance, she surrendered to the giddy rush of elation his compliment brought her.

"Even brighter now." He stared at her with such intent admiration, she was certain he would have kissed her if they had not been surrounded by people.

A moment later, he regained his accustomed brisk manner. "I made some enquiries while you were sea-bathing, about our being able to look over the public rooms in the Pavilion. I am told it can be arranged if you are interested."

"Of course I am." Laura had marvelled at the exotic structure during their stroll on the Steyne the previous evening. "I hardly recognised the place from how it looked when I saw it as a child."

"The King has spent a fortune," said Ford, "having the place enlarged, renovated and redecorated. We have come at a good time to see it, for I'm told the latest work is nearly complete. When do you think you will feel up to going?"

"As soon as you can arrange it. Why? What do you mean *when I feel up to it*?"

It was difficult to tell with Ford's face so darkly tanned, but Laura thought his color rose. "You know." He leaned toward her and lowered his voice. "A tour of that kind will mean a great deal of walking."

A hoot of laughter burst out of her. "Don't fret on that account." She turned to whisper in his ear. "I did not break my leg, only my maidenhead, and the soak in seawater has done wonders for that."

In spite of her reassurance, Ford remained touchingly solicitous of her comfort all that day, insisting their visit to the Pavilion could wait until later in the week. Instead, he took her for a drive through town in a hired curricle, then to a play at the Theatre Royal in the evening. He never mentioned what she had told him that morning, though now and then he seemed distant, making her wonder if he might be thinking about it. Their manner toward one another was cordial but sometimes awkward, as if they no longer knew each other despite the intimate connection they shared.

That night, Laura did not linger over changing into her nightgown. Though she unpinned her hair and shook it out, she did not bother to braid it before going to bed.

The moment she slid between the sheets, Ford reached over and snuffed the candle. "Goodnight. Sleep well."

Without making any effort to kiss or touch her, he settled back on the pillows and lay still.

Laura lay beside him, staring into the darkness, listening to the hiss of her breath and fighting to quell the sting in her eyes. Had Ford sated his desire the previous night, leaving him spent and indifferent? Or was it something else?

She would not weep. She had prided herself on shedding less than a handful of tears since her father's death and one of those had been only this morning. Through years of adversity she had discovered strength within herself and she had cultivated it. Just because her life had taken a turn for the better did not mean she could afford to weaken now. Even as she repeated that personal creed over and over in her mind, her eyes stung harder and moisture gathered in the corners.

"Laura," Ford whispered, turning toward her, "are you still awake?"

Caution urged to keep still and silent, but she could not resist the hushed entreaty of his question. Swallowing the warm, salty liquid that trickled down the back of her throat, she murmured, "Yes. Why?"

"You needn't worry." Ford fumbled in the darkness for her hand. "I will not…bother you again until you're healed from last night. I swear, if I'd had any idea how it was with you, I would have been gentler, taken more care."

His furtive reassurance shattered her defences. A sob burst out of her, mixed with a gurgle of laughter. "So that's what this is about. I thought perhaps you weren't satisfied with me, after all."

"Good Lord, no! What more proof could you want after last night?" Ford pressed her fingers to his lips and raised his other hand to stroke her cheek.

It came out of the darkness so suddenly she could not keep herself from flinching.

Ford groaned as if the breath had been kicked out of him. He lifted his hand from her cheek to rest on her unbound hair, fingers combing feathery furrows through it. "Did Cyrus ever…hurt you?"

She couldn't tell him. She had vowed never to tell anyone. Throughout her marriage she'd gone to great lengths to hide the truth from her family and the servants. It was one of the shameful secrets she had kept hidden away for so long behind the stout walls she'd erected around her heart.

Though she made no reply, Ford seemed to hear through her silence. "He did, didn't he?"

Still not able to say the words, Laura nodded, her head brushing against the tips of his fingers buried in her hair.

"Damn him to hell!" growled Ford as he gathered her into his arms, cradled her head against his shoulder and held her in a powerful, protective embrace.

As they lay there, cloaked in forgiving darkness, their bodies seemed to exchange some wordless communion. Ford's hard, lean muscles tensed with righteous anger, while his smooth, warm skin radiated comfort and his heart pulsed with healing sympathy.

"I swear," he whispered at last, with a depth of fierce certainty that had been lacking in their marriage vows, "I never will!"

Ford held her in his arms all that night, sometimes dozing, sometimes awake and thinking. Hard as it was for him to imagine an old duffer like Cyrus beating a defenceless woman, he knew it must be true even before Laura gave that hesitant nod. It explained so many things that had puzzled him about her behaviour. No wonder she'd been so secretive, so wary…and so reluctant to wed him.

Dear heaven, what must she have feared when he'd barged into her bedchamber after the ball? Ford could not have felt more sickened with shame if he had intended to hurt her.

Whatever she'd done to him in the past and whatever her reasons, she had been punished worse than he had ever wished upon her. Far worse than she deserved. From the parched depths of his heart, he dredged a trickle of forgiveness. It tasted sweeter than he would ever have believed.

When morning dawned, he lay there with Laura in his arms, bathed in a deep, delicious contentment, savouring her warm, soft presence. As on the previous morning, he feasted his eyes upon the innocent beauty of her face, admiring the dainty shape of her nose, the luscious fullness of her lips, the luminous softness of her skin.

For the first time, he noticed a tiny scar to one side of her chin and another extending from the corner of her right eyebrow. How many more scars had Cyrus inflicted on her? How many bruises that had faded from her flesh, but not from her heart? Protective rage swept through him. If only he'd known. If only he'd been there to defend her from his cousin's cowardly abuse, rather than thousands of miles away, wishing her ill.

Just then Laura's eyes fluttered open. In a voice husky from sleep with a subtle shade of wariness she asked, "What is the matter? You look so angry."

Unable to deny his feelings, Ford sought to explain

them instead. "Not with you. With Cyrus…and with myself. When you wrote me that letter breaking our engagement, you hoped I would come looking for you to demand an explanation?"

She caught her lower lip between her teeth and gave a faltering nod.

"It was unreasonable and unfair, but part of me clung to the foolish hope you would rescue me."

How hard had that hope died? Ford shrank from imagining. And what else had died with it? At the very least he owed her an explanation, though it was far too late to change anything.

"I did come looking for you after I got back to England. When I went to your house, your cousin's wife told me you were already married. She did not say a word about your father's death. She made it sound as if you'd been eager to wed Cyrus for his fortune."

"And you believed her," Laura stared into the dark depths of his eyes. "Because another woman you'd loved and trusted had turned out to be a fortune hunter."

The notion left Ford shaken. He had never thought of it that way. Was his father's ruinous second marriage the reason he'd been so quick to condemn Laura as a mercenary fortune hunter?

"I still wanted to find you. But before I could track you down, my creditors descended on me and I had to flee the country."

Her lower lip quivered. "I'm sorry."

"I know." Words he'd never thought he would hear himself say to her fell from his lips. "So am I."

For a while they spoke no more, each wrapped in their own painful memories and regrets. Then, slowly, tentatively, their hands began to move, spreading chaste caresses. Seeking to give comfort and perhaps to find it. But any touch from Laura, no matter how modest, soon had Ford wanting more.

His breath picked up tempo and a hot, thrusting hunger quickened in his loins.

"We should get dressed and go to breakfast." He tried to pull away from her, though every fibre of his body resisted.

"Is that really what you want?" Laura's lips arched in a bewitching grin and the sparkle returned to her eyes again. Clearly she found his predicament amusing.

"You know right well *what* I want to do." He could not resist rubbing against her, sending a shudder of delicious torment through him. "But I promised I wouldn't until—"

"So you did." The melodic ripple of laughter in Laura's voice carried a warm note of sympathy. "And it was kindly done. But I don't feel sore at all this morning and we *are* on our honeymoon, after all."

Ford's body urged him to listen to her and yet… "After everything you've told me about your marriage to Cyrus, I want to prove I can be a different kind of husband."

Her impish grin muted into a bittersweet smile. "You have done very well so far. And I want to be a good wife to you. I hope you don't think because you saw a little blood it meant you injured me. Believe me, I have suffered much wor—"

Perhaps it was the horrified look on his face that stopped her, or perhaps she had not meant to speak of it and could not bear to.

Before he could urge her to unburden herself, Laura

rushed on, "Besides, if you were to woo me as passionately as you did the other night, it would be the opposite of Cyrus. And I do want to stop thinking about him."

Though she had provided him with an ideal excuse to do what he very much wanted, Ford's conscience still nagged at him. "Listen to me. You do not need to prove yourself a dutiful wife by making your body available to me at the slightest sign of interest. Remember how you fought and threatened me on the night of the ball because you thought I was trying to force you? This would only be a different kind of force. Unless you want me as much as I want you, what would be the point?"

The words had scarcely left his mouth before he wondered what had become of his long-held intention to sate himself on Laura's favors until he tired of her. Looking back, he realised his resolve had been eroding by slow degrees ever since he'd returned to Hawkesbourne. The events and revelations of the past few days had placed a greater strain upon it than it could bear.

At last Laura whispered, "I do…want you, that is. I want to feel the way you made me feel on our wedding night."

"In that case—" Ford let his hand stray lower to fondle her breast "—I would be delighted to oblige you."

He set about bedding her slowly and carefully, as if she were made of the most delicate porcelain. Skimming over her skin with his fingertips or his tongue. Drizzling her lips with whisper-light kisses. Employing all his skill and patience, he coaxed her to the brink of release before easing into her. By that time, *his* desire had reached such a hot, pulsing pitch that it took only a few strokes to send them both into shuddering spasms of bliss.

Afterward he held her and stroked her, hoping his body might convey some of the things he could not bring himself to say. He wondered what she was thinking. In the wake of his lovemaking, had memories of her first marriage returned to haunt her? He wished she would tell him more about what she'd suffered from Cyrus. Unburdening herself of those long pent-up fears and hurts might help her begin to heal. But he knew how hard it could be to share such painful secrets.

Perhaps, rather than press Laura to confide in him, he should confide more in her. Caution urged against it, warning him how dangerous that could be. Such revelations put a weapon in the hands of someone he had long mistrusted. Someone he'd given ample cause to use that weapon against him. Someone who had once threatened to destroy him.

As he had several times since their wedding, Ford reminded himself that Laura's *threat* had been nothing more than a hollow, desperate bluff, to which his shameful actions had driven her. She'd denied any intention of jilting him a second time and she had acted true to her word. Even when circumstances no longer compelled her and he had given her good reason to renounce her promise.

Yet, hard as he tried to believe it, some wary part of him remained unconvinced that her threat had been an idle one.

Chapter Thirteen

"Ah, the life of idle pleasure," mused Laura as she and Ford followed their guide through the public rooms of the Royal Pavilion.

The first had been surprisingly subdued, given the Pavilion's exotic exterior. Apart from the octagonal shape and the large oriental lantern suspended from the centre of the tent-like ceiling, its elegant simplicity might not have looked out of place in Hawkesbourne.

"Are you referring to his Majesty or to us?" Ford gave a judicious nod as he glanced around a formal entrance hall that was nearly the size of Hawkesbourne's great ballroom.

"Both, I suppose," replied Laura. "Are you not getting restless, having no matters of business or estate improvements to occupy your time?"

They skirted a tall ladder, on which a workman perched putting the finishing touches to a row of high arched windows painted with golden dragons.

Ford shook his head in answer to Laura's question. "My time has been most agreeably occupied these past few days. Though I will admit there is a stern voice in the back of my mind that grumbles in a disapproving tone now and again. I have been doing my best to ignore it."

"So you have one of those as well?" Laura directed a sympathetic smile his way. "A miserable nuisance, sometimes, aren't they?"

Her disapproving voice had reproached her often during her first marriage, whenever she'd tried to avoid Cyrus or resented his mistreatment of her. It had reminded her how much she owed him and what would have become of her family if not for his intervention.

A searching glint in Ford's eyes made her fear he was going to ask her about it. She quickly looked away and was relieved to find a new subject of conversation opening before them.

"This," announced their guide in a pompous tone, "is the Long Gallery. Quite a spectacular sight, is it not?"

The chamber certainly lived up to its title, for it stretched out a vast distance in both directions. After the subdued colors and restrained symmetry of the previous rooms, this one overwhelmed the eye with clashing shades of bright pink, French blue and rich scarlet.

"A spectacle, certainly." muttered Ford. "A perfect riot of *chinoiserie*. I wonder if there are any porcelain vases left in China."

"I've never seen anything like it." Laura's gaze flew from the life-size figure of a Chinese man to a huge tasselled lantern to a mirrored wall niche that reflected a china pagoda.

"I suppose I should not complain—" Ford paused to survey the huge painted skylight above them "—since my fortune is built on imports from the Orient. Still, I wonder what the Chinese traders in Singapore would make of all this. Wrought-iron bamboo, if you please."

Laura gasped as they emerged from the low-ceilinged gallery into an enormous dining room. The vast dome above them looked to be as high as the tallest part of Hawkesbourne. It was painted to look like a giant tropical tree, viewed from below. A massive chandelier hung down from the centre of the dome, clutched in the claws of a fierce-looking silver dragon.

"That chandelier weighs a full ton," said their guide. "And it is lit by gas, as are the smaller ones in the corners."

"I should be afraid to dine at the table beneath it," Laura whispered to Ford, "for fear the dragon would lose his grip and the whole thing would come crashing down."

She felt rather relieved when they passed into a pink-and-gold drawing room where more craftsmen were busy painting and gilding the cornices.

When they entered the Grand Salon, Ford pointed to a strange round sofa that sat in the middle of the room. Another large chandelier hung above it suspended from the domed ceiling. "I suppose you would not want to sit there, either."

"Quite right." Laura gave an exaggerated shudder. "I'm certain Susannah would go wild for this place—it is so grand and exotic. Does it remind you of India at all? The outside looks like the Indian palaces I've seen in pictures."

"I saw far more of *godowns* and counting houses," said Ford, "than temples and palaces."

"One wouldn't have thought so, to hear the stories you told my sisters when you first came home."

Ford shrugged. "Those few stories account for every

pleasant or interesting moment I experienced during four years in India. The rest were miserably unpleasant or deadly dull. A great many were both."

Laura reflected on his words as they strolled through another elegant drawing room, into the magnificent music room. Whenever she had thought of Ford during his long years abroad, she'd always pictured him in opulent, exotic surroundings like the Royal Pavilion, enjoying thrilling adventures and passionate trysts, while she was trapped in a decaying house with a spendthrift, abusive husband. Though Ford had let slip several remarks to contradict her fantasy, only now did it dawn upon her how wretchedly different the truth must have been.

"You're very quiet," said Ford as they ambled through the Pavilion gardens later. "Were the nine lotus chandeliers in the music room too much for your nerves or were you appalled by his Majesty's extravagance and questionable taste?"

"A little of both." Laura paused to inhale the enticing sweetness of several varieties of lilacs. "I couldn't help wondering how much that gilded clock in the music room cost, or one of those porcelain lamp stands in the dining room."

"Hundreds of guineas, certainly," replied Ford. "A gentlemen at the hotel told me the King has sunk over £700,000 into renovations and additions over the past thirty years. I wonder if he would have made quite so free with such sums if he'd had to earn them?"

Laura gazed back toward the domes and towers of the Pavilion. "If only my father could have been commissioned to work on this—even a single room. Three thousand pounds would have been a pittance to the King."

"Your father's taste was better than this." Ford gave a dismissive wave toward the Pavilion. "He made an excellent job of that garden temple Cyrus commissioned from him. I agree, though, it would have been a fine thing for your family if he'd found greater success as an architect. Then he might have left you all well enough off that you would not have been obliged to marry a man who did not deserve you."

Laura flinched. What had possessed her to mention her father's business? That strayed too far into hazardous territory. She'd already told Ford too much. He was a skilled, considerate lover and a most congenial companion when he chose. That did not mean she dared trust him with any more of her secrets.

"That is all water under the bridge, now." She tried to make light of it. "I am curious to hear more about your time in India. Not the tales you spun to amuse my sisters, but what it truly was like for you."

For a moment she was not sure Ford would answer. He seemed as eager to talk about his experiences in India as she was to talk about her marriage to Cyrus. Then a strange look crossed his face and he began to speak.

"I have nothing against the country itself, for it has many wonders. It is so ancient, so mysterious and such a place of extremes. But I hated it for being so different and so far from home. It did not help that I had no money and was determined to starve before I would borrow any."

"But you found employment?" Laura asked anxiously, then caught herself. "Obviously you must have, or you would never have made your fortune."

Ford nodded. "I would not be here now if I had failed to find employment. Those first years, I often thought I would never live to set eyes on England or you again."

"The work was dangerous?"

"Living was dangerous. The snakes, the weather, the tropical diseases. Big, bold rats that grunt like pigs and will chew a man's hair off while he sleeps."

Laura gave a shudder of revulsion at the thought of such creatures.

"I did find work at the Company factory," Ford continued, "and showed enough initiative that I was soon promoted. The climate didn't sap me of all ambition, like most men."

"I remember you told us about sleeping in the middle of the day because it was too hot to do anything else." She recalled how his talk of lying naked under his bed-netting had made her blush.

Ford gazed out over a swathe of blue forget-me-nots, but his thoughts seemed half a world away. "During the hottest months, it is like having a perpetual fever. Tempers flare over the most ridiculous trifles. I swear there are more assaults and murders during *The Hot* than through the whole rest of the year combined. When the rains first come it feels like sublime deliverance, but you soon discover you've only traded arid dusty heat for the sultry, steaming kind. For a while after the monsoons break the climate is bearable, then everything begins to bake again."

As he spoke, Laura could almost feel that hellish heat. The pleasant June sunshine seemed to bore through her parasol, scorching her skin and parching her tongue.

Once Ford began talking, some long-locked door inside him seemed to open. Only a cautious crack at first, but gradually wider and wider until Laura was not certain he could have stopped if he tried.

He spoke of his employment, so monotonous until he began to understand the workings of foreign trade and to see how he might profit from it. He told of the extreme measures he had taken to save as much of his salary as possible—living in the meanest little room he could find, eating the local food, which was cheap and nourishing but which most other Europeans disdained. How he had fallen ill from a fever and almost died, alone and friendless, thousands of miles from home.

Though he did not mention it directly, loneliness and heartache infused every word of his account, at least to Laura's ears. In a way, she welcomed his willingness to confide such painful memories she was certain he'd never shared with anyone else. She felt herself coming to know him far better than she had during their youthful courtship. She could not help but sympathise with all he had been through and admire the fortitude he'd shown in soldiering on.

When Ford's voice trailed off at last, as if every word on the subject had been wrung from him, she slipped her hand into his and gave it a reassuring squeeze. "The past seven years have not been easy for either of us, have they?"

A shudder went through Ford, as if he were waking from a trance. But he swiftly regained his composure. Tucking her hand in the crook of his arm, he gave a wry chuckle. "You are a mistress of understatement, my dear."

By unspoken agreement, they made their way out of the Pavilion gardens and headed back toward the inn, where a ball was to be held that evening.

After they had walked some distance in thoughtful

silence, Laura ventured to share a little of what was on her mind. "I was fortunate to have the closeness of a beloved family to sustain me and provide a reason to persevere. What kept you going through all your trials to achieve such great success?"

A peculiar expression gripped Ford's features as he considered her question, as if he were torn by several powerful, contradictory emotions, all of which he wished to hide from her.

When he finally answered, his words sounded carefully chosen. "What kept me going? The determination to see Hawkesbourne once more, I suppose. And to make myself worthy of the Kingsfold title, should I be fortunate enough to inherit it."

Laura quelled a foolish yearning to hear that he'd been sustained by an unbidden thought of her or a forlorn hope they might be reunited. Taking care to mask her disappointment, she replied, "You certainly succeeded in your aim. I have no doubt your ancestors would be proud of what you have accomplished."

He gave a gruff chuckle. "Contrary to Lord Henry Dearing's opinion that dabbling in trade disgraces my title?"

"Lord Henry is a proud, foolish old man who could not do an honest day's work to keep himself from starving." Laura wished the gentleman were present so she could give him a piece of her mind. "I sometimes wonder if they aren't half-starving over at Bramberley to maintain that mouldering monument to their glorious ancestors."

"Perhaps the marquis should marry Miss Crawford." Ford held open the door of the inn for his bride. "Before some other debt-ridden nobleman beats him to it."

"That would certainly make Mrs Crawford happy," said Laura as they climbed the stairs. "It might even reconcile her to the disappointment of her son marrying my sister."

"What in blazes is wrong with your sister?" Ford bridled. "She is sweet tempered, kind hearted and a beauty into the bargain. Crawford will be a lucky man to get her. If that jumped-up mother of his thinks otherwise, I shall be only too happy to set her straight."

The thought of such an encounter brought an impish grin to Laura's lips. At the same time, Ford's fierce defence of Belinda warmed her heart. It was clear that, unlike Mrs Crawford and her ilk, he valued personal character above fortune or pedigree.

They continued to make light conversation as they dressed for the evening, then ate dinner. Afterward they passed several enjoyable hours at the ball.

"Here is one more advantage to forfeiting my bachelorhood that I never considered," said Ford as he led Laura through the steps of a jaunty quadrille.

"What might that be?" She sensed a compliment coming.

Ford did not disappoint her. "Being at perfect liberty to monopolise the favors of the most beautiful lady present, without causing a ripple of scandal."

Through the evening, as she danced, partook of the refreshments and basked in Ford's flattering attention, Laura continued to reflect on what he had told her that afternoon. Little wonder he had been so angry with her for causing his exile. he'd suffered far worse than she had.

Cyrus's abuse had left scars, but her life had never

been in danger. She'd remained in familiar surrounding, in the company of her loved ones…most of them at least. In recent years, she'd had to live frugally. But she had not been obliged to labour under harsh conditions to pay off old debts and earn her fortune. All she'd had to do was jilt the poor man she loved and marry a wealthy one instead. And all the while, she'd pitied herself, blaming Ford for the consequences of a decision *she* had made.

Though nothing he'd said today cast the blame for his troubles upon her, Laura felt the familiar weight of guilt settle upon her heart. What irony that while Ford's revelations made her admire and feel closer to him, they also made her understand why he could never forgive her.

"My dears, you are home at last!" Mrs Penrose cried when Ford and Laura entered her bedchamber fresh from their wedding tour. "I know you've only been gone a week, but it has seemed so much longer. I hope you had a lovely time in Brighton."

"We did." Laura rushed to embrace her mother and her sisters, who sat on either side of the bed. "The weather was fine every day but one. The inn was very elegant and Ford arranged a tour of the Royal Pavilion. It is the most fantastical place I ever saw."

Pulling up a chair beside the bed, she launched into a description of the music room and its lotus-shaped chandeliers. Ford hung back, savouring their homecoming and Laura's glowing account of their honeymoon. It appeared he had succeeded in his aim to bring her a few days' happiness. It was little enough compensation for the way he'd treated her since his return to Hawkes-bourne and the seven miserable years she'd suffered with his cousin.

"How marvellous it all sounds!" cried Belinda when Laura paused for breath. "I must ask Sidney to take me to Brighton for our wedding tour."

"Have you set a date for your wedding yet?" asked Laura.

"A fortnight from tomorrow." Belinda raised her hand to show off a ruby ring. "Sidney is getting a special licence so we can have the ceremony here instead of the church. That way Mama can attend. That is, if Ford will not mind?"

Laura glanced back at him with a beseeching look he would have been hard pressed to deny.

"By all means." It was the least he could do to make up for his abominable rudeness to poor Crawford. "And if you will allow me the honour, I should be happy to give the bride away."

"Of course." Belinda flew from her chair to kiss him on the cheek. "Nothing would make me happier!"

Her spontaneous gesture of affection and Laura's grateful smile provoked an absurd rush of elation in Ford.

Mrs Penrose seemed as pleased as her daughters. She looked from Ford to Laura. "The sea air must have agreed with you both. My dear child, I have not seen you look so well in years."

Was it the sea air or their frequent lovemaking? Ford gave a mellow chuckle. "Yes indeed, Mrs Penrose, it was most invigorating."

If Laura guessed his thoughts she gave no sign. "Has all been well while we were away? How have you been feeling, Mama?"

"Wonderfully well," Mrs Penrose insisted, though Ford thought her face looked rather gaunt. "Now that you and Ford have been reunited and Belinda is soon to wed dear Mr Crawford, I could not be happier."

Susannah, who had been strangely quiet, suddenly burst out with news. "All has been well at Hawkesbourne, but not elsewhere in the neighbourhood. Lady Daphne was caught sneaking out to meet your friend Mr Northmore. She has been quite wild about him since they met at the ball, but her uncles refuse to let him call at Bramberley."

"Northmore is no friend of mine, if he would trifle with a young lady's reputation," Ford muttered. "It is a connection his brother might approve, but not if the Dearings object so strongly."

"Perhaps you could talk to them," Laura suggested. "What better match could Lady Daphne hope to make? If she doesn't find a husband soon, I'm afraid she may end up a confirmed spinster like her sister. That would be a shame for she is such a lively little thing."

"I can try, I suppose." Ford did not relish the idea. "Though I doubt Lord Henry or his brother are likely to heed me. The honourable gentlemen seem to think I am a traitor to our aristocratic ranks."

"If anyone can talk sense into them, it is you." Laura cast him a smile that glowed with gratitude and admiration.

They visited awhile longer with Mrs Penrose. Then, as Laura was giving a lively account of her experience sea bathing, Ford noticed her mother's eyes had closed.

"My dear," he whispered, nodding toward the bed,

"perhaps we should go so your mother can rest. We'll want her as fit as can be for Belinda's wedding."

Laura and her sisters rose from the chairs and they all tiptoed out of the room.

Susannah spoke up once they were out in corridor, "I didn't like to contradict Mama, but she has not been quite as well as she claimed. She hasn't eaten much for the past few days."

Belinda did not seem worried. "I'm sure she will improve now that Laura and Ford are back."

A look of concern tensed Laura's features for a moment then eased. "Perhaps you're right, Binny. A few strolls out of doors in her garden chair with Ford will likely restore her appetite."

"I shall be happy to oblige." An idea occurred to Ford. "I wonder if your mother might enjoy a musical evening like the ones you used to put on?"

His suggestion banished a lingering shadow of worry in Laura's eyes. "I think we all would."

Her sisters eagerly agreed.

"May I invite Sidney?" asked Belinda.

"Of course," said Ford. "It is to be a family evening, after all." It would be a perfect opportunity to take his future brother-in-law aside and apologise for his past behaviour.

Laura turned to her sisters. "I almost forgot. We brought you presents from Brighton. A new bonnet each and fans painted with pictures of the Royal Pavilion."

"Where are they?" demanded Susannah, as excited as a child. "Can we see them?"

Laura gave an indulgent smile. "I told Mr Pryce to put my packages in the drawing room."

The girls scampered off in that direction, while Ford and Laura followed.

"I had another idea." Ford felt foolishly hesitant to broach it.

"I hope it is as inspired as your one about the musical evening." Laura's smile glowed with approval. "I am looking forward to it already."

"That will be for you to judge." Ford took a deep breath and ploughed ahead. "I know it is not the fashion for ladies and gentlemen to share a bedchamber, but I rather enjoyed the novelty while we were in Brighton. So I wondered…" His voice trailed off as Laura's brow tensed in an anxious furrow.

"Of course, if that is what you wish." They were the words of a dutiful wife, acceding with good grace to the whims of her husband, whether she agreed or not.

"Only if you wish it, too."

Laura stopped and turned toward him. Ford wondered if she was trying to gauge his sincerity.

"I think we should not make any hasty changes in our arrangements." She lowered her voice to a whisper. "Now that we are married, you will be most welcome in my bedchamber whenever you choose to visit."

The way she glanced up at him through the fringe of her lashes made Ford eager to accept her tempting invitation at the earliest opportunity.

He raised his hand to cup her chin, but regretted the sudden movement when Laura shied from his touch. "If you prefer to keep your quarters private, I could have you come to mine, instead?"

He meant it to be a seductive invitation, but Laura blanched as if it were a mortal threat. "Not that, if you please. Cyrus used to summon me when… That room holds most unpleasant associations for me. Perhaps having joint quarters is the most sensible plan after all."

Ford cursed his cousin. Would the mistreatment Laura had suffered always stand between them? He longed to banish her dark memories and replace them with sweet, wanton pleasure, persuading her what a deliciously desirable woman she truly was.

That would not be the work of a moment, experience reminded him, but patient, steady effort over weeks and months. The struggles of the past seven years had equipped him with the skills and determination he needed to succeed.

He took her hand in both of his. "I reckon your original idea was correct. Worthwhile change does not come quickly. It takes time."

Chapter Fourteen

As her fingers skipped over the keys of the pianoforte to play a familiar lilting tune, Laura felt the past seven years slip away. In happier days, she and her sisters had often entertained their parents with musical evenings like this. Once Ford began courting her, he'd been invited to take part. Belinda and Susannah had tried to revive the custom at Hawkesbourne, but Laura had not encouraged them for fear it would stir up too many bittersweet memories. Perhaps now they could recapture some of the simple joys of the past.

As she ended her piece with a flourish, the audience applauded warmly. It was a select group including her mother and sisters, Ford, Sidney Crawford and Mr Pryce, whom Mama had insisted must join them. Laura rose and curtsied. Then she slipped on to the empty chair beside Ford while Susannah came forwards to play her recorder.

"That was lovely, my dear!" Her mother clasped Laura's hand. "'Gathering Peascods' is one of my favorite tunes. How well I remember dancing to it with your dear papa, God rest his soul."

Laura gave her mother's hand a gentle squeeze. She'd paid a high price so that Mama's fond memories of Papa would not be poisoned, as hers had. If she alone had borne the cost, it would have been worth it. But Ford had paid too, without even the small consolation of knowing what all his years of hardship and loneliness had bought. For as long as her mother lived, Laura could not risk telling him. Even then, she feared he would blame her more than ever.

Not that he behaved as if he blamed her. Ever since their honeymoon in Brighton, he had been as attentive as any new bridegroom. he'd been very understanding about her reluctance to share a bedchamber, though she sensed his disappointment. Often of late, Laura sensed his good humor was sincere, rather than a mask for darker feelings seething beneath the surface. Earlier in the evening, she had watched with some anxiety as he'd welcomed Sidney Crawford to Hawkesbourne, drawing the younger man aside for a private word. But after a quiet, earnest exchange, Ford had offered his hand, which Sidney had taken, looking as happily relieved as Laura felt.

Susannah dashed through her piece a little too quickly and made a few mistakes, but the vivacity of her performance rendered it enjoyable none the less.

Belinda sang next, accompanying herself on the pianoforte. "'Love's a gentle, generous passion, source of all sublime delight.'"

Every so often, during her song, she glanced up at Sidney Crawford with a soft, dreamy expression, which he returned. Laura could not help envy their pure, uncomplicated feelings for one another.

After Sidney led a hearty round of applause for his fiancée, Laura's mother asked, "Who will be next? Ford, you have a fine voice, as I recall. Will you honour us with a song?"

Ford sang very well, Laura recalled, a talent he must have inherited from his late mother, who had been quite a well-known Vauxhall performer before her marriage.

Tonight he shook his regretfully. "I haven't sung a note in ages, ma'am. I should hate to bring down the quality of the evening's entertainment."

Had he sung at all since her mother had last heard him? Laura wondered with a pang. From what he'd told her of his time abroad, he'd had little reason to sing.

"Tush!" cried Susannah. "This isn't Drury Lane. It is only a family musical evening. And, like it or not, you are part of the family now, so you mustn't shirk."

Her words brought a grin to Ford's lips. "As it happens, I very much like being part of this family and I am no shirker. If you can find a familiar piece of music and if my lovely wife will consent to accompany me, I will do my part."

"I'm sure I can locate something." Susannah scurried off to leaf through the stack of music.

"And I would be happy to accompany you, of course." Laura sprang up to help her sister locate a suitable piece.

A few moments later, she and Ford were seated at the pianoforte, his leg pressed against hers, as he sang one of their old favorites in his rich, warm baritone. "'Sweet are the charms of her I love, more fragrant than the damask rose. Soft as the down of turtledove, gentle as winds when zephyr blows.'"

It took every scrap of will-power Laura possessed to concentrate on the notes in front of her, and force her fingers to press the right keys. The way Ford sang those words threw her into as confused a flutter as any callow chit of sixteen with her first beau. It was the same way Sidney looked at Belinda, though it could not be for the same reason. Ford was passionately attracted to her and genuinely fond of her family. If he felt anything deeper, it might be pity for the mistreatment she'd suffered from his cousin.

The sum of those things did not add up to love, though an unsuspecting person might be fooled. Or perhaps a person who desperately wanted to see more than was there. But she was not such a person, surely.

"'Refreshing as descending rains,'" Ford sang, "'on sun-burnt climes and thirsty plains.'"

That final stanza reminded Laura yet again of what he had endured as a consequence of her actions. Perhaps if he knew she'd been trying to spare *him* as well as her family, he might be able to forgive her. Or more likely he would hate her for depriving him of the things he cared most deeply about.

Sweet are the charms of her I love. Ford hummed the tune under his breath as he strode down the east gallery to collect Belinda for her wedding.

Sweet indeed were Laura's many charms, now that he was no longer working so hard to ignore or resist them. During their honeymoon, he'd discovered her touching gratitude for the smallest kindness, and her tender sympathy for anyone in distress. He had first glimpsed the latter when he'd told her about his stepmother's betrayal, but had only experienced its full soothing power when he'd finally brought himself to speak of his early trials in the Indies. True to the words of the old love ballad, her compassion had been as "refreshing as descending rains on sun-burnt climes and thirsty plains".

Yet, for all the appealing, feminine softness of her heart, she possessed a quiet strength that had won his admiration. She'd sacrificed so much for her family. She had endured the cruelty of a violently frustrated husband. She'd given Ford the freedom to make his fortune, even when she believed he had abandoned her. And she'd borne all those burdens alone, hiding them from her family to protect *their* peace of mind.

Just then her voice wafted out of a half-open door ahead of him. "You make a beautiful bride, Binny! I can hardly wait to see Sidney's face when he catches sight of you. It will take his breath away."

"All this is taking *my* breath away," replied Belinda. "I'm so nervous, I fear I'll swoon. *Am* I doing the right thing? Sidney and I have had such a brief engagement, we barely know each other. Perhaps I should call it off."

"And break the poor man's heart?" Laura affected a tone of exaggerated severity. "You wouldn't want that on your conscience, would you?"

Her words stopped Ford in his tracks, his pride stung. He detested the notion that she'd gone ahead with their wedding out of pity and a sense of obligation toward him.

"You're right," cried Belinda. "That would be unbearable!"

"You needn't fret about your brief engagement," said Laura. "I am certain the two of you will have a splendid time getting to know one another better once you are married. So you have no reason to be nervous, do you?"

After a significant pause, Belinda finally answered, but in so soft a voice that Ford could not make out a word.

"Do not worry about *that*, either," Laura reassured her sister. "If you had any idea what pleasure awaits you, I reckon you would fly down to the ballroom and marry Sidney as quick as a wink."

Her voice fell to an intimate murmur, of which Ford could only catch a word here and there. The suggestive playfulness of her tone suggested she was telling Belinda something about the delights of her *marital duties*. He savoured the satisfaction of having altered her attitude so completely on that score.

"I can hardly wait!" Belinda gave a gleeful chuckle. "I assume you are speaking from experience. From the moment you returned from Brighton, I knew you and Ford must have had a blissful honeymoon. You look quite ten years younger."

Ford strained to catch Laura's reply.

"Gracious!" she cried "Look at the time! Where is Sukie? I must go fetch Mama and wheel her into the ballroom."

Stifling a stab of disappointment, Ford made a swift, guilty retreat down the gallery before Laura darted out of her sister's room.

He acted pleasantly surprised to see her, pulling her into his arms. "What shameless behaviour to outshine the bride on her wedding day. Come and take your punishment."

He treated her to a tart, teasing kiss that promised her a night of such pleasure as she'd told her sister.

After a few moments' indulgence, Laura pulled away

with obvious reluctance. "You have not seen the bride yet. I assure you, no other lady has a hope of outshining her today."

"I reserve the right to my opinion." Ford gently tweaked her nose.

"Binny is suffering from bride's nerves," Laura warned him. "You had better hold tight to her arm in case she falls into a swoon."

Ford pretended he was hearing all this for the first time. "I will endeavour to divert her with my sparkling wit."

A few minutes later, he walked back down the gallery with Belinda on his arm while Susannah marched ahead of them. Belinda looked every bit as lovely as Laura had claimed and Crawford was a damned lucky fellow to get her. She was sweet natured, dutiful and obliging with a dash of mischief that saved her from being insipid. For all that, she lacked the spirit, strength and mystery that Ford found so alluring in Laura.

"Don't even think of trying to bolt," he warned Belinda. "If you do, your bridegroom is likely to blame me just when I am anxious to mend fences with him."

"No bolting, I promise." She squeezed his arm. "Laura already reminded me how guilty I would feel if I broke Sidney's heart. I doubt I would be so fortunate as her to get a second chance."

Had they been given a second chance at happiness, as recompense or reward for what they'd endured these past seven years? Ford wished he had done half as much to deserve it as Laura.

He forced those vexing doubts from his mind. "In that case, you had better get it right the first time."

When they reached the entrance to the ballroom,

Ford heard a trio of musicians playing quietly for the assembled wedding guests. Upon the appearance of the wedding party, they broke into a stately march.

As Ford escorted Belinda up the wide aisle between the rows of chairs, he only had eyes for *his* bride. He wished he and Laura could stand up in front of the vicar and repeat their wedding vows. This time he would be able to speak his with a great deal more conviction.

"I wonder how Mr and Mrs Crawford are enjoying Brighton?" said Ford as he and Laura drove to Bramberley in a two-wheeled gig, a few days after the wedding.

It was a fine summer day on the High Weald. A warm wind carried the wild perfume of dog roses and honeysuckle from the hedgerows. In the fields beyond, farmers were cutting their hay.

"I believe you mean, how they are enjoying *each other*." Laura held her hat against a sudden gust of wind. "Tolerably well, I hope. I trust him to treat her kindly, though I worry over his confounded bashfulness."

"You don't suppose he will scoop her up from her dressing table and carry her off to bed?" Taking the reins in one hand, Ford settled the other upon her knee.

His touch, coupled with memories of their wedding night, sent a ripple of heat through her. "I would be very much surprised if he did. Fortunately, I had a little chat with my sister about what to expect on her wedding night."

Ford's dark brows shot up. "That must have been a fascinating conversation."

Laura chuckled. "I hope Sidney will have reason to thank me for it."

They seemed to leave summer behind when they

drove through the Bramberley gatehouse into a court-yard around which the stately old house had been built. The walls were so overgrown with lichen and ivy that several windows were almost completely obscured. Laura half-expected to catch a glimpse of ghosts in ruffs and farthingales peering out from some of the others.

"The Dearings only live in the south range." Laura pointed toward it as Ford reined in the horses. "The rest of the place has been shut up for years."

"They'd be better off renting Bramberley to a rich tenant." Ford swept a critical glance around the moul-dering courtyard. "They could live quite comfortably in Bath on the proceeds. Lord Edward and Lord Henry could take the waters for their health and their nieces would have a better chance of finding husbands."

"That would require putting practicality before pride." Laura squeezed his hand as he helped her out of the gig. "I reckon the Dearings would rather watch Bramberley fall into ruins than rent the place to some *jumped-up nabob.*"

Ford heaved an exasperated sigh. "I have no patience with people who complain of their circumstances, yet resist every means to better their fortunes."

He gave a smart rap with a brass doorknocker in the shape of the Dearing family crest. The summons was answered by a grim-faced porter who looked almost as old as the house itself.

"Lord and Lady Kingsfold," said Ford. "Come to call upon Lord Henry."

The porter took his time looking them over before finally admitting them into a low-ceilinged room lined with linenfold panels.

"Wait here. I'll fetch his lordship." He shuffled to a winding carved staircase at the far end of the room and began to climb it.

"Damned if I would employ such a surly old goat to greet my guests," Ford muttered once the man was out of sight.

"He's probably been with the family for centuries." Laura strolled over to examine a gilt-framed painting of a man in a ruff and doublet playing a lute.

Ford sniffed. "And likely hasn't been paid in half that time."

After many minutes, Lord Henry finally appeared.

"Lord and Lady Kingsfold." He made a slight bow to each of them. "To what does Bramberley owe the honour of your visit?"

His cold expression told Laura he considered their call anything but an honour.

"We came to speak with you about your niece," said Ford. "In particular, her acquaintance with Mr Julian Northmore."

"There is nothing to discuss on that subject." Lord Henry's bushy grey brows drew together. "Have you not made enough trouble introducing that young scoundrel into a respectable neighbourhood?"

Ford's jaw tightened. "Mr Northmore's behaviour is no worse than many others of his age and income. Would you call him a scoundrel if he had a title to excuse his indiscretions?"

"I bow to your superior knowledge of debauchery, Kingsfold," Lord Henry growled. "I would call any man a scoundrel who trifles with the affections of a respectable girl and encourages her to flout the wishes of her family."

Though Ford kept a calm demeanour, Laura knew him well enough to sense his temper rising. She did not want to see an irreparable breach between Hawkesbourne and Bramberley. Casting him a look that begged him to hold his tongue for a moment, she appealed to Lord Henry as a fond uncle.

"Are you certain Mr Northmore means to trifle with Lady Daphne's affections? What if his intentions are honourable? Surely your family would not wish to stand in the way of two young people who love one another?"

"Love?" Lord Henry spoke the word as if it were a bad jest. "How can you give such a name to this shallow infatuation? Once it has spent itself, what have they to look forward to but a lifetime of recrimination and regret?"

Laura flinched from Lord Henry's bitter words. It did not make her think of Daphne Dearing and Julian Northmore, but rather of her and Ford. Was the combustible passion between them doomed to soon burn itself out, leaving only bitter ashes?

"Perhaps if you would permit them to become better acquainted," Laura tried to reason with him, "they might develop deeper feelings for one another. Your niece is much like my youngest sister in temperament. If she is thwarted, I fear she might do something rash. I know you want what is best for her, but if you truly care about her happiness—"

"I will thank you not to lecture me on my responsibilities to my niece!" Lord Henry's craggy features took on an expression Laura had not seen since the last time Cyrus struck her.

"Well, someone needs to!" Ford took a protective

step between Laura and Lord Henry. "My wife is only interested in the young lady's welfare."

"Your wife is the last woman from whom I would expect a lecture on the desirability of a love match." Lord Henry's scathing tone made Laura feel as if her skin were crawling with vermin. "She first secured her comfort by wedding a man for whom she obviously cared nothing. When his death threatened that comfort, she immediately betrothed herself to the new master of the estate, despite her evident distaste."

Laura had long known her neighbours' harsh opinion of her. But to have it hurled in her face, in Ford's presence, was a sickening humiliation. Especially since there was some truth in it. She *had* married Cyrus and accepted Ford's proposal for material considerations rather than love.

Immediately Ford rose to her defence. "My wife's reasons for marrying my cousin are no concern of yours, Lord Henry. Perhaps it is *because* circumstances forced her to wed him that she is anxious your niece is permitted to follow her heart. As for our marriage, she did not pursue me. I persuaded her. If anyone offers an opinion on the subject in future, I trust you will enlighten their uncharitable ignorance."

He offered Laura his arm. "Come, my dear. We have outstayed our welcome, such as it was. If her family are determined to place their superiority above Lady Daphne's happiness, there is little we can do to assist her."

"Go, by all means!" Lord Henry thundered.

Ford shut the door hard, then ushered Laura toward the gig, his arm around her shoulder. "I don't care who his ancestors were. He is no gentleman to insult a lady so. If he were a few years younger, I'd call him out."

Though touched by Ford's indignant defence, Laura could not calm her churning stomach. Just as they reached the gig, the soft rustle of footsteps made her turn to see Lady Artemis hurrying toward them. Her faded olive-green dress and the shadows under her eyes made her look paler than ever.

"Lord and Lady Kingsfold, please forgive Uncle Henry's outburst. I know he can be difficult to reason with at times. You must understand, we Dearings have always preferred to keep family matters private."

Ford helped Laura into the gig. "Then perhaps *you* should speak to him on your sister's behalf."

The lady's fine, dark brows drew together. "You mistake me, sir. Though I regret my uncle's ill-chosen words, I do not disagree with him regarding my sister and that Northmore man. I wish you had never invited him to Hawkesbourne."

Behind those proud words, Laura sensed the lady's sincere concern for her impulsive little sister. Would she feel any different if Susannah imagined herself in love with a man who appeared entirely unsuitable?

"I am sorry you feel that way, Lady Artemis." Ford climbed into the gig beside Laura. "In that case, I fear nothing remains to be said. Good day to you."

He jogged the reins and guided the horse in a wide circle to drive back out through the gatehouse. The sun seemed brighter and the air fresher once they were away from the perpetual November of that gloomy old mansion.

"Do you think Lord Henry has a point?" Laura ventured once the tightness in her throat had eased.

"What point might that be?" A dark scowl still gripped Ford's chiselled features. "That I am an expert in debauchery or that we invited young Northmore to Hawkesbourne with the express purpose of disgracing the Dearings?"

"That we should not meddle in their affairs. I am sorry I urged you to it. I think that I would feel the same as they do if Lady Artemis called at Hawkesbourne to tell me I have not looked after Mama properly or that I should not have let Belinda marry Sidney."

Ford shook his head. "You might resent the intrusion, but you would hear her out at least. And you would not reject her criticism out of hand. If, after considering what she had to say, you recognised some merit in her suggestions, you would act upon them."

"You have a far better opinion of me than I have of myself." His tribute to her character touched Laura more than any praise of her looks. They would fade with time, as would his admiration of them. The other would last. "What makes you so certain I would behave in such an exemplary manner?"

"Because I have observed you in just such a situation. Remember when I first returned to Hawkesbourne and made all sorts of changes to your mother's care?"

Laura squirmed. "As I recall, I raged at you and said you had no right to meddle. But you gave me no choice."

"All the more reason your later change of heart was so gracious." Ford's scowl softened. "For all my good intentions, I *did* overstep my bounds. I should have consulted you first. I know it is far too late in coming, but I am sorry. I hope you can forgive me."

She forgive him? Laura sensed how difficult that was

for him to ask. "Of course! But as I told you then, you were right about Mama. I should not have berated you and questioned your motives. I was afraid you'd become just like Cyrus, making arbitrary decisions to control and frustrate me out of spite."

Ford's hands tightened on the reins.

Immediately Laura repented her hurtful comparison. "Forgive me! I did not mean that the way it sounded. I was wrong. You are nothing like Cyrus."

Ford stared at the road ahead as if driving required his complete concentration. "I have discovered I am far too much like my cousin. My actions with regard to your mother were kindly meant. Others were not. I assumed you must have led Cyrus around by the nose the way Helena did to my father. As a consequence, I was determined to prove I would be master in my own house."

"You thought I…?" How could Ford have believed such things of her, so entirely contrary to the truth, when he'd once claimed to love her?

What had she believed of him, though? That he'd callously abandoned her. That his arduous exile to distant shores had been a carefree adventure. Those had been no nearer the truth than his assumptions about her.

She swallowed her reproaches. "Do not forget, even before you learned the truth about my marriage to Cyrus, you heeded my objections and changed your ways. Today you defended me to Lord Henry. That meant more to me than you can ever know."

"Were the rest of the neighbours like that?" Ford jerked his head in the direction of Bramberley. "All but calling you a fortune hunter to your face?"

His indignation on her behalf eased the sickening humiliation of Lord Henry's attack. "This is the first time I have heard it put into words. But I knew such things were being whispered behind my back. Cyrus did nothing to dispel the gossip. Your tenants and servants were less quick to judge me. Among our neighbours of *quality*, only Lady Daphne and Sidney Crawford showed my family any friendship. Lady Artemis was never uncivil, but I do not think she makes friends easily outside her family circle."

"What you have had to bear all this time!" Pity and indignation mingled in Ford's voice. "If it were in my power to alter the past, I would change yours."

They were now within sight of Hawkesbourne. Laura gazed toward it, struggling to put some of her feelings into words. "We cannot alter the past and we cannot forget it, when we still bear the scars."

"What *can* we do, then?" Ford glanced toward her.

The mask behind which he often hid his true feelings had slipped. Or perhaps he'd deliberately lowered it. Not that it mattered, for what she glimpsed was too confused for her to fathom. Heavy, dark clouds of regret whipped by a tempest of anger and pierced by searing bolts of fear. Was there also a faint, fragile rainbow of hope?

"Perhaps what we are doing now," said Laura. "Trying to see the past through each other's eyes. Owning the mistakes we have made instead of defending our own actions so fiercely. Being willing to share the blame for what happened, rather than holding the other responsible."

With so many unhealed wounds, none of that could be accomplished quickly or easily. They would both have to want it very much and she was not certain Ford did.

Before he could answer, they drove into the stable yard of Hawkesbourne.

Susannah came racing to meet them, as was her habit. Parted from Belinda and forbidden to visit Lady Daphne, she had been at loose ends of late. Laura resolved to pay more attention to her sister.

But as Susannah drew closer, Laura could tell something far worse than tedium ailed her. Her pretty features were crumpled, making her look many years younger, and tears streamed down her cheeks. Ford must have noticed too, for he reined the horses in hard.

Jumping out of the gig, Laura ran to her sister. "Sukie, what's wrong? Not Binny and Sidney, is it?"

Susannah shook her head violently and choked out an explanation between sobs. "It's…Mama. I went to… sit with her after her…nap. But she wouldn't wake up. She's gone… D-dead!"

"That can't be." As ill as Mama had been for so long, Laura found herself unprepared to grasp her sister's fateful news. "She's been so much better lately. Has anyone gone to fetch the doctor?"

Susannah shook her head again. "I just f-found her. Not ten minutes ago."

"I'll go," called Ford, snapping the reins of the gig against the horse's rumps. "Perhaps it is not too late."

Hard as Laura found it to accept the news and much as she longed to seize the scrap of hope Ford offered, deep down she knew there was no need for him to rush after medical help.

Chapter Fifteen

After several minutes working over Mrs Penrose, feeling for a pulse and holding a small mirror beneath her nose to check for breath, the doctor looked up at Ford, Laura and Susannah, who clustered at the foot of the bed. "She's gone, I'm afraid. I am certain it would not have mattered if I'd been at her bedside the instant she expired. There was nothing to be done. If it is any comfort, I can assure you she passed away quite peacefully. Her features are in perfect repose."

Though Ford had witnessed death many times and had not truly believed there was any hope, the finality of it struck him harder than he expected. The same appeared true of Susannah, who had been weeping softly since the doctor arrived, but now burst into fresh sobs. While Laura tried to comfort her sister, Ford thanked the doctor for his assistance.

"We must send for Binny," said Laura once the doctor had departed and Susannah grown calmer. "Poor dear, to get such news on her honeymoon."

She had not shed a tear, though grief ached in her calm, dry eyes. Ford wished he could console her, but he doubted it was within his power. Still, there were practical services he could render.

"I will go to Brighton at once."

"Would you? That would ease my mind a great deal." Laura's look of gratitude almost unmanned Ford, unworthy as he felt of it at that moment.

His face must have betrayed some of that feeling, for when he strode from the room, Laura left her sister to hurry after him.

"Ford?" She caught him by the hand. "What is wrong? I know…Mama, but there is something more, isn't there?"

She had just lost her mother, yet she was concerned for *his* feelings? Did she not blame him as he blamed himself?

"This is my fault." Her quiet sympathy wrenched the words out of him. "Perhaps if I'd left well enough alone instead of taxing her strength with outings and such."

Laura tightened her grip on his hand. "Put that thought from your mind at once. If you had not helped Mama get stronger, she never would have been able to attend our ball or Binny's wedding. These past months were her happiest in many years, and that was thanks to you."

Bobbing up on her toes, she pressed her lips to his in a gesture of tender affection and reliance. With a jolt, Ford realised it was the first time she had initiated a kiss between them.

That kiss warmed his lips and heartened his spirit all the way to Brighton. Somehow it sustained him when he had to break the news of her mother's death to Belinda.

"Oh, dear," she whispered, clinging to her husband's

hand. "I knew something awful must have happened the moment I saw you, Ford. Poor Mama! Attending our wedding must have been too much for her. I should not have been so selfish—"

"Nonsense." Ford knelt before her. "She enjoyed every minute of your wedding and did not appear any the worse for it. You must not reproach yourself."

"P-perhaps not on that account." Tears glided down Belinda's cheeks. "But we should not have come away to Brighton. I might have been with her at...the end."

Ford shook his head. "We were only five miles away and Susannah was there in the house. Yet neither she nor Laura was present when your mother died. I believe that was what she wanted—to slip away quietly."

With a glance, he appealed to his brother-in-law for assistance.

Sidney seemed to understand. "Lord Kingsfold is right, dearest. Even if we'd been at Lyndhurst, or visiting at Hawkesbourne, it would have changed nothing. Besides, your mother would never have allowed us to miss our wedding tour on her account."

Sniffling, Belinda looked from her husband to Ford with a soft, sad smile. "When the two of you join forces, you are very persuasive."

Her words warmed Ford's heart. In recent happy days, he had begun to feel like part of the family. But it was in times of trouble that the bonds of kindred strengthened and new ones might be forged.

"That's the spirit." He rose to his feet again. "Remember, your sisters need you. They both depend on you more than you may realise. Your mother would have wanted the three of you to look after each other."

He addressed himself to Sidney. "My carriage is waiting with fresh horses to take you to Hawkesbourne. I will stay long enough to collect your belongings and take care of any matters that might delay your departure."

Sidney helped his wife up from her seat, then offered his hand to Ford. "Thank you for all you have done, Lord Kingsfold. We are much obliged to you."

Ford shook his head even as he took the younger man's hand. "There is no obligation between family. And since we *are* family now, perhaps we could dispense with formalities if you are willing…Sidney."

"Indeed I am, Ford."

The Crawfords departed at once.

Ford followed a few hours later, so it was long past midnight by the time he reached Hawkesbourne. He went at once to Mrs Penrose's chamber, assuming Laura and her sisters must be sitting up with the body. Instead he found Pryce performing that service. By tradition, the blinds were drawn, the mirrors covered with black crape and the clock stopped.

"Pryce, what are you doing here? Where are the ladies?"

"Gone to bed, sir, at Mr Crawford's insistence." Pryce scrambled up from his chair as if he had been caught doing something mildly scandalous. "I offered to sit up in their stead. The Crawfords elected to stay the night. I put them in the blue room."

Ford nodded his approval of the arrangements. "Very sensible to allow the ladies their rest. I shall invite the Crawfords to remain at Hawkesbourne until after the funeral. My wife and her sisters need to be together at a time like this."

He glanced toward the tiny, lifeless form of his mother-in-law, properly laid out with her hands crossed over her breast. She looked as patient and serene in death as she had in life.

"Mrs Penrose was a fine lady and the most affectionate of mothers," he mused aloud. "Her going will leave an empty place in this house."

And in his heart. From the moment he'd returned to Hawkesbourne, Laura's mother had made him feel sincerely welcome. She had been overjoyed by his betrothal to her daughter, unshakeably certain that his love for Laura had endured the devastation of the past. Had that belief been wishful *naïveté* or insightful wisdom?

"So it will, my lord," replied the butler in a hoarse murmur, his head bowed.

The flickering candlelight glinted on a teardrop that clung to Pryce's craggy cheek. Was there more to his feelings for Mrs Penrose than the devotion of servant to mistress? Not for the first time in recent days, Ford reflected upon the strange, ungovernable force that was love.

Not wishing to trespass on the privacy of Pryce's grief any longer, Ford thanked him for putting the house in mourning and for volunteering to keep the first night's vigil. On the way to his own room, he paused by Laura's door, listening for any sign that she might be awake. But all was as silent as if she were dead, too.

That thought chilled Ford to the quick.

He longed to steal in and assure himself that all was

well with her. But he could not bear to disturb her much-needed sleep or, worse yet, risk giving her a fright. So, reluctantly, he continued on to his bedchamber.

Upon entering, he heard something stirring in his bed. His weary mind harked back to the time in India when he'd found a scorpion on his pillow. But when he raised his candle, its light flickered upon a tousle of long golden hair. Recalling what disagreeable associations this room held for Laura, he was moved to find her here awaiting his return.

He snuffed the candle and shed his clothes quietly in the darkness. Then he slid between the sheets with furtive movements, anxious not to wake her.

But no sooner had he settled himself than Laura edged toward him, warm and soft in the darkness. "I thought you might not return home until morning."

"Would you rather I had waited?"

"Of course not!" She burrowed even closer to him, seeking the sanctuary of his arms. "I have been longing for you."

Laura's need for him penetrated dangerously deep into Ford's heart, but he did not care. He gathered her into his embrace and held her tenderly as she began to weep. Pressing his lips into her hair, he crooned comforting endearments. Not even in the rapturous throes of passion or the lazy bliss after lovemaking had he felt so close and indispensable to her.

Gradually her sobs eased and she grew calm again. At last she confided in a husky murmur, "I hadn't shed a tear until now. I couldn't, even when Sukie and Binny were weeping their eyes out. I cannot tell you how much better I feel for letting my feelings out at last."

Ford's throat grew tight. He did not dare attempt to speak.

Laura spared him the necessity. "You asked me once about my father's death and I refused to tell you. Since then I have wanted to, but I could not while my mother lived."

He'd sensed she was hiding something and it had fuelled his wariness even when he began to wish he could trust her. Why had he never considered she might have an innocent reason for keeping her secret?

"Now that Mama is gone," Laura continued, "I am free to tell you and I cannot keep it to myself a moment longer. I am not proud of what I did, but I felt I had no other choice at the time. I hope you will not judge me too harshly."

Was that another reason she'd kept this secret from him, because she feared he would condemn her? Yet now she could trust him with the truth. Ford tried to reassure her by brushing a soft kiss upon her brow. He could not think of any words that would be adequate to the task.

Laura took a deep breath and her body tensed, as if she were preparing to plunge into cold, dangerous waters. "I must go back a bit first, so you will understand and not think badly of poor Papa. You see, a few years after Susannah was born, my mother suffered a stillbirth and was very ill afterward. The doctors warned Papa that any attempt to bear another child would surely kill her."

Laura paused to swallow several times. "That left only we three girls, who could not inherit his small estate. That was why he took up the practice of architecture, to earn extra money for our dowries."

"I remember," said Ford. "We first met when your

father was designing that garden temple and Cyrus invited your family to visit Hawkesbourne. I counted it a brilliant stroke of luck that I was here at the time."

He'd been trying to dun his cousin for money to pay off his gambling debts, Ford recalled to his shame. Laura Penrose had seemed to embody every wholesome virtue he craved. She'd made him want to mend his profligate ways and do something useful with his life.

"A brilliant stroke of luck?" Laura sighed. "I know you've had reason to think otherwise many times since then. I hope what I have to tell you will not make this one of them."

Though he yearned to assure her that was impossible, Ford could not. Would the secret she was about to reveal destroy the fragile happiness they'd begun to reclaim? Perhaps he should silence her with a kiss and remain in blissful ignorance. Not for the first time, he reminded himself that what he didn't know *could* harm him.

Perhaps Laura sensed his feelings, for when she spoke again she sounded more troubled than before. "Though he worked hard, Papa did not have a head for business. Cyrus advised him that an architect could make more money by providing workmen and materials to construct the buildings he designed. Since that required capital, which Papa did not have, Cyrus helped him find an investor."

Had his cousin been trying to insinuate himself with Laura even then? Ford wondered. After everything Cyrus had done for her family, it was no wonder she had turned to him for help. "The last time I saw your father, his business prospects were looking up. He had a commission for some nabob's country house."

"The client was in a great hurry," replied Laura in a tremulous whisper. "So Papa purchased stone and marble and fine wood. He engaged labourers. But when it came time to sign the contracts, the man changed his mind. Papa's investor heard of it and demanded his money back. My family knew nothing of all this at the time, though Mama was worried that my father did not seem himself and spent all hours at his office."

Ford had some inkling of the pressure Mr Penrose must have been under. He had experienced the anxiety of creditors clambering for money he did not have. How much worse must it have been with vast sums at stake and the future of a beloved family threatened?

"One evening Papa did not come home for dinner so Mama sent me to fetch him. I f-found him in his office…hanging from a beam. Sometimes, in my nightmares, I can still see his face."

The instant he heard the word *hanging*, the bottom seemed to drop out of Ford's stomach. Until then, he'd expected Laura to tell him of the fire Belinda claimed had killed their father. Bad as that would have been, the truth was a thousand times worse for the family Mr Penrose had left behind.

"My poor darling!" He held Laura tighter, offering comfort that was seven years too late in coming. "I would give anything to have spared you that sight."

"There's more."

More than finding her father dead by his own hand?

"I couldn't let him be found like that. I couldn't! Do you know what becomes of suicides? It would have killed my mother to see Papa buried by a crossroads with a stake through his heart, as if he were some wicked monster rather than a good man driven to despair. The disgrace would have ruined my family. And how would we have begun to pay his debts with all Papa's possessions forfeit to the Crown?"

It was a wonder the shock and strain had not driven Laura mad. "What did you do?"

"I knew I must go home before Mama sent someone after *me*. I don't know how I kept from breaking down. I suppose part of me refused to believe what was happening. I decided to say Papa had to work late again. After the others went to bed, I planned to steal out of the house and go find you. I was too dazed to think how I would get all the way from Newington to Piccadilly on my own, at night, with no money. I only knew I must try. I had this absurd belief you would be able to make everything all right."

He couldn't have, of course. Yet Ford wished with all his heart he'd been there to try. But he had been abroad, pursuing an unexpected business opportunity that had promised to turn his fortunes around. It had come up so suddenly he hadn't even had time to tell her he was going.

Laura carried on with her account in a flat, distant tone, as if she were reliving the whole ordeal. "When I arrived home, Cyrus was there. He'd got wind of Papa's difficulties and had come to offer his assistance. I was never so relieved to see anyone in my life. I gave Mama some sort of excuse for accompanying Cyrus to Papa's office, hoping I could persuade him to take me to you. When he told me where you'd gone, I broke down completely. The only reason I could imagine for you going to Spa was to gamble. I felt you had forsaken me."

She began to weep again and Ford stroked her cheek,

whispering soothing words in spite of his own agitation. How had Cyrus found out he'd gone to Spa?

After a few moments, Laura mastered her emotions enough to go on. "When I burst into tears, Cyrus asked what the trouble was and promised to do everything in his power to assist me. I had no one else I could turn to for help. So I told him everything. He was shocked, of course, but full of sympathy. He agreed that if Papa's suicide became known, it would kill my mother and ruin the family. But he had an idea how that might be prevented, if I would trust him."

Understanding dawned on Ford. "Cyrus set fire to your father's office?"

"He never told me so and I could not bring myself to ask, but I believe he must have. When my family were woken in the night with news of the fire, I was finally able to vent my horror and grief over what had happened. No one else was hurt in the fire, thank God. And no one suspected my father's death was anything but an unfortunate accident. But after that, I began to be afraid what Cyrus might be capable of.

"My mother was quite shattered by my papa's death and losing our home to his cousin. I had to protect her and the girls. If I'd been the son my parents needed, we would have been in no danger from the entail after Papa died. There would have been no need for him to enter the treacherous world of business, which destroyed him."

"None of that was your fault!" Ford protested, though he knew too well how such feelings of guilt defied reason. He had long blamed himself for urging his widowed father to wed that grasping baggage, Helena.

"I know it must sound foolish." Laura sniffed and wiped her eyes with her hand. "But now that I am free to tell you all this, I need you to understand why I acted as I did. I was grateful to Cyrus for protecting my family, yet I feared he might reveal the truth if I crossed him. My family had nowhere to go and Papa's debts to repay. Cyrus said the only means he could devise to assist us was to wed me. He would provide my mother and sisters with a home and make me a settlement sufficient to repay Papa's debts."

So that was what had become of the money Ford had been so certain she'd frittered away. A barbed shaft of shame pierced deep into his conscience.

"I tried to think of some other way." An echo of her desperation tightened Laura's voice. "I begged Cyrus to make *you* a settlement instead, so we could marry and take care of my family. He told me you had changed your mind and hoped I might tire of our long engagement, releasing you from your obligation to me."

"Damned lies, all of them!" The intense emotions building inside Ford ignited. "I was never inconstant in my feelings for you. How could Cyrus say such things about me? How could you believe them?"

"Do you think I wanted to?" Laura shrank from his outburst. "It was not your behaviour that persuaded me it must be true, but *my circumstances*. The more I thought about it, the more reasonable it seemed that a man with your prospects and personal attractions could not possibly be content with a penniless girl from a family of no distinction."

For so long Ford had been convinced she'd cast him aside with contempt. Despised him as unworthy of her love. Even used him to further her ambitions for a more advantageous marriage. Everything he'd done in the past seven years, all his business accomplishments, the fortune he'd amassed, had been a way of proving to himself and the world—and especially to Laura—that he *did* deserve her.

What bitter irony that one of her motives for marrying his cousin had been the mistaken belief that she was unworthy of him. Understanding fell like gentle, quenching rain on the blaze of Ford's anger.

"A penniless girl from a family of no great distinction?" He took her hand and raised it to his lips. "I never once thought of you that way. I swear it."

How bitterly he regretted many far worse things he *had* thought of her since then.

"I wanted to believe that." Laura clung to his hand as if she feared he might change his mind and disappear at any moment. "But after I received no answer to my letter breaking our engagement what was I to think? When I heard you'd sailed off to the Indies, I thought it proved the truth of everything Cyrus had said."

What had made her doubt him? Perhaps the shock of her father escaping *his* responsibilities at the end of a rope, foisting those burdens on to her shoulder?

"We both made mistakes." Somehow the concealment of darkness made it easier to admit. "Both erred in our judgement of each other. Then we had seven long years for bitterness to fester and resentment to harden. Even with all that, we were not entirely able to forget what we once meant to one another. Were we?"

"I tried to forget." She sounded weary of the effort it had cost her. "When you returned, the last thing I wanted to be reminded of was the man you'd once been and the feelings I'd had for you. Yet I resented that you had changed. Perverse of me, I know."

Forgetting she could not see him, Ford shook his head. A barely audible chuckle rustled in his throat. "I love perverse women."

"Including this one?" Laura sounded hesitant, perhaps afraid, to ask.

What could he say? His feelings for her were so intense and volatile, so raw and baffling. Could he reliably give them as simple a name as love?

But he sensed it was what she needed to hear, so he pulled her close and whispered, "*Only* this one."

Chapter Sixteen

Ford still loved her. Or he had learned to love her again. Perhaps a little of both.

During the difficult days after her mother's death, Laura held his reassurance in her heart. It comforted her to believe Mama had known the truth all along. Perhaps, content in the certainty that her elder daughters had found security and happiness at last, she had been able to let go of her feeble hold on life and slip away.

But she did not slip away unnoticed. Ford made certain of that.

"What a magnificent funeral cortège." Susannah peered out of the dark-curtained window of the mourning coach she shared with her sisters, as the procession set off to St Botolph's. "There must be thirty carriages. I didn't think Mama knew that many people."

Wearing black crape gowns and bonnets swathed with veils, the Penrose sisters rode immediately behind the hearse. Four horses, draped in black velvet with silver-trimmed harness, drew their carriage. Ford and

Sidney rode in the next coach with the other pallbearers. Those included the Marquis of Bramber, the local magistrate and Hawkesbourne's butler, Mr Pryce. Some people might consider it an odd assortment, but to Laura it seemed fitting. Her mother had never cared about titles or fortunes, treating everyone from countess to chambermaid with the same gentle courtesy.

Dear Mr Pryce had looked after them all as best he could after Cyrus died, when money was so very scarce and conditions at Hawkesbourne far below their former standards. He could have got a better position elsewhere without any difficulty. Laura suspected his devotion to her mother had prevented the butler from deserting them. Yet she might never have considered asking him to be a pallbearer if Ford had not suggested it.

That was only one of the many things, great and small, Ford had seen to since her mother's death. Laura could not imagine what she would have done without him.

"It is all very splendid." Belinda raised her handkerchief to her brimming eyes. Perhaps because she was most like their mother in temperament, she had taken it hardest. "Sidney told me Ford hired a great many mutes and that the church will be ablaze with candles. It comforts me, somehow, to see a fuss made over Mama at last."

Laura agreed completely.

"Poor Papa's funeral was such a small, hasty affair," added Belinda. "I always regretted that, though it could not be helped at the time."

Any sort of Christian rites was more than her father had been entitled to, Laura reflected with a pang of conscience over her part in concealing the manner of his death.

"There could be twice this many mourners," said

Susannah, "and we still would not have to worry about running out of food for them. Ford bade Cook spare no expense and she took him at his word, bless her. She said she would make the refreshments worthy of a duchess, though she would far rather cook for a wedding than a funeral."

"Ford has been as kind to Mama in death as in life." Laura murmured, more to herself than to her sisters.

"Not only to Mama." Belinda reached for Laura's hand. "I cannot thank you enough for sending him to bring me word in Brighton, when you most needed him to console you. No one could have been more sympathetic or considerate. I don't know how I would have borne it otherwise."

Laura squeezed her sister's fingers. Beneath the pall of her grief, a sense of sweet, long-denied fulfilment uplifted her. Hard as she found it to believe, Ford's actions convinced her of the love he had professed. Now with that assurance, she could take the frightening but wondrous step of allowing herself to return his feelings without reserve.

The time had come to destroy the weapon she'd kept for her defence. A weapon that now threatened her newfound happiness.

As Ford stared at the portrait of his cousin on the diningroom wall, he wished Cyrus was standing there alive and he had a weapon in his hand. All the anger he'd once felt for Laura now found its rightful target. Unfortunately, Cyrus was beyond the power of human judgement.

Pryce had just filled Ford's cup with coffee. Now he asked, "Is there anything else you require, my lord."

"There is." Ford pointed toward his cousin's portrait.

"I want that taken down at once and burned. Find something else to put up in its place. Where is the portrait of my grandmother that used to hang there?"

"In the west attic, I believe, sir." Pryce did not appear surprised at Ford's order or reluctant to carry it out. "I will have it brought out at once and restored to its rightful place…with pleasure."

The almost bloodthirsty relish in the butler's voice prompted Ford to ask, "Did you have any idea how my cousin was treating her ladyship?"

"*Mistreating*, I believe you mean, my lord?" Pryce stared up at the portrait of his former master. "I swear I never saw him raise his hand or voice to her, but then he always kept very private. And her ladyship was good at concealing any sign of trouble. I suppose she didn't want to worry her family. All the same, I felt there was something not right."

Somehow, the butler's subtle intimation of trouble made the truth even more real to Ford.

"I've often regretted not saying something to him… or to her ladyship." Abruptly Pryce met Ford's gaze. "I did not keep silent because I was afraid of losing my place—at least not on my own account. I feared it would only make things worse for the mistress and for Mrs Penrose, God rest her soul."

"Do not reproach yourself." Ford drained his coffee. It was not half as bitter as his regrets. "You acted with the best of motives in an intolerable situation. Her ladyship told me what sterling service you rendered her family after my cousin's death."

Pryce did not seem convinced. "If that will be all, my lord, I shall see about removing that painting."

After the butler had gone, Ford found his eyes drawn back to his cousin's portrait, almost against his will. Those stony features and guarded eyes seemed to ask if he was so much better a husband to Laura. Perhaps he'd never struck her, but that did not mean he hadn't hurt her.

In spite of the love he'd once professed for her, he'd been despicably quick to brand her a heartless fortune hunter and spend seven years blaming her for every ill that had befallen him. When his opportunity had finally come to learn the truth and seek some reconciliation, what had he done? Stormed into her life with veiled accusations, predatory advances and threats to evict her family.

An empty threat! Ford sprang from his chair and strode to the window, turning his back on the painting. he'd never had any intention of removing the Penrose family from Hawkesbourne. It had been leverage to induce Laura to accept his proposal. That kind of thing was common practice in business.

Though he could no longer see his cousin's face, Ford could hear Cyrus's voice in his thoughts. This had not been business, it reminded him. And it did not matter that Ford knew his threat was hollow. Laura had believed her family was in as much danger as they'd been seven years ago. She had felt forced into marriage once again by another domineering, suspicious and potentially dangerous man.

So many incidents from the past months rose to reproach Ford as he interpreted his words and actions from Laura's point of view. She must have thought him no better than his cousin. Now he began to suspect she was right.

Laura seemed to have found it in her wounded heart

to forgive him. But Ford feared the day might come when he would have to answer for his actions.

The soft tap on her bedroom door sent a jolt of alarm through Laura. She knew it must be Ford, of whom she no longer had the slightest fear. What she feared was the brittle, yellowed slip of paper in her hands—the one she'd attempted to destroy several times since her mother's funeral. There was a small tear on one side, where she had tried to rip it to pieces. The opposite corner was charred where she had held it over a candle flame. Each time, her conscience had intervened at the last instant.

"Is that you, Ford?" she called, not because she had any doubt, but to give her time to return the paper to its hiding place.

Lifting her Bible from the bed beside her, Laura let its pages fall open. Her gaze fell on a familiar verse of scripture. *And ye shall know the truth, and the truth shall make you free.*

That had certainly been true for her and Ford, she reflected as she slipped the marriage certificate back between the pages. Only by sharing painful truths about the past had their hearts been set free from prisons of secrecy and mistrust to rediscover love.

But this secret was different. Laura slammed the Bible shut and stuffed it into the drawer of her bedside table. It would shame Ford and rob him for ever of the title and estate that mattered so much to him. If all that was not bad enough, it would poison the few happy memories he had of his early life and perhaps destroy his newfound willingness to trust any woman.

"Why?" Ford called back in a bantering tone. "Were you expecting someone else? May I come in?"

Destroying that paper would not change what had happened, Laura reminded herself as she flew to her dressing table and picked up her hairbrush. Nor would it remove *all* evidence. For the rest of her life, she would be dogged by the fear that someone else might discover and expose the truth.

And what about the rightful heirs to Hawkesbourne? A distant relative, perhaps, living in need while Ford had a comfortable fortune of his own? It had been so much easier to justify keeping this secret when her family's welfare depended upon it and when she was only *concealing* evidence, not destroying it.

"Of course." She strove to keep her voice from betraying the tension quivering inside her. "I am almost ready. You can help me choose which dress to wear."

They had been invited for a quiet family dinner with the Crawfords at Lyndhurst, one of the few social events condoned during mourning.

"How much difference can there be between one black gown and another?" Ford stole up behind her, lifting her hair off her shoulders to bestow a warm kiss upon each. "I am certain your mother would not wish you and your sisters to go about in black for months on end on her account."

"Neither do I." Laura nuzzled her cheek against his hair. "But we would not want the neighbours to think we have ceased to grieve for her so soon."

"Indeed." Ford tilted his head to cast a doting gaze at her reflection in the dressing-table mirror. "Still I vow that once you are out of mourning I will buy you a new gown in every color of the rainbow and half a dozen in as many shades of pink as can be found."

"Half a dozen pink gowns? You will spoil me." Catching hold of his hand, Laura pressed it to her cheek. "As long as I have you, I would be content with one old black dress and a single gold ring."

Ford gently pressed his finger to the tip of her nose. "That would be a crime against beauty. And what is wrong with a man spoiling his wife a little, pray? You are long overdue, by my reckoning. But, come, put on your black gown and pin up your hair before I lose all self-control and whisk you off to bed instead of to Lyndhurst."

With a chuckle, Laura bounced up from her chair, trying as hard as she could to forget about the ominous slip of paper concealed between the pages of her Bible.

After she had dressed and done her hair, they drove over to Lyndhurst. There they enjoyed a pleasant dinner with Belinda, Sidney and Susannah, who had been visiting with the Crawfords since their mother's funeral.

"Have you had word from your mother and sister?" Laura asked Sidney. "Do they find Bath to their liking?"

He had been clever to suggest the trip so that Mrs Crawford and her daughter would not have their social lives curtailed while Lyndhurst was in mourning.

"Very much." Sidney looked vastly pleased with himself. "We've had several letters from Mama. She writes that they have made a number of new acquaintances, including one or two gentlemen she thinks might do very well for Arabella."

"Reading between the lines," added Belinda, "I believe Mrs Crawford may have an admirer, too."

"Excellent news all around!" Laura raised her glass. "Romance seems to be contagious lately."

"I wish I could catch a fevered case of it." Susannah sighed. "If I could find a beau half as agreeable as my new brothers, I should be very well satisfied."

Ford struck a pose like some handsome actors did to let audiences admire their looks. "I suppose there might be a few fellows around who are *half* as agreeable as Sidney and me. But to find any of those who are half as handsome would be a rare stroke of luck indeed."

Susannah made a face at him. "If I thought for a moment you were serious, I would say marriage has made you abominably vain. Does Laura spend all her time telling you how wonderful you are?"

"Not *all* my time!" Laura entered into the spirit of their banter. "Never more than six or seven hours a day."

"Is that all?" Sidney winked at Belinda. "My darling wife spends at least ten singing my praises."

Belinda smiled back at him. "I could very easily and not stretch the truth a jot."

Ford set down his wine glass after taking a deep draught. "I am pleased to hear it. That must mean none of your wedding day worries amounted to anything."

"What worries might those be?" asked Sidney. "Is there anything I should know?"

Laura shook her head. "Before the ceremony, we had a little chat about the joys of marriage. Belinda was worried she might not be able to make you happy. I assured her there was no danger of that unless she called off the wedding."

"Quite right. She has made me as happy as a man can be and more so every day." Sidney managed to tear his eyes off his wife long enough to shift a glance at Ford and Laura. "Speaking of which, part of the reason we invited you here this evening is to share some news that has redoubled our happiness."

"Oh, Binny!" Laura glanced from the dinner her sister had scarcely touched to Belinda's radiant face. "You have a baby on the way? This is happy news indeed!"

Decorum brushed aside, she and Susannah scrambled from their seats to envelop their sister in joyful embraces. Meanwhile, Ford offered Sidney hearty congratulations and the two men drank a toast to the happy news.

The rest of the evening flew by in an excited buzz of conversation about how Belinda was feeling, when the birth was expected, what preparations would be needed and what names were being considered.

Later, when they drove home to Hawkesbourne, a subdued silence settled over Ford and Laura. Tempted as she was to bear her private worries in stoic silence, Laura knew this was not her concern alone. Besides, she had learned the relief and comfort to be found confiding in Ford.

"Belinda and Sidney certainly seem pleased to be starting their family so quickly."

Ford nodded. "If they keep going as they've begun, Lyndhurst will soon be filled to the rafters with small Crawfords."

Laura gave voice to what she suspected they were both thinking. "Did you get the feeling they hoped we would take the opportunity to make a similar announcement?"

"Quite distinctly." After a moment's hesitation Ford

added. "I don't suppose there is any chance we might? In another few weeks, perhaps?"

"I'm afraid not." Laura pulled her wrap tighter around her shoulders. The early autumn evenings were growing cooler. A sense of foreboding chilled her more. What if she was barren as Fate's punishment for the wrongs she'd done? Or perhaps as a divine balance so the rightful heirs of Hawkesbourne would one day inherit?

"No matter," Ford insisted in a hearty tone that struck a false note with Laura. "We are not in any hurry, after all. I am quite content to have you to myself for a while before a parcel of young Barretts come along to demand all their mama's attention."

"But what if they never come?" she could scarcely bear to ask. "Cyrus often hit me in places where the bruises would not show. What if I am barren on account of that? When you proposed to me, you said you wanted an heir."

"You mustn't fret on that account." Ford pulled the reins into one hand, freeing the other arm to slip around her shoulders. "Did I also not say I was done with love and wanted a wife who would be content with a marriage of convenience? I hope you have discovered how little I meant that."

She longed to believe him. But after all that had happened, it was not easy. "Are you saying you do not want a child? A son? An heir to Hawkesbourne?"

Ford thought for a moment before answering. "I must admit, it would be hard for me to contemplate not passing Hawkesbourne on to my descendents. But I would rather have you, with or without a child, than any number of heirs by another woman."

Laura rested her head against his shoulder, savouring the warmth and strength of his embrace. His words reassured her…to a degree. But she could not forget what he'd said about wanting to pass Hawkesbourne on to his descendents.

She could only imagine how it would devastate their marriage for him to discover he had no right to the estate and title he treasured.

Chapter Seventeen

Returning from a brief business trip to London one late October evening, Ford felt a warm tug of homecoming when he rode on to Hawkesbourne lands once again. Every familiar landmark seemed to welcome him home. He inhaled a deep draft of bracing autumn air, redolent of wood smoke, curing meat and the sweet pungency of windfall apples. He would not trade those homely scents for all the perfume and spices of the East.

A satisfying sense of accomplishment filled him as he reflected on the improvements he'd made to the estate in the six months since his return. Unproductive marsh had been drained for cultivation, new breeding stock had been introduced, long overdue repairs made. He could not take credit for the good harvest, but his tenants acted as if he were personally responsible. Of all the changes around the estate in the past six months, the improved attitude of his tenants was the most unexpected and might prove the most valuable in the long run. They were more receptive to his ideas, less tied to the past, more optimistic about their future.

Much of that was due to Laura. The tenants had come to know and respect her during the past seven years. So when she endorsed Ford's plans and told them that their prosperity was his chief concern, they listened. In turn, she'd persuaded him to listen to their ideas and concerns. That had turned out to be as useful an education in estate management as all his reading on the voyage from Singapore.

The thought of Laura made Ford urge his mount to quicken its pace. The three days he had been away from her felt like three months. It was the longest they had been apart since his return to Hawkesbourne and some invisible cord, stretched tight by their absence, seemed to pull him back to her.

Riding into the stable yard, his gaze flew toward her window. A light glowed from it, welcoming and inviting. He could not wait to answer its summons.

Striding into the house, he pulled off his hat, gloves and greatcoat, which he handed to Pryce. The butler greeted him warmly and inquired if he should have Cook prepare a late supper.

Ford shook his head. "I ate before I set out. Tell me, has her ladyship been back from Lyndhurst long?"

"About an hour my lord," replied Pryce. "She retired soon after that. Can I fetch a drink to warm you after a cold ride? Brandy, perhaps, or arrack?"

The nights were growing chilly. Ford expected they would be seeing frost before long. But he could think of something much better than brandy to warm him up.

"Not tonight, thank you, Pryce." He charged up the

stairs, two at a time, and raced down the corridor. When he reached the bedroom door, he threw it open, desperately eager for a glimpse of his lovely wife.

He was well rewarded, catching sight of her clad in her nightgown. After weeks in the dull black attire of mourning, she looked achingly beautiful in white linen with a modest trimming of lace. There was nothing modest about the way the firelight from the hearth outlined her body's enticing curves. Ford crossed the threshold, closing the door behind him.

His abrupt entrance made Laura jump. But the next instant she raised one hand to her breast and let out a breathless chuckle. "Ford, you startled me!"

"Forgive me." It pained him to think he'd frightened her and to wonder how often he'd done it in the past. "I was so eager to see you, I forgot to knock."

"And I am very happy to see *you*." She flew toward him, slipped her arms around his neck and pressed upon him an ardent kiss of welcome. The flicker of desire Ford had felt at seeing her ignited into full fire. Yet something gnawed at the fringe of his thoughts, refusing to let him fully immerse himself in passion.

"Laura." He gently stroked her cheek with his thumb. "There's something I should have done long ago. I've never begged your pardon properly for my behavior the night of our engagement ball. It was infamous, despicable, especially after what Cyrus had put you through, damn him."

Laura frowned. "But you had no idea then what Cyrus had done. For all you knew, I was an experienced woman, eager to welcome your advances."

That was perfectly true. Though looking back, with the knowledge he now possessed, it did not soothe his guilt.

She took both his hands in hers and tugged him toward the bed. "For my part, I had no idea the pleasure you meant to give me. If I had, things might have gone differently that night."

Ford tried to draw consolation from her words, but he recalled too clearly his predatory advance and his request for a kiss that must have sounded like a veiled demand. "I cannot tell you how often I've wished I could go back and change what happened that night."

"That is not possible." Laura came to rest against the bedpost and pulled him toward her, trapping one of his legs between hers. "But perhaps we can do the next best thing. I have a confession to make."

That made Ford uneasy. Her previous revelations had all shaken his world.

Pressing her warm, fragrant body against his, Laura stretched up to whisper in his ear. "When you came here that night, you were convinced I wanted you."

Ford nodded. It seemed a pitiful excuse now. The signs of her reluctance and fear had been so obvious to anyone not determined to ignore them for his own selfish reasons.

"I did." Her ragged whisper made him forget his shame. "Part of me at least. Wary and ignorant as I was of such things, I wanted you. Looking back, I wonder if I was more frightened by the intensity of my own desire than I was of you."

She grasped one of his hands to place over her sweetly rounded bottom and the other upon the tantalising swell of her breast.

"Now I know exactly what I want." She brushed her lips across his cheek, bringing them to rest against his.

Ford's self-control crumbled like a tower of cards. Seizing her in a lusty embrace, he proceeded to sate his hungry hands and mouth upon the rich sweets she offered. To his delight, she responded with equal fervour, rubbing her thighs against his and tugging up his shirt so her hands could range over his chest. She stoked the blaze of his lust until he felt in danger of bursting into flame.

Ever since their honeymoon, Ford had been careful to keep his lovemaking restrained and gentle. After her mother's death, he'd been even more solicitous. He had been rewarded with intense satisfaction from those encounters, but this fierce, urgent love play promised something more.

As they exchanged fevered caresses, Laura began to turn as if performing a figure in some wildly sensuous dance. Ford was only too happy to let her lead. A moment later, he discovered her intent when she pushed him backward upon the bed, landing on top of him in a thrilling reversal to what happened on the night of that ball.

Laura straddled him, her parted thighs poised above his loins. Her hands rested on his chest, restraining him even as they fondled. A cascade of tousled golden hair framed her flushed, eager face.

"Tonight—" she leaned toward him and ran her tongue over his lips, pulling back with tormenting playfulness when he tried to kiss her "—I hope you will give me—" she pressed her parted thighs against his straining rod and he could feel her sultry heat clear through his buckskin breeches "—what I want!"

Her thrilling demand sent a jolt of lust searing through him.

Once again she taunted him with her mouth, daring him to ravish her…and risk being ravished in return. "Are you man enough for the challenge?"

"I will show you what I am man enough for!" Ford spoke in a hoarse whisper as he strained to claim her lips. Thrusting his hands beneath the hiked-up hem of her nightgown, he fondled the firm, rounded lobes of her bottom.

She wriggled on top of him with wanton abandon, returning the scorching heat of his kisses until neither of them could bear the urgency of their need. He tore off his upper clothes while she fumbled his breeches open and tugged them down.

He tried to pull off her nightgown, but only succeeded in getting his head inside the billowing folds. There, the sight of her bare breasts proved too compelling a temptation for him to think of anything else. As he kissed and lapped and suckled with greedy gusto, Laura guided him inside her. At once they embarked on a glorious, wild ride that sent them bucking, writhing and crying out in a frenzy of savage delight.

Spent and sated, they barely had the strength to crawl between the sheets.

"Another like that—" Ford sighed as his whole body pulsed with waves of satisfaction "—and we are apt to set the bed on fire."

"Let us save that challenge for next winter." Laura nestled against him, planting a kiss on his breastbone. "It would be a great help with the coal bill."

With a drowsy chuckle, Ford drifted toward the

tropical shoals of sleep, thinking he could not possibly be happier. Then Laura showed him otherwise.

"Speaking of winter and warmth," she murmured, "I think it would keep us both much warmer this winter if we share a bedchamber."

For a moment, Ford was too overcome to speak. He knew what a difficult step it must be for her to forfeit a place of her own to which she could retreat. In its way, this was a deeper, more courageous commitment to their marriage than going through with the wedding ceremony.

"A capital idea," he replied at last in a husky whisper. Recalling a jest he'd made on their wedding night, he added, "For better for worse, for richer for poorer...for hotter for colder."

This time Laura laughed, a sound as warm and sweet as mulled cider on a frosty night. That laughter poured from her lips, straight into Ford's heart, until it was so full, he wondered how it could keep beating.

Laura froze on the threshold of her bedchamber. As she stared at her Bible in Ford's hand, time seemed to stop and her heart along with it.

She'd just returned from a visit to Lyndhurst, her spirits lighter than they had been in weeks because she had finally hit upon a solution to her dilemma. She would entrust the marriage certificate to a lawyer along with a letter of explanation and directions that it should only be made public after Ford's death. It might not be the proper thing to do, legally or morally, any more than concealing the true manner of her father's death had. But weighed against the personal cost to those she loved most, it was the best compromise she could live with.

But a higher power appeared to disagree. Had this been some sort of test, which was now being taken out of her hands because she had failed?

After a moment that seemed to stretch on and on, Laura forced herself to move and speak. "Ford, what are you doing here? What is going on?"

Hard as she tried to keep her tone neutral, her words came out sharp and tight. She had not spoken to her husband like that since their honeymoon. Lately they had both gone out of their way not to provoke each other. Now her abrupt entrance and peremptory questions seemed to strike Ford the wrong way.

"Is it not obvious?" He gestured toward the two housemaids who had been bustling about collecting Laura's belongings. "I am having your things moved to our new quarters. I thought I would surprise you by getting all the work done while you were away. You are earlier than I expected."

Though she knew he'd meant it as a thoughtful gesture, an expression of his eagerness to be closer to her, Laura could not quell a flash of irritation. Once again, Ford was taking charge of her life, invading her privacy without let or hindrance. And he made it sound as if she was in the wrong for acting contrary to his expectations.

"Belinda was indisposed so I did not stay long." She reached to take the Bible from his hand. "I wish you had told me what you were planning. I would just as soon have done this myself."

She tried to pull the Bible away, but Ford refused to surrender it. "It would not be much of a surprise if I told you. I was only trying to save you a little work. I did not think you would take such exception to my offers."

Discretion warned Laura not to make such a fuss. It would only rouse Ford's suspicion. But this secret had been preying on her peace of mind, stalking her newborn happiness, threatening to destroy all her hopes. How could she remain calm while its exposure hung by a thread?

Laura pulled harder on the Bible just as Ford suddenly let go. As she staggered backward, flailing to catch her balance, the Bible slipped from her hand and dropped to the floor. The folded paper fell out.

With trembling hands, Laura seized it, then scooped up the Bible and thrust the paper back inside. As she rose from the floor, she glanced up Ford. The cold glint of suspicion in his gaze made her heart sink, even as it pounded a frantic beat in her breast.

He turned to the housemaids who stood about awkwardly in the middle of their work. "That will be all, thank you."

The two girls fled as if the room had caught fire. Laura feared it soon might.

Once the housemaids' hurried footsteps had faded in the distance, Ford fixed Laura with a wary gaze and held out his hand. "What are you trying to hide from me now?"

She could not let him see that paper, especially under such suspicious circumstances. He had hated her once when he thought she'd tried to steal his inheritance. How would he feel now, knowing she had cost him not only his lands and title, but his very name and his mother's reputation? She had given seven years of her life to ransom this secret. She would not surrender it now without a fight!

The last thing in the world he wanted was to think ill of Laura. For so long, the lurking serpent of suspicion had poisoned his feelings for her. Every one of those suspicions had proven false. he'd vowed never to let them threaten his and Laura's happiness again. But as he gazed at the Bible in his wife's hands, the corner of a paper protruded from its pages, mocking his trust.

Trust cut both ways, he reminded himself. He'd assumed everything was open and understood between them now and Laura was keeping no more secrets. How could he ignore her blatant efforts to hide something from him? How could he ignore the memory of her threat to destroy him, which now echoed in his mind?

"Hide from you?" cried Laura in a pitiful pretence of indignation. "Don't be ridicu—"

"Is *this* ridiculous?" Ignoring her squeak of protest, Ford strode toward her, wrenched the Bible from her hands and pulled out the scrap of paper pressed between its pages. "What are you so determined to prevent me from seeing?"

When he tried to unfold the paper, Laura seized his wrists with surprising force, holding his hands apart. She gazed up at him with a pleading, panic-stricken countenance. "It is…a letter my mother left…for my eyes only. I will thank you to return it to me."

He wasn't sure which enraged him more. That she would tell him so blatant a lie? Or that she thought him daft enough to believe it?

"What kind of fool do you take me for?" He slipped into his old glacial severity like a familiar greatcoat he had put away for the summer, but now found himself urgently needing. "If this is from your mother, as you claim, you should have no objection to my unfolding it enough to view her signature. If it is hers, I will return it to you with my sincerest apologies."

Laura gripped his wrists even tighter. "Do you suppose any apology would be sufficient to excuse such an intrusion?"

"I will take that as a refusal." Ford's lip curled. "Which surprises me. I should think you would be eager to prove your innocence."

"I resent having to prove anything to you! Especially after all we have been through. Very well, it is not a letter from my mother. It is something you are far better off not knowing. Now please, if you care about our happiness, give the thing to me so I can destroy it. Then we can put it out of our minds and—"

"And what?" Ford demanded. "Go back to ignorant bliss? I fear that will not do for me. You talk about our happiness, but how am I to be happy with a secret like that between us?"

With each word his voice grew harsher. His hands balled into fists, the right one still gripping the paper. He shook his arms, shaking Laura as she clung to them. "You might as well wish me pleasant dreams, then put a scorpion in my bed!"

Sensing he was in danger of losing control altogether, Ford froze and dropped his voice to a murmur. "I thought we were done keeping secrets. They have caused nothing but trouble between us."

His sudden icy calm seemed to affect Laura more than his passionate outburst. "Any secrets I kept were to protect the people I love. That is what I am trying to do now. Do you think I should have told my mother the truth about how my father died or the way Cyrus mistreated me?"

"I am not like your mother. I do not need to be shielded from the slightest unpleasantness. Tell me, is this the instrument of my ruin you threatened me with the night of the ball? Would you try to protect me by destroying it? Or do you plan to keep it as a weapon to use against me some day?"

Laura recoiled from his charge. He thought she might crack, but she was made of sterner stuff. Disappointed and enraged as he was, Ford could not stifle a flicker of admiration for her spirit.

"Go ahead then!" She threw her hands up, releasing his. "I can see you will not rest until you know, even if it means destroying everything we were beginning to build. I want you to know one thing first. I paid a high price to protect this secret even when I believed you had forsaken me. If you cannot believe that, you can never trust me. And if you cannot trust me, you cannot love me as—" her voice broke "—as I deserve to be loved."

Ford ached to rip the paper to shreds as he might throttle a venomous snake that menaced Laura. He pictured her tearful smile and her arms held open to forgive him the doubts he had fought and conquered for her sake.

But the paper seemed to burn his fingertips, mocking him with its vile mystery. How could he protect himself against a phantom peril? If life had taught him one harsh lesson, it was that what he did not know could harm him most.

"Forgive me." He unfolded the paper and stared at its contents, surprised to discover it was not a letter, as he'd supposed, but some kind of document. "I have to know."

Chapter Eighteen

Ford peered at the words, struggling to make sense of them. "What in blazes is this?" he muttered. "It looks like—"

"A marriage certificate." Laura finished his sentence in a flat, dead tone. Even if Ford could forgive her for destroying his life, she was not certain a marriage so blighted by suspicion and past hurts was worth saving. "Don't you recognise any of the names?"

"My mother's—her real name. Her family didn't approve of her becoming a paid entertainer and since Italian sopranos were all the fashion, she took the stage name Alicia Forelli."

Why did Ford bother to explain all that? Laura wondered. Was he desperate to postpone the moment he must acknowledge the shattering truth? "I know. Cyrus told me. He said your father's family was not happy about the marriage. Cyrus decided to investigate your mother's background. He found…that."

Ford read the words over and over, as if trying to

devise some meaning he could bear to believe. "It says she was married on the third of November, seventeen hundred and eighty-five, to a Daniel Witheridge, hostler of Dartmoor parish. That's four years before I was born. I never knew my mother was a widow."

"For God's sake!" cried Laura, "Do you suppose I would have tried so hard to keep this from you if she'd been a *widow*? Cyrus got this certificate from Daniel Witheridge himself, six months after your parents were married! He meant to show it to your father, but when he returned to Hawkesbourne he learned your mother was expecting a child."

A child whose parents were never legally wed because his mother had a previous husband still living. A child whose birth was therefore illegitimate, barring him from holding the family title and estates.

"Why have I never heard a whisper of all this in thirty years?" The significance of what it meant seemed to be dawning on Ford at last.

"Your grandfather dreaded the scandal it would make. He forbade Cyrus to reveal it. By the time Cyrus inherited the title, your mother and father were both dead, as was Mr Witheridge. I suppose he felt there was nothing to gain by dredging up the past and humiliating you unless…"

"Unless what?" Ford shook the marriage certificate at her. "And how do you come to have *this* in your possession?"

"You might call it a wedding present," said Laura. "Along with the money to pay off my father's debts. I know you despised me for putting your inheritance in jeopardy by marrying your cousin, but I never wanted to do that. When Cyrus first offered to give my family a home and pay my father's debts in exchange for marrying him, I refused. It would have been as bad as stealing money from you to provide for my family." Her voice trailed off.

Ford continued to stare at the paper in his hands. Was he gazing into the abyss of ruin that had suddenly opened before him? Or could he not bear to look at the agent of his destruction?

Though Laura doubted he would believe a word she said, she still felt compelled to explain. "When I told Cyrus why I could not marry him, he said it did not matter because you would never inherit Hawkesbourne. He said if I bore him a son, there would be no need for anyone to know your mother's secret—least of all you. If I refused to marry him, he threatened to make the scandal public. As proof, he gave me the marriage certificate."

Ford said nothing. He did not have to. Desolation was written on his face in deep, cruel strokes. Part of Laura yearned to comfort him, though she feared he would never accept. Another part still burned with anger that he had brought this upon himself and her with his insidious mistrust. Again and again she'd proven his worst suspicions about her false—that she was a fortune hunter, that she had betrayed him, that she had schemed to jilt him for Sidney Crawford. Yet when she had given him an opportunity to trust her at last, he had tossed it aside with scorn.

"I suppose you wonder why I kept the marriage certificate all these years. While Cyrus was alive, I almost forgot I had it. But when you returned from abroad and proposed, I thought I might need it as security, something

I could use against you if you ever tried to hurt me as Cyrus had. The night of the ball, I thought that was what you were trying to do. But when you swore you would not force me and when I realised how much my past actions had hurt you, I could not go through with it."

Ford looked up at her at last with haunted eyes. "You took pity on me?"

Angry as she was, she pitied him now. And she pitied his tenants if they should lose him. Whatever his failings, he had been a better lord than his cousin, who had every legal right to the title. "Yes, I suppose I did."

For all the havoc this revelation had wreaked upon them both, Laura experienced an unaccountable sense of relief once the burden of that lurking secret no longer weighed upon her conscience. It no longer stood like an invisible but impenetrable barrier between her and Ford. It had emerged from the shadows to be acknowledged and sorted out somehow.

And perhaps to be overcome?

Laura opened her mouth to ask Ford how they would go on from here. But before she could get the words out, he spun away from her with his mother's marriage certificate still clutched in his hand. Then he strode to the door and marched away without a backward glance.

That night, in a room at the Brighton inn where he and Laura had spent their honeymoon, Ford sat staring at his mother's marriage certificate in horrified fascination. The thing seemed to devour his identity as Lord Kingsfold, master of Hawkesbourne and the son of a virtuous woman, making him feel like a hollow shell of himself.

His first desperate instinct had been to doubt it was

real. From Laura's bedchamber, he had gone straight to the one they were to have shared, where all his belongings had already been stored. He'd opened a small but handsomely carved box of teakwood—the one possession he'd taken with him to the Indies and kept close throughout his exile.

It held an old playbill from Vauxhall with his mother's name listed as featured soloist, along with some items cut from newspapers of the day, which lauded her divine voice and dusky beauty. There was also a gold locket engraved with two A's entwined, for Anthony and Alice. Inside the locket were miniatures of his parents, painted at the time of their marriage. Ford had tossed these and other treasured trinkets aside until he found what he sought—a letter written by his mother to his father during their courtship. She had signed it twice, with her stage name and her birth name.

Comparing that writing to the bride's signature on the marriage certificate, Ford gasped as his brittle bastion of denial was smashed to splinters.

Scarcely aware of what he was doing, he'd thrust the marriage certificate into the box, seized a few articles of clothing and ridden away from Hawkesbourne without any clear idea where he was going. Finding himself on the Brighton road, he'd decided that was as good a destination as any. In mid-November, the seaside resort would be deserted by society, giving him the solitude he craved to grasp this devastating development and decide how to deal with it.

The account Cyrus had given Laura dovetailed so perfectly with what Ford knew of his mother. Little wonder she and his father had eloped to Scotland—no doubt at her insistence. She must have feared any publication of banns might reach the ears of someone who knew about her earlier marriage. It also explained why Ford knew so little about her family, except that they'd lived in Devon and had not approved of her singing career. In light of the evidence, her taking of a foreign stage name was suspicious too. His father's second marriage proved he'd been an easy dupe for designing women.

Taking out his mother's locket, Ford flicked it open and stared at the tiny likeness of her. How he wished he could have her alive for an hour to demand an accounting for what she'd done. No matter what she told him, he doubted he would understand. His sympathy lay with Daniel Witheridge, the man whose wife had deserted him to build herself a new life upon a precarious foundation of lies.

That thought nudged a memory of something Laura had said when he'd pressed her for information about her father's death. *If you start digging now, everything you have built on those foundations may come tumbling down.*

At the time, he'd suspected it was threat. Now he sensed it had been a warning, issued for his own good.

Casting aside his disillusionment and self-pity, Ford contemplated Laura's role in all of this, though he could hardly bear to. For seven long years he had reviled her for jeopardising his inheritance. From the moment of his return, he had sought to punish her in dozens of subtle ways for what she'd done, while all the time she had been suffering his cousin's cruelty in order to protect him from a far worse fate. And when she'd tried to protect him again today, pleading with him to trust her, he had repaid her love and sacrifice with vile suspicion.

Ford thrust his mother's locket and marriage certificate back in the teak box and slammed the lid on them. He did not need that damning piece of paper to prove he was a bastard—his contemptible behaviour spoke for itself.

When morning dawned at last, Ford put on his hat and greatcoat and spent several hours roaming the chalk cliffs, listening to the remorseful lament of the sea. He tried to rally his spirit with the reminder that he had faced ruin once before only to overcome it.

Then he recalled what had saved him before—his intense twisted passion for Laura, his obsession with reclaiming her and proving himself worthy of her.

That very objective proved quite the opposite. No man who viewed the woman he professed to love as a possession to be won or lost could truly be worthy of her. Least of all if that woman was Laura. From the depths of his exhaustion and anguish, the dark siren song of despair urged Ford to hurl himself to the rocks below. That way Laura would be free of him, as she deserved, and he might escape the disgrace and loss of everything that made living worthwhile.

He might have gone through with it if he had not reflected on what it would mean for Laura. She would be engulfed in scandal, the object of malicious gossip. With Hawkesbourne gone to its rightful heir and his fortune forfeit to the Crown, she would be dependent on the Crawfords' charity. Worst of all, she might hold herself to blame for his death, her spirits forever shrouded in unmerited guilt when she deserved all the happiness in the world.

In the end, he concluded there was only one way he could begin to repay Laura for every contemptible thing he'd done *to* her and every good thing she had tried to do *for* him. Now that he knew the truth, he could not continue to live at Hawkesbourne and carry a title that rightly belonged to someone else. But he would not entangle Laura in his disgrace, or encumber her with a husband who never had been, and never would be, worthy of her.

If she had any sense, she would walk out on him now without a backward glance. But she had given him too many undeserved opportunities to redeem himself in the past. He could not take the risk that she might find it in her bountiful heart to forgive him one time too many.

The greatest kindness he could do her now would be to make her hate him.

Ford must hate her, as she'd been certain he would. Laura stifled a yawn as she picked at an array of her favorite foods Cook had prepared for tea. But must he torment her by riding away with no hint of his destination or when he intended to return…if ever?

She had scarcely slept or eaten since he'd gone. She walked through the house with quiet steps, seldom raising her voice above a murmur. It felt almost as if she were holding her breath, waiting for the storm to break or the axe to fall.

Of course she had only to send word and her family would have rallied around to offer their support. But she could not face Sidney's bafflement, Belinda's grieved looks or Susannah's probing questions. They were so happy again after many years of grief and worry. She could not bear to spoil it. Besides, she was accustomed to shouldering her troubles alone.

But not altogether alone.

The servants knew something was wrong, as they might have guessed during her marriage to Cyrus. But they did not intrude with questions or unsought advice. Instead they went about their work as quiet as ghosts, closing ranks protectively around her. Cook prepared the most tempting dishes at mealtimes while Mr Pryce hovered nearby, more solicitous than ever. Though he never presumed to intrude upon Laura's privacy, his manner invited any confidence she might wish to share.

When, three long days after Ford's abrupt departure, Mr Pryce entered the dining room with a brisk, purposeful stride, Laura sensed he bore some news. She tensed, waiting to hear it.

"Lord Kingsfold has returned, my lady." There could be no mistaking the relief in the butler's tone. "He awaits you in the drawing room, at your convenience."

Laura let out a shaky breath. At least Ford was alive. After the shock of discovering that he was not the legitimate heir to the Kingsfold lands and title, she'd feared he might do something desperate. But his request to see her in the drawing room, like a stranger come calling, did not bode well. Surely if he understood why she'd acted as she had, he would have come to her himself, without any formality.

A vindictive impulse urged her to keep him waiting while she changed into her finest clothes, dressed her hair and perhaps resorted to a subtle application of paint to hide the dark shadows beneath her eyes. Perhaps if Ford spent an hour pacing the drawing room, wondering when she would come, he might have a taste of what the past three days had been like for her.

But she was tired of playing tit-for-tat. It had never done anything but build thicker walls between them. With their marriage hanging in the balance, there had never been a more vital need to show forbearance.

"I will come at once." Laura rose from her chair and smoothed out her skirts. With her insides constricted as tight as they'd been on the day Ford first returned to Hawkesbourne, she headed to the drawing room.

Seven months after that first encounter, the place looked altogether different. The furniture had emerged from beneath its dust covers to stand proudly, all cleaned and polished. The new window curtains were open, letting in plenty of pale November daylight. A fire burned in the marble hearth, taking the chill off the air.

But when Ford turned from the window, he looked far too much like the cold, enigmatic stranger who'd returned from India with unknown plans for her.

"Welcome home." Laura tried to make her greeting sound warm and sincere, but the sight of him roused all her old wariness. "Are you hungry? Cook made twice too much for tea and I fear I have not done it justice."

"Later, perhaps. First there are some matters we must settle." Ford strode toward her, coming to a halt two arms' length away. From behind his back he drew a paper Laura recognised from its charred edge. Grasping one corner between his fingertips, he held it out to her.

She was able to take hold of the other side without any danger of their hands touching. "What do you want me to do with this?"

Once the paper was in her possession, Ford lowered his arm and thrust his hands behind his back. "Precisely what you have done so well for the past seven years, for a little longer."

"I don't understand."

"I am surprised. I thought a clever woman like you would have worked out what must be done now. I want you to keep my mother's marriage certificate away from prying eyes until after the New Year, by which time I will be on a ship back to Singapore, where the scandal will scarcely signify."

"And after that?"

"Oh, please don't be tiresome. After that you will present this evidence of my bastardy to the Court of Chancery, so the Kingsfold title and estates can be given over to their rightful heir. In exchange for this service, I will put a sum of money on deposit for you with a reputable London banker, which should keep you in comfort for the rest of your life. I will also give you your freedom. You need not feel bound by the marriage vows neither of us meant. I certainly will not. In a few years, once the scandal has died down, I can return and sue for divorce, if you wish to remarry."

The word *divorce* jolted Laura out of her daze and unlocked her lips. "I do not want a divorce and I do *not* want your money! Do you think I kept this so I could blackmail you with it?" She held the paper away from her as if it were contaminated with some horrible pestilence.

Ford ignored her question, addressing himself to her denial instead. "If you do not want money or your freedom, what in blazes do you want?"

Had the shock and disillusionment of the past few days made him forget the sweet, fleeting happiness they'd found together?

"I want *you*." Laura struggled to hold on to her memories of a very different man than the one who stood before her now, making such a repugnant offer. She had to believe the other Ford was inside him somewhere, imprisoned by pride or pain. For both their sakes, she must try to reach him. "I want us to be happy together again, like we were before…this. We can be again, now that everything is out in the open and there are no more secrets between us."

She searched his eyes for a glimpse of the man who had made her mother's last months so rich and full. The one who'd ridden out in the rain to find her and fetch her home. The one who'd defended her against Lord Henry's insults. The one who'd demonstrated so delightfully how a man's hands could bring her pleasure instead of pain.

But he had disappeared behind a hard, cool wall of jade green.

Perhaps for ever.

Never had Ford needed his iron self-control more than at that moment. He prayed it would hold long enough for him to do what he must.

Lifting his chin, he forced himself to stare at Laura. Memories of their brief happiness tormented him, but he channelled his pain into a glare of arrogant hostility. "You are mistaken in supposing no more secrets remain between us. Now that yours has been disclosed at last, I believe the time is ripe to reveal mine."

"I knew there must be something. How dare you condemn me for keeping secrets when you had your own to hide?" Laura steeled herself against the expected blow. "What is it, then?"

He wished he could spare her any further suffering, but it was the only way to spare her a lifetime of shame and regret. "The true reason I wanted to marry you, of course. Never quite satisfied with my explanations, were you? You should not have been so easily diverted. More than once I feared you might worm it out of me."

"Worm what?" Laura looked dubious. He would have to make his performance very convincing. "What reason?"

"Revenge, of course." He rolled the word around on his tongue as if it had the sweetest flavour, rather than the most revolting. "Revenge for jilting me and stealing my inheritance. I spent seven years laying my plans and making my fortune in order to carry them out."

Strained and tired as she looked, Laura did not flinch. "Marriage to you was supposed to be my punishment, was it? I fear you miscalculated there. After my marriage to Cyrus, these past weeks as your wife have been like heaven. Until now."

Her words caught him like a cricket bat to the knees. He did not want to hear that he'd made her happy. Neither could he bear to be reminded of the dizzying, delicious joy she'd brought into his life. Such thoughts only made it harder to do what he must.

"I will be the first to admit my revenge has not gone entirely according to plan. There have been a number of unforeseen departures." Ford ground out the most agonising words he'd ever had to speak. "My original intent was to wed you so I could take control of the money you'd inherited from my cousin. I did not plan on finding it gone."

"That was Cyrus's doing!" Laura's heavenly eyes flashed with pure, righteous anger. "I only took a pittance to provide for my mother and sisters. And what I needed to pay my father's debts."

"Spent is spent." Ford shrugged with what he hoped was convincing scorn. "Though I calculate I have taken sufficient pleasure in your bed to compensate me for the monetary loss."

No matter how great the necessity, it would be impossible for him to deny their rapturous passion. The best—or the worst—he could do was pretend the pleasure they'd shared had meant nothing more. Even that taxed his resolve to its limits.

Two bright spots flamed in Laura's cheeks. "If you expect me to be flattered by that despicable remark, you are the most loathsome scoundrel who ever deceived a woman."

She squared her shoulders and skewered him with an icy glare. "You can have nothing more to say that I wish to hear. I am going to Lyndhurst. As far as I am concerned, this wicked fraud of a marriage is over."

He had achieved his purpose. But he could not take the chance that Laura might relent at some later date. Or was he only seeking to steal one last precious memory with which to torture himself?

"Must you go?" Seizing her by the wrist, he pulled her into a forceful embrace. "The other compensation I sought from you was an heir. It hardly matters now, I suppose, that the child would have no title or estate to inherit. Still, I might as well salvage what I can from this *wicked fraud of a marriage*."

The black depth of his cruelty must have shocked her speechless. Or perhaps, in spite of everything he had done to destroy her feelings for him, a wayward spark of desire still smouldered. For an instant, Laura froze in his arms, mute and yielding.

Before she had time to recover her wits, Ford forced a harsh, blistering kiss upon her. Thrusting his tongue between her lips, he scoured her mouth, desperate to drive her away for ever. And to brand the taste of her upon his memory.

The next instant he felt a stinging pain as she struck him on one cheek, then the other. Again and again. Harder and harder.

"You wretched, selfish brute!" She punctuated her words with a rain of blows. "I never did anything to deserve such treatment from you! You should thank me on your knees for trying to protect you! How could I have been such a daft fool to trust you? You are *worse* than Cyrus. At least he never tricked me into loving him!"

With no more warning than when she had launched her attack, Laura stopped. Turning away from him she wrenched the drawing-room door open, then slammed it shut behind her.

Ford dropped to his knees, where Laura said he belonged. He'd succeeded in making her hate him. And it had been much easier than winning her love. Though a crushing sense of loss engulfed him, he clung to a small shred of satisfaction. He had done the right thing at last, giving Laura the freedom and independence she deserved. He would make certain word got about that he had deserted her. That way, once the scandal of his illegitimacy broke, she would not share in his disgrace, but instead be an object of public sympathy.

He only wished that, in order to save her, he had not been obliged to hurt and deceive her.

Chapter Nineteen

⁓⁓⁓

"I think Ford lied to you," announced Susannah with stubborn certainty, the morning after Laura had arrived at Lyndhurst, pale and distraught.

Belinda had asked no questions the night before, but put Laura to bed after making her drink a saucer of sweetened cream mixed with brandy. The potion had done its job, lulling her into a deep, exhausted sleep. But when she woke and recalled what had happened, she began to weep in harsh, jagged sobs that she was powerless to control.

Someone must have heard her, for Belinda and Susannah soon burst in. Still wearing their dressing gowns and nightcaps, they clambered on to the bed, offering comforting words and embraces.

The moment she was calm, however, Susannah demanded information. "What has Ford done? You must tell us. I know you probably think I am too young to understand, but you're wrong."

"Sukie," Belinda pleaded, "give poor Laura some privacy. She will confide in us when she feels the need."

"And when will that be?" Susannah glared at them both. "When pigs fly? I am sick of secrets and tiptoeing about, pretending nothing is wrong when it's clear something is dreadfully wrong. If you don't tell me, I will go straight to Hawkesbourne and badger the truth out of Ford."

Her sister's protest took Laura aback. Something about it echoed the complaint she'd made to Ford about being denied power over her life. By trying to protect her sisters from distressing truths, had she denied them the power of knowledge and the power to help?

"You will do no such thing!" cried Belinda. "You are under my roof, remember. And I forbid—"

"Sukie is right." Laura wiped the tears from her cheeks. "I am sick of secrets, too. They are like mould, festering in the dark. It is no use trying to explain what happened between Ford and me without telling some other things I have kept to myself for far too long."

An hour later, an exhausted hush lay over the room. Her sisters were pale and subdued but Laura felt strangely at peace.

"I think Ford lied to you," said Susannah at last. "In fact, I'm certain of it."

"Of course he did." Laura hugged her bent knees to her chin. "Every time he pretended to care for me."

"Not then—last night! Put your hurt feelings aside for a moment and think. Is it easier to deceive someone day and night for months on end or for a few minutes in the heat of an argument? And which speaks louder, actions or words?"

Every instinct for self-preservation urged Laura to

ignore her sister's opinion. All the more because of how much she wanted to believe it. She could not afford to live in a false world of rosy delusions as her mother had. Life had treated her too harshly for that. All she wanted now was a little hard-won peace.

Yet a stubborn vein of reckless spirit still pulsed within her heart, unbowed by her past ordeals. One that had gloried in the sheer tempestuous adventure of loving a man like Ford Barrett. Against her caution and better judgement, it made her say, "I understand what you mean. But why should he tell me such a terrible lie—one that was sure to make me leave him?"

No sooner had the words left her mouth than a possible answer presented itself. But did she dare believe it?

"My lady!" Mr Pryce looked as if he wanted to throw his arms around Laura when she returned to Hawkesbourne later that day. "I was going to call on you this evening at Lyndhurst, though his lordship told me to wait at least a week."

"Wait for what?" Laura strode into the entry hall. "And where is his lordship? I have a few things I wish to say to him."

"He's gone, ma'am. I have no idea where. I was hoping you might. He went this morning, taking all his belongings. He said you were to have charge of the estate for as long as need be. I was to go to Lyndhurst in a week's time and inform you. The way he took his leave of me, I felt his lordship did not ever mean to come back."

"I don't believe he does, Mr Pryce."

Why had Ford quit Hawkesbourne so soon, leaving his whereabouts such a mystery? Laura wished he were there so she could demand an answer to that question and many others. Had he fled to escape her questions because he dared not answer them truthfully?

"Begging your pardon, my lady." Mr Pryce studied her face with fatherly concern. "Master Ford didn't harm you, did he? I always regretted ignoring the signs when Master Cyrus mistreated you. I was afraid I would only make things worse for you and for Mrs Penrose."

"That was the very reason I kept silent," replied Laura. "I can hardly blame you for doing the same. I thought I had succeeded in hiding my troubles from the rest of the household. I should have known nothing would escape your efficient scrutiny. Master Ford did not harm me. Indeed, I believe he may be trying to protect me, but he is going about it in quite the wrong way."

"The two of you seemed so happy together." The butler sighed. "I wonder if this house is cursed, like the Scripture says about visiting the iniquities of the fathers on to the third and fourth generation?"

"Iniquities?" said Laura. "Cyrus, you mean?"

Mr Pryce shook his head. "That was only the fruit of it, my lady, not the seed. Forgive me. It is not my place to speak out of turn about the family."

His remark piqued Laura's curiosity. "I know you would never comment about the Barretts to outsiders. But since I am a member of the family, I do not think it would be out of place for you to tell me. Perhaps over a cup of tea in your pantry?"

Mr Pryce seemed torn between discretion and a

desire to oblige her. But after several moments' reflection he nodded. "You look as if you could use a cup of tea, my lady, and I know I can."

He led her below stairs to the butler's pantry, a snug little room that smelled of boot-blacking and silver polish. A long narrow table stood against one wall, overlooked by a row of windows just below the ceiling. There were two chairs, of which Mr Pryce offered Laura the upholstered one by the hearth, while he pulled up a plain wooden one for himself. Then he bustled off the kitchen, returning a few minutes later with a tea tray.

"So tell me," said Laura as she poured the steaming tea into their cups, "what sort of curse hangs over Hawkesbourne? If there is such a thing, I have been as much its victim as anyone. Perhaps if I know what I am dealing with, I can find a way to break it."

She didn't really believe in curses, but she had seen for herself how wrongs from the past, especially those shrouded in secrecy, could ripple out to cause harm for years afterward. Might Mr Pryce tell her something to help her find Ford and make things right? Or would it convince her that a fresh start held the only hope for Hawkesbourne, Ford and her?

Mr Pryce took a sip of his tea. "I reckon you know, ma'am, that Master Cyrus was descended from old Lord Kingsfold through his first wife and Master Ford through his second."

Laura nodded. "That was why Cyrus was so much older than Ford."

"Indeed, my lady." Pryce glanced around the room. "When I came here as a boot boy, many years ago, I heard it said the old master's first marriage was arranged by his father and not at all to his liking. When he inherited the title shortly after his son was born, he sent the child and his mother to live in Bath and seldom saw them again for the rest of their lives."

Though she could not help but sympathise with anyone forced into a loveless marriage, Laura could not condone the actions of Ford's grandfather, particularly toward his son.

"Master Cyrus's parents must have died young," the butler continued, "for he was living with his grandmother in Bath when she died. Old Lord Kingsfold sent the boy away to school, but he came here on his holidays. They were never close, but it got worse after his lordship remarried—for love this time—and Master Ford's father was born. His lordship doted on his second son and made no secret of wishing he and his descendents would inherit Hawkesbourne instead of Master Cyrus."

Was that why Ford had felt the family title and estate were his rightful destiny? Laura wondered. Because his grandfather had drummed it into his head from childhood? As for Cyrus, a reluctant flicker of pity stirred in her heart for him. Hearing an echo of it in Mr Pryce's voice, she sensed how his loyalties must have been bitterly divided through the years.

The butler paused for a drink of tea, then carried on his story. "It went beyond talk, too. Old Lord Kingsfold tried to keep Master Cyrus from finding a wife. Meanwhile he showered his younger son with the best of everything and encouraged him to wed young, for love."

Mr Pryce's account explained so many things that had long puzzled Laura. She could see precisely how past slights and wrongs had sown the seeds of more recent ones. Would it ever end?

"Master Cyrus had good cause to resent his grandfather's second family, but he never let on. I used to think he must have a very forbearing nature. Now, I reckon he was nursing a grudge and biding his time."

It all made such perfect sense, except…

"I beg your pardon, Mr Pryce. Did you say old Lord Kingsfold *encouraged* his younger son to wed for love? Surely he could not have been pleased to have a Vauxhall singer for a daughter-in-law?"

Mr Pryce thought for a moment. "The neighbours gossiped and slighted young Mrs Barrett, but Lord Kingsfold praised her to the skies—said Master Cyrus hadn't a hope of getting a bride half so lovely."

"That is quite at odds with what Cyrus told me," Laura mused. "Though he might have gone digging into Alice Ford's past on his own."

"I beg your pardon, ma'am?"

Laura started, suddenly aware that she'd been speaking aloud. Was she grasping at straws? Or was she beginning to glimpse the truth at last?

"I appreciate your candour, Mr Pryce. Now there is something I must share with you." She reached for her reticule and took out the long-hidden paper. In a few words she described how it had come into her possession. Then she handed it to the butler. "Do you think it is possible this marriage certificate might not be genuine?"

Mr Pryce examined the document closely. "It looks in good order, my lady. I reckon there is only one way to be certain."

As he explained, Laura listened, nodding. It would not be a pleasant undertaking at this time of year, but she must know the truth. She could only hope it might set her and Ford free from the dark thrall of the past.

As Ford stood at the taffrail of the brig *Lady Grace*, a raw January wind ruffled his dark hair in a brisk farewell caress. The ship had just eased through that last crook in the meandering Thames known as The Hope, on its way to the wide mouth of the river and the Straits of Dover beyond.

Did this mean he was leaving hope behind? Ford asked himself with a rueful grin. Perhaps that was how he should feel. But, strangely, he did not. The last time he'd quit England, he'd been driven from his homeland, disillusioned and heartbroken, consumed with helpless rage. Today he left of his own accord, on his own terms. His poorly healed heart had been broken yet again, but that was his own damned fault and he would not have had it otherwise. His bittersweet interlude of happiness with Laura had been worth the price.

The crew of the *Lady Grace* swarmed the vessel's tall masts, unfurling sails and adjusting rigging, but Ford paid them little heed. His spirits resonated to the shrill, mournful cries of the gulls that glided and wheeled in the sky above. Sky that was the clear, constant blue of Laura's eyes.

Eight years ago, he had fled these shores feeling cheated, betrayed and deceived—all entirely misguided. Now he knew the truth, about himself and about Laura. The former had been a bitter blow, but in the end, the latter had saved him.

Now he was sailing off on a great adventure to become a better man—a man whose nobility came not from titles or estates, but from living a worthwhile life. Throwing back his shoulders, standing taller than he had in years, he inhaled a deep draught of bracing, briny air.

But what was that he smelled? A whiff of warmer climes—the wholesome, tangy sweetness of orange blossoms.

Ford spun about to find a woman standing behind him. She wore a black cloak over a black gown. Her bonnet was swathed in a dark veil, making it difficult to distinguish her features. Surely it could not be…

The lady raised her delicate, gloved hands and drew back the veil to reveal a beautiful, beloved face.

"Laura?" Ford clutched the taffrail to keep from pitching overboard. "Good God, what are you doing here?"

His question seemed to cast a shadow over the angelic purity of her features, but she did not flinch. It suddenly occurred to Ford that true angels could not be the fragile, helpless creatures they were so often portrayed, but valiant, resolute beings, prepared to wrestle darkest evil to reclaim a man's soul. That was how Laura looked now—fearful of the outcome, perhaps, but still undaunted.

"Why should I not be here?" she asked. "This is a public vessel and I am a paying passenger. If you object on the grounds of propriety, you should know I have brought my lady's maid and a respectable man to serve as my escort." As if it had slipped her mind, she added, "And, of course, my husband is travelling aboard this ship."

"You know perfectly well what I meant." Ford clutched his hands behind his back to keep from reaching for her. "I thought our marriage had served my purpose and was ended in all but name."

The falsehood burned on his tongue, and all the icy waters of the North Sea could not cool it.

Laura considered for a moment, gazing deep into his eyes. Never had Ford wanted more desperately to conceal his true feelings from her. Yet never had he felt them so naked for her scrutiny.

"I thought that, too, at first," she replied. "But then I began to wonder if your sudden claim of marital revenge might have been invented to spare me from scandal."

When Ford tried to deny it, Laura held up her hand for silence. "Let me finish, please. I promise you the last word."

Such was her gallant authority that Ford could not bring himself to defy her wishes. If only he had spent the past eight years making himself worthy of her love, what a man he would be!

"Upon reflection and heeding some wise advice," Laura continued, "I began delving into your family history and made several discoveries of interest to us both. That is one of the reasons I have come here. It was easier to discover which ship you had booked passage on than track you down in London. Besides, I thought it more likely you would hear me out if the alternative was swimming to shore."

"Sound strategy." Ford cast a glance at the choppy grey waves. "This is not the best time of year for sea bathing. So…what did you discover."

It would make no difference as far as he and Laura were concerned. Ford quelled any foolish flicker of hope. But the ship was due to make port briefly on the

Kentish coast. If he let Laura have her say, then persuaded her she would be much better off without him, she could go ashore there with no harm done. In the meantime, he would have the precious torment of seeing her one last time.

"To begin with," said Laura, "your grandfather used his first family very badly."

As she told him how old Lord Kingsfold had exiled his first wife and son, Ford's first impulse was to think what a dreadful thing his grandfather had done. Then, with a sharp pang of conscience, he remembered it was not so different from what he'd once planned for Laura.

"Later," she continued, "your grandfather made no secret of wishing the descendents of his second family would inherit Hawkesbourne, rather than Cyrus."

Much as he wished it were not true, Ford recalled how often as a child his grandfather had assured him he would one day be Lord Kingsfold. Could that be why he'd felt such an absolute right to his inheritance and considered himself robbed of it by Laura's marriage to Cyrus? Everything he'd heard made him feel sorry for his cousin, which was the last thing he wanted.

"What does any of this matter now?" he demanded.

"I believe it matters a great deal, if that was what made Cyrus so anxious to prevent you from inheriting. He added a vicious little twist of his own, by stealing the woman you intended to marry."

"Stealing? You mean he...?"

"I believe he contrived to ruin my father to coerce me into marriage. He may even have arranged that convenient business opportunity for you in Spa."

"I wondered how he knew I'd gone there." Ford cursed himself for underestimating his scheming cousin.

"One thing Cyrus did not anticipate," said Laura, "was my reluctance to deprive you of your inheritance. He was forced to improvise by forging—"

"A sham marriage certificate?" Ford could have sworn the ship suddenly lurched into a deep trough between two massive waves.

Why had he been so ready, even eager, to believe his beloved mother a bigamist and himself a bastard? Could it be that, with every new proof of Laura's innocence, the guilt over how he'd treated her had built up inside him until he could no longer bear to go unpunished?

"It was a sham," said Laura. "I travelled down to Devon and examined the parish register with my own eyes. There was no entry that remotely corresponds to the names and dates on the forged certificate. I also spoke to some cousins of your mother. They assured me she was not married when she went off to find fame in London. There is not a shred of doubt, you are the rightful Lord Kingsfold."

She had done all that to redeem him from scandal and disinheritance after everything he had done to her? He might be legitimate by birth, but Ford knew he was still a selfish bastard at heart…the last in a long line, by the sound of it.

Laura seemed puzzled and cast down by his subdued response to her news. "I was a fool to accept the story Cyrus told me and the *proof* he offered. I should have questioned it, then. How different our lives might have been if I had!"

"No!" Ford's iron restraint shattered. He seized her

hand and clung to it like a life rope in a storm-tossed sea. "You are not to blame for any of this! I never questioned the lies Cyrus told you, and I had far more reason to suspect his motives. Far more reason to believe in my mother's honour.

"Besides," he continued, making no effort to hide the depth and intensity of his feelings for her, "you have already suffered far too much trying to protect your family and me. You put yourself through years of hell and braved my undeserved hatred to keep a secret you knew would destroy me. My only regret is that I have proven myself so unworthy of your sacrifice."

He forced himself to release her hand. But Laura captured his between both of hers and refused to let go without a battle he did not have the will to fight. "Let me be the judge of that. As for sacrifice, I believe you made up that story about wedding me for revenge to spare me from being tainted by the scandal of your birth."

Her words snatched Ford's breath away, like the gust of a North Sea gale. He had only to recant that wounding falsehood and he could reclaim the elusive happiness he'd once found with her. But he could not offer her anything less precious than the truth, even if it cost him the joy of a lifetime.

"Perhaps I did not spend seven years planning revenge, but my true plans were little better. I believed you had stolen my inheritance and I was certain you had stolen my heart. I thought if I married you and possessed you, like some unfeeling object, I would soon tire of you and break the hold you had upon me."

Ford saw the hope in her eyes die a martyr's death and his mangled heart took a fresh wound. He longed to say no more, fearing it might revive her hope only long enough to give it a mortal blow. But he had sworn never again to deceive her and he could not break that vow.

"If it is any consolation, my plans failed miserably. The moment I saw you again, something began to change inside me. I started to doubt all the things I'd spent seven years believing. I found myself caring for the strong, stubborn woman you'd become. I am not proud of the fight I put up to resist every impulse of admiration and forgiveness. And I regret every moment of anger or fear or sorrow I gave you. But when I stood beside you at the altar on our wedding day, I meant the vows I made to you more sincerely than I knew."

Even after he had confessed the wrongs he'd done her, Laura did not release her grip on him, though it slackened a little. Now Ford could feel her hands trembling. Her eyes were misted with brine that came not from the cold sea, but from the warm springs of her heart.

"You must be freezing." His voice rasped with emotion. "You should go below to the cook's galley for a cup of mulled wine to warm you. When we make port at Deal, you can go ashore."

Slipping his hand from her grasp, Ford drank in one final look at her. In the days to come, that memory would warm and cheer him and assure him he had done the right thing at last. He turned to go below decks.

Behind him Laura's voice rang out, sweetly defiant. "If you expect to get rid of me that easily, my dear husband, I am afraid you are mistaken. I know you believe you are doing what is best for me. But you are going about it in your old way—charging decisively ahead without asking my opinion or giving me a choice. In matters of love, that will not do. Power must be shared, compromises made. Do I not deserve some say about our future?"

Her words rocked Ford. Was that what he'd been doing? Making arbitrary decisions about what was best for her? Taking all the power over their relationship out of her hands? Leaving her with no choice but to endure the consequences of his actions?

Seven years ago, neither of them had a choice. They'd been pawns at the mercy of cruel forces from the past. Was he so determined to seize control of his fate, that he would rather accept the certainty of an empty future than risk his heart on Laura's choice?

He turned to face her once again. "There can be no question of you deserving whatever your heart desires. Tell me then, what is your opinion?"

Though the rest of her features were composed in serene fortitude, the beginnings of a smile kindled in Laura's eyes. "I believe if you persist in trying to punish yourself, you will punish me, too. I do not think you want that."

"Never!" The power of his conviction pushed Ford a step toward her.

As if taking part in a halting but vital dance, Laura took a step toward him. "Then rather than punishing ourselves for the mistakes of the past, would it not be better if we atone for them by dedicating ourselves to each other's future happiness?"

The power of her presence drew Ford another step closer. "You make it sound so simple."

Standing toe to toe, Laura gazed up at him. "Perhaps

the best and truest things in life are simple. That does not mean they are easy."

Slowly he raised his hand to her cheek. "I trust that you can do whatever you set your mind and heart to."

Leaning in to his caress, Laura raised her hand to mirror it. "And I have every confidence in you."

Ford could not decide whether he was in a blessed dream or more truly engaged in life than he had ever been. "Then I reckon we can reach a mutually satisfactory agreement. What would you say to a second honeymoon in the Canary Islands?"

She gave a sigh of sweet fulfilment like Ford had often heard in the wake of their lovemaking. "I would say it sounds like heaven."

He bent toward her as she stretched up to meet him. The delicious warmth of her lips was like a long-awaited homecoming.

Epilogue

St Valentine's Day, Tenerife, the Canary Islands

Laura had one more secret to tell Ford and this time she could hardly wait.

"I feel as if I've gone to heaven." She sighed, fanning her face with a palm frond. "Though I had to go through hell to get here, it was well worth the ordeal."

She and Ford sat in the shade of the wide balcony that overhung the inner courtyard of their rented *casa*.

"If this is heaven, you belong here." Ford peeled a banana and offered her a piece, accompanied by a doting smile. "For you are an angel."

Laura gazed into his dark eyes as she nibbled the soft fruit from his fingers, savouring its mellow sweetness— and his. In some ways Ford seemed an entirely different man from the cold, severe avenger who'd descended upon Hawkesbourne the previous spring. But she recognised many fine qualities she had glimpsed in him since then. Having reconciled the past, he had begun to balance all the best aspects of his old and new selves. He had amply justified her faith in his basic goodness.

"An angel is a fine consort for a saint." Her gaze flickered over his striking features with ardent appreciation. "You showed all the patience of a saint, the way you tended me on our voyage from England. I was afraid I would die of seasickness before we reached these blessed islands. If it had not been for you holding my head while I retched, bathing my face afterward and all the time diverting me with stories from the Indies, I do not know what would have become of me."

"You would have survived." Ford assured her as he offered her another morsel of banana. "For all your tenderness and compassion, you have a core as stout as oak. But if I was able to ease your suffering in the least, I count it a privilege."

An anxious look tensed his handsome face and he made no effort to conceal it. "Your appetite has not improved as I hoped it would, once we put ashore here. You are still too thin in spite of all the delicacies I bring from the market to tempt you. Must I send to Hawkesbourne for Cook? She would not rest until she fattened you up."

"Am I too scrawny to rouse your desire?" Laura gave a husky chuckle that was anything but angelic. Having eaten the last piece fruit from Ford's hand, she closed her lips over his fingers, caressing them with her tongue.

He reacted with a soft gasp of pleasure. His dark eyes shimmered like molten pools of passion. "If you do not know the answer to that already, I shall be delighted to demonstrate when we retire for our *siesta*."

"I certainly hope you will," she whispered. "You cannot complain that my appetite for *you* is less than it should be."

"No indeed." Ford slipped from his chair with predatory grace and moved to kneel beside hers. He began to drizzle exquisite kisses up and down her neck, fuelling the sultry heat that seemed so easily stirred of late. "If you dined with the same gusto as you dally in bed, I would not have a moment's worry."

The ache of concern beneath his lusty banter touched Laura. Much as she savoured the joy of her precious secret, she must not keep it from him any longer. Reaching back, she closed her hand over his and raised it to her bosom.

After scanning the courtyard and the balconies to make certain none of the servants was about, Ford fondled her breast with such deft skill she almost forget what she meant to tell him.

She tilted her head back to whisper in his ear. "In another few months, these should be plump enough to inspire your lust rather than your worry."

Reluctant as she was to interrupt his thrilling attentions, she tugged his hand lower, to rest over her taut belly. "It was more than heavy seas that made me sick on our voyage."

For a moment Ford froze so completely, she feared he had stopped breathing. Then a drop of warm liquid fell upon her neck and trickled down her shoulder.

"My angel!" Ford lowered his head to rest upon her bosom, while his hand stretched over her belly in a protective, adoring caress. "I thought you could not possibly make me happier than on the day we sailed from England."

Laura knew exactly what he meant. Delighted as she was to be carrying her beloved husband's child, she was grateful she'd sought this reconciliation *before* she knew about the baby. She stroked Ford's hair as her heart overflowed with love and happiness.

The reality of what she had told him seemed to take possession of Ford.

"We cannot go on to Singapore now!" He pulled himself upright and cradled Laura's face in his strong, deft hands. "We must go back to Hawkesbourne for you to have the baby. Or would you rather stay here until after the child is born?"

"We still have plenty of time to decide." Laura prepared herself for the most wondrous kiss she had yet received from him. "Wherever we go, as long as we are together, it will be heaven."

* * * * *

MILLS & BOON
Historical

On sale 6th August 2010

IN THE MASTER'S BED
by Blythe Gifford

To live the life of independence she craved, Jane has
disguised herself as a young man! But she didn't foresee
her attraction to Duncan – and the delightful
sensations stirring in her very feminine body...

OUTLAW BRIDE
by Jenna Kernan

Bridget Callaghan is desperate to save her family stranded
in the Cascade Mountains. But the biggest danger is trusting
the only man who can help them – he's dark, dangerous
and condemned to hang!

TRIUMPH IN ARMS
by Jennifer Blake

Reine Cassard Pingre feels trapped: the only way to keep
her beloved home is to accept 'Falcon' Christien's bold
proposal of marriage. Reine cannot dissuade him
from wedding...and bedding...her!

MILLS & BOON

MODERN™

The Drakos Baby

An enthralling linked-story duet by best-selling author

LYNNE GRAHAM

*A Greek billionaire with amnesia, a secret baby, a convenient
marriage...it's a recipe for rip-roaring passion,
revelations and the reunion of a lifetime!*

PART ONE

THE PREGNANCY SHOCK

On sale 16th July

Billie is PA to gorgeous Greek billionaire Alexei Drakos.
After just one magical night together, an accident leaves
Alexei with amnesia and Billie discovers she's pregnant –
by a man who has no recollection of having slept with her...

PART TWO

A STORMY GREEK MARRIAGE

On sale 20th August

Billie's baby has been born but she hasn't told Alexei
about his son's existence. But her return to Greece
and their marriage of convenience will lead to
a shocking revelation for Alexei...

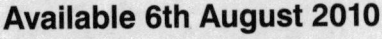

2 FREE BOOKS
AND A SURPRISE GIFT

We would like to take this opportunity to thank you for reading this
Mills & Boon® book by offering you the chance to take TWO more
specially selected books from the Historical series absolutely FREE!
We're also making this offer to introduce you to the benefits of the
Mills & Boon® Book Club™—

- **FREE home delivery**
- **FREE gifts and competitions**
- **FREE monthly Newsletter**
- **Exclusive Mills & Boon Book Club offers**
- **Books available before they're in the shops**

Accepting these FREE books and gift places you under no obligation to buy, you may cancel at any time, even after receiving your free
books. Simply complete your details below and return the entire page
to the address below. You don't even need a stamp!

YES Please send me 2 free Historical books and a surprise gift. I
understand that unless you hear from me, I will receive 4 superb new
books every month for just £3.79 each, postage and packing free. I
am under no obligation to purchase any books and may cancel my
subscription at any time. The free books and gift will be mine to keep
in any case.

Ms/Mrs/Miss/Mr ———————— Initials ————————

Surname ————————————————————

Address ————————————————————

————————————————————————

———————————— Postcode ————————

E-mail ————————————————————

Send this whole page to: Mills & Boon Book Club, Free Book Offer,
FREEPOST NAT 10298, Richmond, TW9 1BR